Wrath of the Lemming Men

Toby Frost

MYRMIDON

www.myrmidonbooks.com

Published by Myrmidon 2009

A catalogue record for this book is available from the British Library.

ISBN 978-1-905802-35-7

Set in 11/14pt Sabon by Falcon Oast Graphic Arts Limited,
East Hoathly, East Sussex

Printed in the UK by CPI Group (UK) Ltd, Croydon, CR0 4YY

3 5 7 9 10 8 6 4

To all the readers, but especially to Alex

I'd like to thank my friends, family and everyone who bought the first two books for their support. Once again I ought to thank Verulam Writer's Circle and Leighton Writers, as well as John, Owen and Ed for their comments on the manuscript. As ever, particular thanks must go to my parents, who throughout have been Mission Control to this adventure in space. Hurrah!

Toby Frost 2009

Contents

Prologue:

The Battle of the Tam Valley

'By dawn it was clear to General Young that General Wikwot's drive to capture Varanor had ground to a halt. The Colonial Army had displayed remarkable courage in the face of a frenzied assault. Yet the lemming men pressed on. Unable to disgrace himself with acts of self-preservation, General Wikwot threw his reserves into the fray as the 112th Army prepared to strike the death-blow. . .'

The Official History of the War Against the Lemming Men, Galactic War Office

'Many and arrogant were the Yull, sure that their early success would bring them certain victory. Yet we M'Lak made ready, and our humans too, and fiercely the Yull were met among the trees. Not cowardly were our warriors, and not light the grievous slaying in that gory vale. For severed heads, piles of lemming men, the squeaking of fallen rodents: these are pleasing things to us. . .'

The Saga of Varanor, Verse 613

TOBY FROST

'In an unprovoked act of self-defence, the offworlder scum turned on our friendly and entirely non-genocidal army. The dirty foe fought unreasonably for their lives, and urgently the splendid General Wikwot ordered our reserves under noble-born Colonel Vock to attack from the north and mercilessly butcher the enemy – for their own good, of course. . .'

Final (Terminal) Report of Lieutenant-General Prang, Divine Amiable Yullian Army

*   *   *

Agshad Nine-Swords leaned back in his deckchair and studied the sky above. It was a clear, hot day, and the sun streaked through the high trees, throwing bars of light across the glorified pillbox that he called home. The sun made Agshad feel strong and keen. It was a good day for adventurous deeds, and so he had taken the accounts books into the garden.

He sat outside on a deckchair, calculator on his lap, sleeves rolled up, occasionally looking up from his books to frown and stroke his mandibles and chin. Later on, he decided, he would lock up the little fort, take the jeep across the bridge and say hello to the main garrison five miles east, at Tambridge.

A running figure appeared at the far side of the bridge. Agshad shielded his eyes and peered: it was a man in army uniform, his arm in an improvised sling. He vanished behind one of the great timber pillars of the bridge, reappeared, looked behind him, stumbled, rose and lurched on.

Perturbed, Agshad got up and strode out to meet him. As he looked down the length of the bridge he recognised the man.

'Eddie?' he called. 'Are you alright?'

Eddie half-collapsed on him. 'They're in the trees!' he gasped. 'They're coming!'

'Who's coming?'

'Them! The Yull!'

'But the Yull are miles away, Eddie.'

'No, no.' Unable to speak, Eddie bent over and panted. 'The garrison's down,' he managed. 'All dead. Yull came – thousands of them. They killed everyone – Brian, Clarrie, even Old Joe. Tambridge is fallen!'

'Oh my ancestors,' Agshad said.

'We fought to the last man. Can't let 'em get you, the bastards. They sent me – to warn you.'

'How many –' Agshad began, and as if to answer him high voices pulsed through the forest beyond the bridge, a hard, impatient chant: '*Yull, Yull, Yull!*'

'It's an army,' Eddie gasped. 'We've got to warn HQ!'

Drums and gongs through the trees, the sound of wild shrieks and cracking whips. '*Yull, Yull, Yull!*'

'We're too late!' Eddie cried.

Agshad rooted about in his pockets and took out a key. 'I'll deal with this,' he said. 'Take the jeep and go and warn headquarters. I'll delay them as long as I can.'

Eddie looked hard at him for a moment, then nodded. 'Alright. Good luck, Agshad.'

'You too,' Agshad said mildly, and as the battered jeep coughed into life behind him, he strolled onto the empty bridge.

The Yull rushed over the horizon like a tidal wave of fur. A thousand sleek bodies slipped between the trees. Axes glinted, forage-caps bobbed, banners flapped, human skulls grinned and shook on banner poles. And amid the horde came the squeaky voices of the looting, murdering lemming men of Yull.

They poured down the hill, squeaking and yelling, the officers beating their maddened soldiers on to the river's edge. Agshad picked up the broom he used to sweep the bridge.

Suddenly a voice barked '*Huphup! Harp-huphephop!*' and the lemming men stopped dead. They halted at the edge of the bridge in a crowd, desperate to pour across but lacking the orders to do so. The army stretched along the opposite bank as far as Agshad could see. To the right, a lemming man pointed into the swirling waters of the Tam and made excitable sounds until a sergeant tripped him and tore out his heart. The Yull did not tolerate indiscipline.

The horde parted before Agshad and a figure stepped onto the bridge. He wore the cuirass, helmet and enormous shoulder-pads of a high-ranking officer, but Agshad could have told his status had he been naked. The puffed-out chest, the swaggering walk – the Yullian officer class were not only vicious sadists, but insufferably pompous as well.

'You!' the officer barked. 'Dirty offworlder!'

'Morning,' Agshad said.

'Harruph! I am Colonel Mimco Vock of the sacred army of Yullia! The war god of the Yull, in his divine wisdom as interpreted by the high-priests of the Yull, has

12

decreed that it is to be the Yull who will rule this galaxy.'

'There's a surprise.'

'*Shup!* This bridge is now the property of the Greater Galactic Happiness, Friendship and Co-operation Collective – so beat it, M'Lak trash, or I will torture you to death!'

Agshad reached out and tapped a small brass plaque fixed to the timber. 'I think you will find that this bridge is the property of the army of the British Space Empire. I represent their accounts department and, as the highest ranking officer present, I forbid you to make use of it.'

'British Space Empire? Pah!' Vock snorted, hands twitching towards the axe at his waist. 'I am not here to speak with animals! How dare you address me so, human coward lackey! Surrender at once so I can tear out your still-beating–' a look of rudimentary cunning stole across his whiskered face and he calmed himself with a shudder '–liberate you from the yoke of serving the British oppressor.'

Agshad shook his head. 'Sorry, no. I refuse to join an army which practices human sacrifice and has no adequate pension plan. We M'Lak are wise to you. Which, incidentally, is why we are helping the humans trounce your army downriver.'

'Lying offworlder who is lower than a beast and smells of cheese! The Divine Migration cannot be halted by scum like you!'

'Then why are you here with all these reinforcements? The truth is that your furry legion came down to the woods today, and you got a big surprise. Not a picnic any more, is it?'

13

'Nobody compares me to a soft toy!' Vock yelled back. 'Dirty weak offworlders get nothing but death! You are lucky if I kill you quick, big smelly coward! You will die slow, yes – slow!'

Agshad thought of Eddie, and imagined him tearing down the dirt road in the jeep. He would probably have reached the main camp by now: perhaps he was in a tent with General Young herself, pointing out the Yullian advance on the map. He smiled.

'You smirk at me? If you had whiskers I would pull them out, nice and slow! I will wear your kneecaps on my. . .' Vock paused, speechless with fury, 'On my knees!'

Agshad shrugged.

'But you are brave, for an offworlder,' Vock hissed. 'Most would have begged for mercy by now.' He leaned forward, and spoke more gently. 'I will give you something for your defiance. If you turn away and leave now, I will let you live. And when we are done killing your allies as gradually as possible, I will reward you and make you a retainer of my house. A fair offer, I think.'

'Indeed.' Agshad leaned in as if to reply quietly. 'It sounds good, but–' He tilted his head back, sniffing the air.

The lemming frowned. 'But what?'

'I smell a rat.'

For a moment, Agshad thought Colonel Vock was going to pop. The Yull drew back as if struck, shook violently, turned on the spot and punched one of his lieutenants in the eye. 'Right! That's it!' Vock gestured to his men. '*Hup-hup!*'

Agshad glanced over his shoulder. Sixty feet beneath the

bridge, the waters of the Tam slapped and broke upon the rocks. Agshad thought: they would be three abreast on the bridge, and it would be hard for them to fight the urge to jump. He could keep them back – for a while.

A Yullian knight shouldered his way through the horde, a fat brute in blue plate armour. He braced himself, raised his axe over his head like an executioner, screamed a battle cry and charged.

'*Yullai!*' he shrieked – and stopped dead as the bristle end of Agshad's broom struck him in the mouth. He made muffled noises, chewing at the bristles in his rage, and Agshad turned and deftly shoved him over the railings. Vock's champion dropped into the rapids, whooping with demented glee. The Tam had claimed its first victim.

Agshad felt tranquil and absolutely confident, as if the sun had risen anew and bathed him in its rays. He was where he was meant to be. His whole life had been leading to this moment: decades as a warrior, followed by the rigorous discipline of accountancy. He looked down at the river, where the body of the Yull bumped against the bank.

'One,' Agshad said.

The Yull poured howling onto the bridge. Agshad whirled the broom, braining one and knocking a second flat. The third lemming man fell over the second, and Agshad leaped up and kicked a fourth in the snout. The bodies of the Yull began to pile up and more clambered over them. Agshad pressed on, tallying his kills as he waded into the foe.

It was turning into a beautiful day: a morning's bookkeeping and then a fight to the death, all in very clement weather. One could not have wished for a better end to life. Agshad's only regret was that his offspring could not see him; they would have been quite impressed. He kicked a lemming man over the railing.

'Fourteen!' he cried. 'Ancestors of mine, children of mine, watch me now, for this is how I die!'

Suruk the Slayer was suddenly awake. He had been sleeping in the traditional way, squatting on a stool like some great bird of prey – in one movement he sprang down from his perch and landed softly in the middle of the room, silent except for the hiss of the blade as he slid it from its sheath.

He stood there in a fighting-crouch, tasting the air, his shrewd eyes flicking around the room. I felt something, he thought. Something was here. . . something very wrong.

'Who is there?' he asked softly, speaking the language of his forefathers for no reason he could understand. 'Father? Is it you?'

The shadows did not answer.

'It must have been the curry,' Suruk said, and he shrugged and went back to sleep.

1

The Fur Flies

It was a photograph of a young woman, taken in holo-type. She was in her early thirties, pretty, slim, with a vague, pleasant smile. She wore a short top that exposed her tanned midriff, and a cloth band across her forehead to pull her dreadlocks back. She was up to her waist in tea plants. As Isambard Smith rocked the picture back and forth in his hands, the girl waved: she was making the sign for a victory, or for peace.

The picture made Smith tired, then angry. No point keeping the bloody thing. He tried to rip it: the photo did not tear but stretched, and the plastic at the top of the picture warped and whitened above Rhianna Mitchell's head.

'Bollocks,' Smith said. He'd been trying to forget the girl; now he'd given her a halo. He tossed the picture onto the desk, turned it face down and Rhianna disappeared. I wonder where she is now? he thought. Probably with some bloody man, some smart fellow, doing something more important and exciting than she'd ever do with me. 'Well, better get on with this commando raid,' he said, getting up.

He picked up the .48 Markham and Briggs Civiliser and

holstered it. He checked his sword and put on his coat. Then he took his rifle from behind the door and left the room, bumping his head on a model Hampden bomber hanging from the ceiling as he stepped into the corridor.

Polly Carveth was in the cockpit, leafing through a copy of *Custom Model*, the fashion magazine for androids. 'Alright there?' she said as he entered, not looking up. She leaned over and consulted a brass-edged dial fixed to the dashboard by screws and tape. 'We'll be in drop range in. . . oh, two minutes.'

'Good work, Carveth. Keep us steady.'

She looked around. The light from the consoles tinted her face a sickly green. 'Still going with the others?'

'Yes.'

'You know, when I want to forget my troubles, I just go shopping.'

'I told Wainscott I would, Carveth.'

'Well, don't cock up. I wouldn't want you to get hurt, boss: you've always been. . . well, not bad.'

'Thanks, Carveth. I appreciate that.'

'Not a prob. I'll see you off once we're in position.' She turned to the controls again: a counter, which for all Smith knew might have been removed from a fruit machine, had begun to spin. He left her to it.

The Deepspace Operations Group waited in the hold. There were five of them, armed with grenades, pistols, knives and Stanford machine-guns. Major Wainscott, the commander of the group, was demonstrating something to Susan, the team's beam gun operator.

'So I snapped it in two and rammed one end up his nose, straight into the brainpan,' Wainscott said, making a vicious thrusting gesture. 'Killed him stone dead.'

Susan nodded. 'And the rest of the Kit-kat?'

'I ate that for elevenses. Ah, Smith. Still going down with me, are you?'

'Yes.'

'Good man.' Wainscott was scruffy, slight, clever and quick, and probably the bravest and most dangerous man that Smith had ever met. He was also, according to rumour, a former resident of the Sunnyvale Home for the Psychologically Uneven. 'Now, men: here's the state of play. The filthy lemmings have fifty Kaldathrian beetle-people down there, and they've promised to start pulling their legs off the moment they detect any ships in orbit – hence we're using assault pods to slip through the radar. We need to rescue these fellows before our main force goes in and plasters the fluffy bastards from on high.

'The captives are spread between three forts, each with its own codename. We will be dealing with the first fort, codenamed Theodore. Two commando teams from the Indastan army will be taking the other two forts, Simon and Alvin. The Kaldathrians are too big to get on board, so we've got a medical shuttle set to follow us down once it's safe. What's the word from Polly Pilot, Smith?'

'We're lined straight up with the drop zone,' Smith said. 'From the looks of it we'll land in the courtyard of this fort of theirs. The lemmings haven't detected us, but as soon as they know we're there, I gather they can be relied upon to go absolutely bananas.'

'Exactly,' said Wainscott. 'So, priority one is to find our people and secure the area so the medic ship can put down and get them away. Priority two is to smash the place up.

Wreck it.' Wainscott grinned. 'Plus, there's a bonus. General Wikwot himself is believed to be in one of the forts, probably on a visit to do over the prisoners in person. If he's down there, we Shanghai the fat sod and drag him back for trial. Understood?'

There were nods of assent from the Deepspace Operations Group.

'Everything you've heard about the lemming men is true. These are the cruellest and most depraved creatures in the galaxy. You are to expect demented resistance. Now, I know the Kaldathrians may not be British citizens, or even human, but its time the Yull learned that nobody messes with the beetle people. They belong to us!' He nodded towards the row of long sealed boxes at the far end of the hold. Each was the size of a telephone booth, held in a cradle ready for launch. 'Ever use an assault pod before, Smith?'

'No,' said Smith.

'How about a khazi?'

'Many times.'

'Very similar principle,' Wainscott explained, 'except this time it's the ship that drops its load, not you.' His laugh was hard and barking; arguably indicative of the man as a whole.

From the doorway Carveth said, 'We're in stable orbit, ready to go. So just sit tight and wait for the movement to stop.'

'Good. Now, where's that alien chap of yours?'

Suruk the Slayer dropped from the rafters, landing with a soft thump between them, like a kitten.

The resemblance stopped there. He stood up, and his

mandibles opened to reveal a large, hungry grin. He wore his armoured vest, and there were knives strapped to his belt, arms and boots. Suruk wore a couple of his favourite skulls and the sacred spear of his ancestors was strapped across his back. 'Greetings, friends,' he said. 'Not long now until our blades run red with lemming blood. We shall accost them on their doorstep like the carol singers of doom!'

They climbed into the pods. Inside Smith's cubicle it was small and smelt of plastic. There were a few controls: a dispenser to his right would print out copies of the mission objective and landing zone; at his shoulder, a chain controlled the emergency door release.

Carveth looked into the pod. 'I'll be waiting up here. Good luck,' she said. She slammed the door and Smith was suddenly alone. He leaned back against the padded seat and strapped himself in.

He felt grimly nervous, like a man with bladder trouble at the start of a rollercoaster ride. The pod shook and fell onto its side, ready to be shot out of the back of the ship – or else Carveth had pushed him over for a laugh. If she has, he thought, there'll be hell to – and then suddenly the hold sprang open and the assault pods flew out like pips from a squashed fruit.

He was in space, hurtling towards the landing zone. Bloody hell, he thought, what *am* I doing? The Empire's work, he assured himself. Bashing the Furries. He flicked on the radio, hoping to pick up the others, or at least the Light Programme.

'. . . have to break contact until we hit the ground,' Wainscott was saying. 'Remember: if you can't get back,

21

make sure they don't take you alive. Use your pills. Or better still, a grenade. Hello Smith. Raring to go, are we?'

'Something like that,' said Smith. 'Has anyone heard from Suruk?'

'I am here, friends,' Suruk growled over the intercom. 'I was indulging in a brief slumber prior to slaughtering our foes. Are we nearly there yet?'

''Absolutely!' Wainscott said. 'Now, listen: we'll cut radio once we hit the upper atmosphere. As soon as we hit ground the comms'll come back on. Everyone work towards each other and regroup. And keep an eye out for those captives as you do. They're about the size of a horse, so they shouldn't be too hard to find. Remember: if you see anything with whiskers and a twitchy nose, kill it. Got me?'

The Deepspace Operations Group understood.

'Loud and clear,' said Smith.

'Best of luck,' Wainscott said, and the radio went dead.

Smith sat in the rocking, rattling pod, the window too high to look out of. A counter under the door lock began to roll, clicking down. Not long, he thought. The pod lurched and white fire licked at the window.

He closed his eyes and leaned back. It's just a khazi, he told himself. Just a khazi in a hurricane. And besides, who else is here to do this, if not me?

It was no time to be afraid. The lemming-men didn't know fear: for them, the only sin was self-preservation. The Yull were not afraid of coward humans.

'I'll show them cowards,' Smith said. Something at the side of the pod went *clunk* – decoys being launched, hopefully, and not the steering vanes falling off – and it shook more than before. Smith checked his rifle again. He felt a little sick.

The counter was whizzing now, too fast for the eye to take in. Smith thought about Rhianna, a billion miles away, working with the secret service's psychic department and gone for good from him. Then about the *DKR Clauswitz*, the vast UE troop carrier that the Yull had rammed to announce their entry into the war. And then the city of Neustadt: overrun and burned to the ground in the same night. The lemming men had rushed headlong from their forest homeworld deep into human space. They called it the Divine Migration: to everyone else, it was merciless war.

'Final descent commenced,' said the pod.

The Marshall of the fort was strutting across the courtyard, axe swinging at his side, when the Ghast advisory officer strode over to meet him.

'*Hup-hup*,' said the Ghast, out of courtesy.

'*Ak nak!*' the Marshall replied. They switched to English, each finding the other's language difficult to pronounce.

'I hear that you wish to bring the prisoners into the courtyard,' the Ghast said, rubbing its antennae together.

'Yes!' the Marshall puffed out his chest. 'The General wishes to test his axe. Perhaps he will sacrifice some of the beetle people. Most amusing!'

The Ghast scowled. The left side of its jaw had been badly burned during the street fighting on New Luton. Behind the scars, its malevolent eyes studied the Yullian Marshall with contempt. 'Your petty sadism is inefficient.

Drawing attention to this base with a massacre will result in our secrecy being compromised, and that will *not* be tolerated. Were the humans to attack—'

'Humans, attack? Ant-soldier, you speak rubbish! They would be stupid enough to want to rescue the captives, but they would not dare try. Offworlders are too cowardly to protect their own, let alone these dung-rolling Kaldathrians. Hahaha! We noble Yull will slaughter all stupid talking insects – er, present company excluded, of course.'

'Foolish. Do not say that you were not warned.' The Ghast pulled its coat tight around its body, stamped and turned on its heel, rear end bobbing behind it in time with its steps.

Even *they* are cowards, the Marshall thought. When Earth is enslaved and the M'Lak dead, we shall turn on the Ghast Empire. They may be mighty, but none can stop the Yu—

An armoured telephone box dropped out of the sky onto his head, bursting him like a water-bomb. The box fell open and Wainscott sprang from it like a showgirl popping out of a novelty cake, a machine gun blazing in either hand.

'I am a khazi in a hurricane,' Smith told himself, and the bottom of the pod smacked into something, rocked, stopped, shot straight down ten feet and stopped again.

He sighed. Well, that hadn't been too bad. He'd had worse journeys on British Monorail. The window exploded and a spear shot through like a bolt of light. Smith threw himself down as it slammed into the headrest. He yanked the chain and the wall in front of him flew off and hurled the lemming man behind it into a pile of crates. It squeaked feebly and died.

Smith looked around him. He had landed in a bunkroom, crudely hacked out of the rock. Sunflower seeds lay in a pile on the floor; pictures of what looked like dormice in suggestive poses were pinned up beside the bunks. The drop-pod stood in a shaft of light where it had crashed through the roof, as if sent down from heaven.

Shadow flicked over the light and a figure dropped onto him. Six feet of rodent hit him in the chest with a ragged screech and Smith staggered back, sprang forward and shouldered the Yull as it fumbled for its axe. Its slim, hard paws swiped at his face – he dodged and the two of them were scrabbling at one another in the dim room, knocking each other's blows aside.

The Yull stank of sawdust and pee. 'Filthy offworlder!' it snarled, which struck Smith as pretty rich. 'Now you die!' It tried to gouge his eyes, he twisted aside and claws raked his cheek. Smith knew Fighto: he dropped his weight and knocked its legs aside, and as it lost balance he grabbed it round the neck and drove it head-first into the wall. It fell and he brained it with his rifle-butt.

Now what? He paused, listened, and checked the console strapped to his wrist. No signal. 'Damn,' he said, and he started down the tunnel.

He reached the end of the passage and peered around the corner: crude striplights turned the corridor into a patchwork of shadow and stark light. There was a doorway up ahead, and in it a Yullian officer holding a club stood with its back to him.

'All into the courtyard!' he barked, addressing someone in the room behind. 'Move, scum!'

The sword made almost no sound as Smith drew it. He ran and thrusted, the needle-thin tip slipped through the officer's back. Smith twisted the blade and pulled it free, and the lemmingoid gargled and dropped into a heap of dead fur, like a stack of pelts.

He stepped into the room. Like jewels in dirt, dozens of huge eyes stared back at him. A beetle-person lurched out of the dark; its six legs wobbling, its carapace scorched and grimy. Slowly, as if remembering something from long ago, it looked down at Smith, raised a limb and saluted.

Smith saluted back. 'Hello,' he said, sheathing his sword. 'Isambard Smith, pleased to meet you. I'm here to get you people out of here.'

'The army?' a voice buzzed from the floor. 'The army's come!'

'Well, not the whole army,' said Smith. 'There's only seven of us. But don't worry, it's enough. Now, can you all walk?'

'Some cannot,' said a third Kaldathrian, clambering upright. 'Those monsters beat us and stole our dung to stop us from rolling it – and they call *us* savages!'

'Don't worry, old chap, we're fixing them. Are there any more guards?'

'There is a room just down the corridor,' the beetle who had saluted said. 'It is where they lurk and plot.'

'Stay here,' said Smith. 'Lock yourselves in. I'll be back in a moment.'

He stepped back into the corridor and nearly walked

into Suruk the Slayer. 'Blimey! You scared me there, Suruk!'

The M'Lak carried his spear in one hand, and was pulling a laden trolley with the other, draped in a cloth. 'What's on the trolley?' Smith said.

'Heads,' Suruk said, lifting the cloth. 'My pod landed in their mess-room, an appropriately-named location.'

Smith outlined the situation and together they strode up the corridor. There was a large metal door ahead. Smith cocked his Civiliser and Suruk turned the handle and gently pushed the door.

They looked into a laboratory. Machinery lined the walls, both human computers and alien biotech. Ghast science officers fussed over ceiling-high stasis tanks, dictating into bio-transcribers. A pair of Yullian guards watched sullenly. There was a table in the middle of it all, and beside the table was a man dressed like a chauffeur: in boots, black jacket and a cap with false antennae protruding from the brim.

'A Ghastist!' Smith cried. 'Gertie-loving traitor!'

He fired and the Ghastist fell across the table. The Yull moved: Smith blasted one and Suruk's spear flew into the other's chest. One of the Ghast scientists reached into its lab-coat for a pistol and Suruk hurled a machete, hitting it right between the eyes. Smith shot the second Ghast. Suruk grabbed the third and threw it through the glass of the nearest tank, then dragged it out and repeated the process to make sure.

'Good lord,' Smith said, looking around. 'They must have been researching something really important here – no wonder HQ didn't want us to bomb it.'

'Top secret, it seems,' Suruk said, readying his spear. 'Now the smashing begins!'

Something moved behind them and Smith turned, gun ready, to recognise one of Wainscott's men. 'Craig?'

Craig was slim and pale, the Deepspace Operations Group's disguise expert. At the moment he looked like himself. 'Careful, Captain! You could have my eye out with that.'

'Sorry,' said Smith. 'I've found the prisoners; they're down the corridor. They're pretty roughed-up. How's things up top?'

'Busy. Listen: we need to be away in five minutes. I'll get the beetles out; you give us a hand clearing the courtyard topside.'

'Righto,' Smith nodded, and Craig jogged out of the room. 'Just coming.'

Smith would never know what made him reach over the dead Ghastist and pick up the man's lever-arch file. Perhaps it was providence, or destiny, or just that the file had shiny metal bits on the front. But he had only flicked through a couple of pages before he knew that he was dealing with something very serious indeed. 'Good God,' he whispered.

'What have you found, Mazuran?' Suruk demanded.

'I'm not sure. . . it's in Ghastish. Let's see. . . *Hak natsak* – that means surgery of the reproductive organs – *smak Vorlak* – attacking the Vorl?' He looked up. 'Suruk, this is vital information. We have to get it to W at once. This lever-arch file could contain the destiny of the universe!'

Suruk looked doubtful. 'A small, flat destiny, it seems.'

Major Wainscott ran through the warren with a gun in one hand and a knife in the other, killing all before him. He booted a door open, saw a Ghast advisor getting up and shot it as it drew its pistol. A Yullian soldier leaped out of nowhere: Wainscott dodged its axe, sprang in and sank his knife into the rodent's throat.

The lemmings were fighting to the death. Good, he thought: he'd never liked them anyway.

He searched the room but there was nothing to destroy or kill. Wainscott sighed, somewhat disappointed, and stepped back into the corridor to come face-to-face with the biggest rodent he had ever seen.

It was a mound of solid fat on solid muscle that blocked off the passage as if poured into it. There were black circles around the eyes; the brute's left pupil was dead and white. The beast shook its chops.

'General Wikwot,' Wainscott said.

The general snarled. He raised his huge paws; steel hooks were strapped to his fists. His voice was coarse and hard. 'Well, well, the offworlder bigwig. But are you big enough to fight me, eh?' Wikwot took a step closer, teeth bared. 'This warren is mine!'

Smith emerged into smoke and dazzling light. The courtyard was empty and burning: black fumes billowed from a row of Yullian ramships standing against the far wall. The guards, at least forty of them, lay across the yard as if scattered by a sower's hand. The air was full of fluff.

Susan and Nelson had set up the beam gun behind a pile of sacks. Smith strode forward to meet them, Suruk by his side, pushing the trolley – and a figure jumped out

29

from the battlements. Smith whirled, raising his pistol, but the Yull had already fallen into two pieces, neatly bisected. Susan lowered the beam gun.

Something moved on one of the ramships. An explosion had cracked its wing, and its pilot ran down the length of the fuselage, straddled the nose and began to unscrew the nosecone.

No-one seemed to have noticed. Puzzled, Smith watched the pilot as it took a small mallet from its jacket.

'What on Earth is he doing?' Smith said, more to himself than anyone else, and the end of the nosecone fell off to reveal a plunger and a large red button. Howling something to its war-god, the pilot leaned back and swung the mallet down, towards the button –

'Bloody hell!' cried Smith as he flicked up his pistol. The gun kicked in Smith's hands and the Yull shrieked, stiffened and slid off the nose. The courtyard was suddenly quiet.

A side door burst open and a crowd of beetle-people scuttled out. Wainscott struggled into the courtyard after them, dragging what looked like a pile of fur coats behind him. His knuckles were bloody and split. 'Good work, Smith!' he said, dropping his burden on the ground. 'Here's the General – and a fat bugger he is too. Rather a successful trip so far, don't you think?'

'Yes, very good. Looks like we cleaned out the whole fort.'

A grappling hook sailed over the wall. Smith raised his rifle, looked down the sights and waited for the furry head to appear – and thirty more hooks followed it. 'Oh hell,' Smith said. 'They're climbing the wall!'

A howl of mingled rage and glee rose up from a

thousand voices outside the fort. 'Bugger,' Wainscott said. 'Everyone take places and prepare to hold!'

The first Yull appeared in Smith's sights. He fired: it squeaked and fell out of view. Beside it two more lemming men popped up, and then the Yull were swarming over the wall, clambering onto the battlements. Smith glanced left, then right, then behind, and saw furry bodies scrambling over the wall on all sides.

Guns rattled and cracked from the courtyard. The Yull leaped at them from the battlements, unable to resist the urge to jump. 'That's a lot of lemmings!' Wainscott called over the stuttering roar of his gun.

Smith shouted into the radio. 'Carveth! Where the devil are you, woman?'

'I'm coming, I'm coming,' her voice crackled back. 'You know what a bugger this ship is to park.'

Smith had a sudden uncharitable mental image of her, boots up on the console, leafing through *Custom Model*, reading 'My boyfriend ran off with my RAM upgrade'.

Howling war cries and waving axes the Yull poured in from all sides. Smith aimed his pistol and put one down at twenty yards; the next got five yards closer before he dropped it, the third reached ten. . .

'Soon they will be upon us!' Suruk declared, twirling his spear.

'Smith,' Wainscott called, 'where's our transport gone?'

'Up there!' Smith said, pointing, and in a rush of engines the *John Pym* dropped down as if from the sun itself, the hold door open. Behind it, a medical ship, specially armed.

Lemming men rained down around them from the walls. Suruk killed two with his spear.

The *Pym* landed, legs creaking under its weight, and Carveth ran down the ramp.

'Did you find them?' she shouted over the engines.

'Yes,' Smith shouted back. The beetle people were climbing into the medical ship, supporting one another. he saw that several were missing legs and fury rushed through him like an electric charge. 'Bastards,' he snarled, and he raised the rifle to shoot another lemming dead. Wainscott's men were pulling back to the ships, closing in as they neared the ramp. The Yull fell like a breaking wave, covering the courtyard in fur. But they kept coming.

Carveth yanked Smith's sleeve. 'Let's get the sodding hell out of here!'

'Are you deranged?' Suruk demanded as he bounded up the ramp, pulling his trolley behind him. 'They have hardly reached us yet!'

Three minutes later, the Empire sent in a formation of Hornet light bombers and blew Fortress Theodore to bits. An hour and a half after that the *John Pym* reached the Fifteenth Fleet, slipped between the great dreadnoughts and docked with the transport ship *Edward Stobart*. It took half an hour before they were cleared to open the hatches, allegedly owing to bioweapon quarantine procedures but really, Smith suspected, because the dockers had lost the paperwork.

Smith leaned back in the captain's chair, sipping his tea as he watched the warships drifting round the *Pym* like sleeping whales. He had hoped to see some Hellfires dart between them, but only a post shuttle trundled from one craft to another. After a while the boarding light turned green and at the airlock they said goodbye to the Deepspace Operations Group.

'That was damned good work,' Wainscott said, leaning back against the wall. Behind him Susan and Craig carried the unconscious General Wikwot, who looked like a bear in a breastplate. 'Easy in, easy out. Well done, Smith.' Wainscott leaned in and ruffled Carveth's hair. 'You too, pilot girlie.' He glanced at Suruk, clearly considering whether it was wise to ruffle his mane. 'And you,' Wainscott added, deciding against it.

'All in a day's work,' Carveth said, hooking her thumbs over her belt. Glory did not often come her way. She pulled what she imagined was the sort of face tough, competent pilots had. 'Whatever the mission, you know we're big enough to take it on.'

'Which is exactly why I'll be using you next time,' Wainscott said, and the smile faded somewhat from Carveth's face.

'Next time?' she squeaked, and Wainscott turned to Smith, oblivious.

'Cheerio, Smith.' His eyes narrowed. 'Hope you don't mind me asking, but where's that floaty bird who used to be with you? Funny sort, smelt of herbal tea?'

'Rhianna,' Smith said. 'She – well, she doesn't work for us anymore. I – well, I suppose she had trouble being sufficiently committed.'

'I've had trouble with commitment myself,' Wainscott said, and his eyes widened. 'I'm not going back in there. You can't make me!'

Susan tapped him on the arm. 'That's committal. It's alright, Boss.'

'Oh, I see.' Wainscott shrugged. 'Well, bad luck about that. Still, she never seemed *quite right*, you know? Anyway, can't stand here making jaw forever. Come along Susan, we've got a war to win.'

'Us too,' Smith said, and he turned the wheel and the airlock swung open with a sharp, rusty creak. Wainscott gave them a little wave and wandered out into the transport ship, his men chaperoning him like students around an elderly don.

'Tea?' enquired Smith.

They took tea in the living room, together with some scones they had picked up on Proxima Secundis. The radio played light music. Smith poured cups for Suruk and Carveth, then sat down.

'Well done, men,' he said. 'We got everyone back intact, bagged loads of furries and got all those poor beetle people into good medical care. Excellent.'

'With Rhianna and most of our drugs mysteriously gone, I ought to brush up on my first aid,' Carveth said, taking a deep draught of tea. 'I've not been in a medical facility since we refuelled at the Free States.'

Suruk snorted. 'It said MASH on the roof and you thought it was a pie shop.'

'Well, you don't even have an anatomy. The day I entrust my health to someone with a face like a lobster bonking a pasty is the day—'

The Elgar on the radio suddenly broke off and was replaced by a military band playing 'Lilliburlero'. Then a crisp voice declared: 'We interrupt this programme to deliver an important message. News has reached us of victory on the world of Varanor! For the first time, Imperial troops have completely defeated the Yull!'

'Excellent!' Smith cried. 'Turn it up!'

'Yesterday afternoon the enemy attempted a full-scale assault, seeking to encircle and destroy the 112th Imperial Army. They were met with heroic resistance from human and Morlock forces fighting under the British flag, and their advance has been completely shattered in what is fast becoming known as the Battle of the Tam Valley. Thousands of disgraced lemming men have flung themselves into the river. General Florence Young and Asrath the Vengeful, Commander of Colonial Beings, have pledged to take back Varanor and teach a stern lesson to the Yull. Forward the Empire!'

'Good Lord!' said Smith. 'We've thrashed them!'

Suruk chuckled, which was always a bad sign for somebody.

'Great!' said Carveth. 'How's about I break out the Malibu? It's naval Malibu,' she added, pre-empting a disapproving look from Smith.

'We'll have a gin and tonic once we've engaged the autopilot,' Smith said. 'In the meantime, scones all round.'

Carveth took an extra scone, breaking off a piece for Gerald the hamster. She jogged up to the cockpit, and Smith leaned back in his seat and sighed.

So, the Yull were not as tough as they'd thought. The Empire had met them head on and bloodied their twitchy noses. This was victory, and perhaps the beginning of the end for the Galactic Happiness Collective. He felt proud of his Empire. If only Rhianna was here.

Stupid woman. Why couldn't they stay together? Why was the galaxy too much of a distance to keep their relationship going? They had been *right* together, had made each other happy. It had been a good week, and then she'd gone and spoilt it all by dumping him on Sunday afternoon. Should have got myself an Imperial girl, he thought glumly. Someone called Harriet with big thighs and a Labrador. It was too bad that Rhianna had opened his mind to more exotic things, with her herbal biscuits and her 'Belly dance to fitness' tape. That was too pleasant a memory to be entirely bitter.

On the far side of the table, Suruk scratched a mark into the handle of his spear. Smith felt a sudden twinge of envy. Suruk had no sex drive, felt no affection beyond comradeship, no need to feel the pain that seemed the inevitable result of falling for a girl. Against his better judgement, and the better judgement of the Empire, he wondered if the M'Lak might have got the whole evolution thing down pat.

'Ah, sharp implements,' Suruk said. 'Brilliant, eh?'

Perhaps not, Smith decided.

The doorbell jangled and Smith strode to the airlock with his mug in hand. A man in blue and red stood on the threshold, a cap on his head and a satchel over one shoulder.

'Captain I.D.W. Smith, Miss P.R. Carveth, Mr S.T. Slayer?' he said. 'Post for you.'

He passed Smith a wad of envelopes and departed. Smith closed the airlock and called Carveth down.

'Postman's just come,' he said. 'This one's for you. And

this is for you, Suruk,' said Smith, handing the alien a letter, 'and these are for me.' He pressed his thumb onto the security seal and the postmark turned from red to green. Smith tore it open and read the note inside. By the time he had reached the bottom, the top had started to disintegrate.

'Carveth,' he declared, dropping the letter into the galley sink, 'we're having some time off. Set a course for Paragon on Albion Prime. We're to meet W down there and have a couple of days leave. Normally, I'd be reluctant to take leave while there's aliens to fight, but we've done well.'

Smith left Suruk in the living room and joined Carveth in the cockpit. He dropped into the captain's chair just in time to see her disconnect the *Pym* from the *Edward Stobart*. The grey flank of the *Stobart* seemed to slide off the left side of the windscreen as they pulled away. Swift and unarmed, the *John Pym* split from the fleet, Carveth humming the *Blue Danube* as they flew.

Once the course was locked into the helm, Carveth looked round. 'So, what's in your other package, then?'

'I'm not sure. Perhaps it's an Airfix catalogue.' Smith pulled out a dog-eared magazine and a video. 'What's this? There's a note. . . it's from my friend Carstairs, back home:

Dear Smith, sorry to hear about your funny bird buggering off. This should keep your spirits up. Carstairs.

It must be an Airfix catalogue,' he added, lifting up the magazine. '*Red Hot Fillies*,' he read. Puzzled, he opened it up – 'Ruddy hell,' he said.

Smith glanced at the video, but too late – Carveth

snatched it and, smirking, held it up to the light. '*Emma and Verity's Super Jolly Hardcore Pimms Party*,' she read. 'Tut-tut, Boss!'

'I didn't ask for this stuff, you know,' Smith said, aware that he was turning red at the edges of his moustache. 'I don't find this at all amusing, Carveth. What did you get, anyway?'

'Oh a letter from the manufacturers, checking my warranty. And they've sent me a birthday card. Too bad the Leighton-Wakazashi translation department's seems to be on holiday.'

The card showed a happy robot under a rainbow emblazoned with the Leighton-Wakazashi logo. In sparkly letters the card read: *Birthday greetings synthetic friend – happy robotty love!*

'Nice of them to try,' Carveth said. 'The L-W offices are on one of New Albion's outer moons; they must have sent it across from there. Only three months out of date, too.'

Suruk strolled into the room. 'We are travelling to Albion Prime?' he said.

'Yep,' Carveth said.

'Good.' He folded the spare seat down and crouched on it. 'And is it a good place?'

'God yeah,' the android said. 'It's posh frock time down there. Party capital of Imperial Space. The English may take their pleasures sadly, but on Albion Prime they take them sadly and *big*. So, Suruk: I got a card, the captain got a fistful of smut – what did you get?'

'News,' Suruk said.

Smith peered through the dim light of the cockpit at his friend. The alien looked thoughtful rather than ferocious, less like a gargoyle than a crouching child. 'Is something wrong, old chap?'

'Indeed,' Suruk said. 'My father is slain.'

The airlock opened and a Ghast praetorian guard lumbered into the hall. Its antennae twitched as its tiny eyes surveyed the room.

'462,' it growled.

Thirty metres away, on the far side of the hall, was a tiny bench. Amidst the statues, speakers, screens, surveillance cameras and posters, holograms and busts of Number One, the bench looked like an afterthought.

A clock ticked. Somewhere outside, marching music played.

'462!' the praetorian roared.

The sole occupant of the bench lowered a copy of *Legions of Annihilation Weekly*, tossed it onto the table and stood up. Slowly, deliberately slowly, 462 pulled his trenchcoat tight around his meagre thorax and started across the room.

His limping steps rang across the polished marble floor. As he drew close, his sole eye squinted at the praetorian.

'*Commander* 462,' he said. 'Your insolence is noted, Praetorian. Sleeve!'

The praetorian's arm flicked out. Quick as a trap, 462 leaned forward and used the guard's sleeve to polish the tiny camera that had replaced his right eye. 'Sleeve done,' he said, and the arm was whipped away. He lurched through the airlock and it closed behind him with a biotechnological squelch.

Two more praetorians stood guard inside. They led 462

down the corridor, opened a set of double doors and ushered him into the presence of the mighty Number Eight.

It had been a normal morning for Eight. He had risen at dawn, run twelve miles, composed a violin concerto and, while still weeping at the beauty of the music, strangled a pit-bull and fed it to his ant-hound, Assault Unit One. He then sent Number One a surveillance report on Number Two and Number Two a surveillance report on Number One.

Now, however, he was sitting behind a desk. As 462 entered he stood up, all six feet nine of him, and smiled as pleasantly as a Ghast could. He was a remarkably fine specimen, the stern perfection of his features marred only by a long scar on either cheek. For a prototype, he was quite impressive.

'One moment,' he said, nodding towards a seat.

462 sat down. On the vidscreen a minion was blathering excuses. 'We will triple our efforts!' the underling pleaded, 'quadripple them!'

'You had better,' Eight said. 'My superior, Number Two, is less. . . stable than I. I need two divisions hatched and subliminally indoctrinated by next Thursday.' He flicked off the vidscreen and sat down. 'So,' he said, '462. Make yourself at home.'

There was a drinks machine in the corner. 462 leaned over and fixed himself a cup of pulped underling.

'Now,' said Eight. He opened a file on his desk and read from the top sheet. '*462 is a ruthless, vicious sociopath, willing to sacrifice his minions in the name of efficiency and entirely unencumbered by conscience, sanity or remorse.* Quite a reference.'

'Thank you,' said 462.

'I take it 157 was reluctant to part company with you, then?'

'Indeed. But then nobody enjoys being sent to the Morlock Front, especially by their own adjutant.'

'No doubt. I'm interested in having you in my legion, 462. I appreciate that you had problems on Urn, but they were vitiated by your recruitment of the Yull. Even now our degenerate, disposable allies are doing excellent work in depleting Earth's supply of ammunition.' He paused. 'You know a lot about humans, don't you? Humans took your eye, didn't they? And gave you that limp and the scars. Or perhaps I should say. . . one human in particular.'

462's scarred lip rose into a snarl. 'Isambard Smith. That Earthlander scum-pig dogs my every move! I can hardly annex anything without seeing his stupid moustache in front of me!' He shook his fist, a gesture he had picked up from Number One. 'He must be utterly destroyed!'

'Quite. If you work for me, 462, I guarantee you'll have the opportunity to dispose of him in whatever unpleasant manner you choose.'

'Truly? What must I do, mighty Eight?'

'What I have to tell you is classified. It may strike you as. . . unconventional. But I can assure you that it is in the interest of the Ghast Empire.'

462 nodded. Whatever was said, he would be taking it in carefully. If it was useful, it could further his career. If it was subversive, he could shop Eight to the authorities and it would still further his career. Sometimes the Ghast Empire was an excellent employer.

There was a large portrait of Number One behind Eight's desk. The Great One was in mid rant, arms flailing as if about to topple off a cliff. Eight stood up and turned the picture to the wall, disconnecting a listening device fastened to the back. He sat down again. 'I have important information on the human race,' he said. He pressed a button beside the desk, and the vidscreen flicked back into life. A planet appeared on it, three quarters blue and a quarter green: a fat, weak, juicy world, plump with resources, tasty with citizens.

'Earth,' said Number Eight. He pointed with one of his pincers. 'Do you recognise that land-mass there?'

462's antennae twitched. 'Europe, seat of the Franco-German Alliance.'

'And this set of islands?'

'Britain. Isambard Smith was created there in some sort of slackly-run breeding programme.'

'Correct.' Eight reclined in his biochair, and it crawled back from the desk. 'It is no surprise to me that you have found Isambard Smith such a difficult opponent. He is the culmination of two thousand years of military training and pig-headed arrogance. While we dismissed them as weaklings, the humans hid their greatest military secret under a veil of soggy mediocrity. But my superior mind has uncovered the truth – the island we dismissed as a rainy little pisshole is in fact an ancient offshore facility for the breeding and indoctrination of humanity's shock troops!'

If he had wanted a reaction, he hardly got one. 462 nodded. 'I am not surprised,' he said. 'We need more soldiers.'

'No. We need *better* soldiers.'

'Well, we could shoot some officers. That tends to encourage them. Until you run out of officers,' 462 added, recalling a nasty incident where he had nearly encouraged his troops by ordering them to make an example of himself. He had promoted a minion to lieutenant just in time. The worst of it was that it really had perked his soldiers up.

'No!' Eight slapped the desk, sending a little trophy rocking. 'Not that! I am suggesting an overhaul of the praetorian DNA structure.'

'But their DNA is perfect. They are custom-engineered for fighting humanity. There's no more DNA we could splice. . . none except the Vorl.'

Eight's mouth split open in a huge smirk. There could be no doubting his praetorian heritage; rows of teeth gleamed. 'My science-drones have been carrying out preliminary survey work at a laboratory hidden deep in Yullian territory. The pathetic drivel that makes up Yullian myth includes a number of references to the Vorl – most usefully, their location. The laboratory was destroyed a few days ago, but there is enough information to go on and I have plenty more science-drones. All we need is a little more work and it will be done.'

'How may I obey?' 462 inquired.

Eight put his fingertips together, and then his pincertips. 'You are the only ranking officer to encounter the Vorl and survive. I gather your last target – one Rhianna Mitchell – turned out to be less an all-conquering superhuman than an amateur folk-musician with a hemp fixation – but do not worry: this time, you will not be looking for an individual but an entire planet.'

'You wish me to find the home world of the Vorl?'

'Yes. All indications suggest the edge of Known Space, where our territory overlaps with that of the lemming men. Which is why you will travelling with the Yull.'

462 shuddered. 'The Yull? Those savages? But, Glorious Eight, they are idiots! The Yull are worthy of a freak show,' he added, crossing his legs around his stercorium. 'I see no reason why a Ghast officer should have anything to do with a bunch of arrogant little animals who have learned how to talk!' He ran a hand over his antennae. 'Must I lower myself to working with creatures like that again?'

'You brokered the deal with them.'

'Only so we could break it, Mighty Eight. The Yull are imbeciles and barbarians. *And* they will make my spaceship smell.'

'Your contact will be a Yull with a name to get back – one disgraced in recent combat with Earth. A Yullian officer would eat its own litter to gain status with its miserable kind.'

462 thought about it. He had no love for the lemming men: the Yull were wretched beings, continually jostling to improve their position in their worthless society. On the other hand, Eight might give him a promotion for this.

Eight said, 'Once the enemy find out our plan, they will make every effort to beat us to the Vorl. They may even send Isambard Smith against you. He has already given you facial scars and a serious limp – who knows what he may do this time?'

462 shuddered.

'Our species must be refined.' Eight struck an orator's pose, his vicious little eyes squinting into space. 'Through genetic engineering we have become the galaxy's most effective fighting force: by removing our ability to breed we have orchestrated ourselves entirely.'

462 nodded keenly. Eight seemed to be talking about music, which he regarded as human frippery, but it was important to look enthusiastic.

'Each of us is fitted for his role,' Eight continued, 'much like an instrument in the concerto I was writing shortly before you arrived. The drones are our percussion, the praetorians our horns, we commanders the wind section. But now we must move in harmony, if you will, each of us a muscle in the body politic, each of us straining his utmost to further our species' mighty movement!' He paused. 'We are the instruments of destiny, you see: I am the conductor, and you are—'

'All aboard!' 462 barked, throwing a swift salute.

Eight winced. 'Yes exactly. 462, here are your orders: you will be provided with a mixed team of Yullian warriors and modified praetorians, custom-rigged for maximum ruthlessness. You will allow nothing to stand in your way. You will hunt down the Vorl and we will make their psychic power ours. And once we have the Vorl – we shall have Earth!'

'Oh my God, Suruk, I'm so sorry,' Carveth said. 'Oh my God.'

'I'm really very sorry to hear that, old chap,' said Smith. 'He was a good sort. Did he, ah, go properly?'

'He died well,' Suruk replied. In the bad light of the

cockpit he had to peer at the letter. Smith swung the map light down on its arm and flicked it on. 'He fell fighting our old enemies, the disgraceful Yull. Forty-six foes fell to his broom, and many more leaped to their deaths rather than face his rage. He held up the Yull advance, it says, buying time for the army to prepare a counter-attack and stall their ambush.'

'Forty-six?' Carveth stared at Suruk.

The alien nodded. 'Let me see. . . *outstanding bravery*, it says.' Suruk chuckled. 'So, my father died well! I am honoured to be the spawn of so great a warrior.'

He hopped down from his seat, passed the letter to Smith and strode to the front of the cockpit. Carveth glanced at Smith, about to offer Suruk a tissue: he shook his head quickly, and she stayed still.

His mandibles parted and, smiling, Suruk pushed his nostrils against the glass. 'Out there, among the stars, Agshad dines in the halls of my ancestors. Even now my father exchanges noble stories with Aramar the Wise, and punches with Gob-Gob the Less Wise. I shall miss him, but I am proud. I wanted him to be a warrior as well as a sophisticate, and he heeded my words.' Suruk looked around. Some of the fierceness faded from his eyes. 'And yet he always wished me to be a professional: a lawyer, or a doctor perhaps.' He moved towards the door and Smith handed him the letter as he went. 'I must think,' Suruk said. . . and then he was gone.

2

Indifferent Engines

The *John Pym* dropped from high orbit into the atmosphere of Albion Prime, and smog reached out and covered it like a shroud. Carveth flew by the instruments – a risky business for all concerned – and like a fly in the smoke of a bonfire they sank towards the city. Suddenly, as if a magician had pulled a tablecloth away, the smog parted.

'Look!' Carveth cried, excited as a child.

They were above a million lights that studded the sides of towers and chimneys that rose up like spines from the back of a hedgehog. Huge statues of Imperial heroes towered over the city as if wading through a sea of houses. Towers, spires and huge cranes studded the skyline, many tall enough to disappear into the smog. Airships drifted around the *Pym*, their windows smeared by the myriad noses of legions of day-tripping citizens, all gazing in awe at the might of Paragon.

As they descended Smith made out the great civic buildings: The Imperial Planetarium, Chetworth's Domes of Sensorial Delight, The Municipal Orphan Repository, the huge bell on top of the galaxy's largest test-your-strength machine.

An airship swung down low, its propellers nearly flicking the *Pym*, and Carveth waved at the families on board until an oik gave her the finger. Order was restored when Suruk, who had slipped into the cockpit unheard, held up a skull from his room.

'Little scamps!' said Smith.

'Indeed,' Suruk growled. 'They should be devoured in a basket with chips.'

Panels slid back in the huge glass roof of the spaceship hangar, and the Pym sank into the aperture. The landing legs hit the ground and the radio crackled into life.

'Good day, ladies and gentlemen! Welcome to Paragon!'

Smith glanced at the others, then at the door. 'Well, shall we?'

They emerged into the sound of creaking metal. Above them, great mechanical arms unfolded from the wrought iron roof and slotted into the ship, scanning and refuelling it.

'It hasn't changed much,' Smith said.

Carveth glanced at him. 'You've been here before?'

'We both have,' Suruk said. 'It is much as it was, except that I was wearing a paper bag on my head last time.'

As they climbed down the uneven metal steps, a door opened in the side of one of the dock offices and a gang of gravvie engineers hurried towards the *Pym*, tools in hand. They were short and stocky, the result of high-gravity and inbreeding, and looked almost like another species as they swarmed over the ship, as though it were infested with gnomes.

A tall stick of a man paced behind the technicians like a teacher on a field trip. He wore a jacket with patches at the elbows and smoked a thin cigarette; his long face was lined and weary, as if bought second-hand. Only his thick hair and pencil moustache looked healthy, but there was a surprisingly vibrancy in his eyes, at once kindly and tough.

He coughed as he approached and stuck out a hand. 'Smith.'

'W.'

They shook and the master spy looked over Suruk and Carveth. 'I heard about your father, Mr Slayer. My condolences.'

Suruk nodded. 'I thank you. It is a comfort to know that my father died smiting the Yull.'

'Good. And well done everyone on your work against the lemmings. Now,' he added, 'Wainscott mentioned some sort of lab in his report, staffed by Ghasts. Is that right?'

'Yes,' Smith said. 'There was something down there. It didn't look like Yull stuff – it didn't smell of sawdust, either. I took this file off a dead Ghastist: it mentions the Vorl. Whatever was going on there, it was dirty alien business, that's for damned sure.'

He passed the file to W. The spy opened it and ran a bony finger down the page. 'Let's see. . . *hetuphikup* – that's a Yull word meaning the risk of error caused by excessive enthusiasm. Smith, you're right – this does seem to be about the Ghast Vorl research programme.'

'Vorl?' Carveth said. 'Aren't they those ghost things that Rhianna's mum copped – that Rhianna's descended from?'

'We thought the Ghasts had given up trying to contact

the Vorl. I need to think about this,' W said, 'over tea.' He looked troubled, more than usual. 'Take the evening off, and come and see me tomorrow. I'll be ready to discuss this then. Oh – and Smith?' he added.

'Yes?'

W fished an envelope out of his jacket. 'This may be of interest. I leave it to you what you do with it.' He turned, coughed again and strode off, the smoke from his cigarette curling out behind him. 'Carry on, everyone.'

'A night off, eh?' Smith mused, studying the towers and domes of the skyline. He slipped the envelope into his pocket. 'And the whole city to explore. So, men: who'd like pie and mash?'

'Right then,' Carveth said, spooning jellied eels into her mouth, 'Who wants to take in a show?'

They sat in a branch of Halbury's Galactic Pie Emporium, the remnants of their dinner around them like the debris of an explosion. It was half-nine and the shop was deserted apart from a young couple in fleet uniform and a wallahbot that rolled around and tried to sell them flowers.

'Hmm?' Smith had been thinking about Rhianna. How he wished she were here with him now. Well, he thought, looking at Carveth's gravy stained face whilst Suruk inflated his throat and let out another belch, not *right* now.

'A show, boss.'

Full of meat pie, Smith picked up the local newssheet and turned it over.

'*Private Parts on Parade*,' he read. '*A Revue on matters*

topical, historical and comical, to be given by Young Actresses of Prominent Talent in celebration of our recent Victory on Varanor. Followed by the renowned Major-General Choudhury speaking of his Manly Exploits up the Purdang Basin and Music from Miss Lily Tuppence, the Nightingale of Mars. That sounds promising.'

'Indeed so,' Suruk said, poking around in a polystyrene cup. 'I have several of Miss Tuppence's records. If possible, I should like to get a souvenir from her.'

'Oh?' Smith said, remembering the sort of souvenirs that grinned from Suruk's mantelpiece.

The M'Lak offered his cup around. 'Is it true that whelks are made from French people?'

'No. The whelk is actually a small, slimy invertebrate that lives underwater, whereas your Frenchman lives on land. You see–' He leaned across the table, gesturing with his little wooden fork, and W's envelope fell out into his mushy peas. Smith picked it up and broke the seal. 'Hmm.'

'What's it say?' Carveth demanded.

Smith unfolded the letter. '*Dear Smith*,' he began. '*I am writing this sub rosa, as it were: you and your people have done good work for the Service and I believe in paying back a service rendered*. That's nice,' he said.

'Is it a raise?'

'Let's see. . . *Use this information as you will. Your crew includes an alien and a girlie, so you may find it appropriate to keep this under your hat, as it were, in case they get excitable.*'

'It *is* a raise!' Carveth cried.

'Agshad Nine-Swords did not die in combat: he was murdered by a cowardly blow struck from behind.'

Suruk raised his head from his cup of whelks. 'What is this?'

'My army contact tells me that around ten a.m. orders were given by General Young herself for Third Armoured Brigade to travel to Tambridge as quickly as possible. The garrison on the other side of the Tam had been overrun. The Yull meant to cross the bridge and attack from the North. It was vital to retake the bridge or destroy it to stop the Yull getting across.

'I am informed that the raiding party were greeted by a scene of destruction: the sides of the bridge were smashed open, and there were dead Furries all over the shop. In the middle of it all was Agshad Nine-Swords. He was holding a broom and covered with wounds. The men realised that it was him who'd been holding the Yull back, and refused to detonate the bridge until he was rescued.

'The report states that on hearing the vehicles of the armoured column, Agshad looked around. At this point, a Yullian officer, previously held at bay by Agshad, leaped on him and struck him in the back.'

Smith stopped. They looked at him. He took a swig of tea.

'I am informed that the raiding party rushed the bridge, rescued Agshad and pulled back, detonating the bridge supports as they withdrew. Agshad died on the way to the brigade HQ.'

'Roses, luverly roses, get 'em 'ere!' the wallahbot called, and with a whine of servos it rolled to the next table. 'One fer two pahnd, three fer a fiver!'

'I see,' Suruk said. Smith and Carveth watched him

carefully. He raised an eyebrow-ridge. 'Proceed, Mazuran.'

Smith nodded. '*The Yull headman is called Colonel Vock. Even for one of the Furries he's known as a savage, merciless bastard. He was the ground officer at the Burning of Neustadt.*'

'And my father?' Suruk said. 'What of him?'

Smith said, '*Agshad spoke to the medic just before he died. He expressed* – Look, Suruk, I'm not sure—'

'I am.'

'Alright: . . . *he expressed the wish that his son had taken up a proper job.* Then W says I can do what I like with the information.' He tossed the letter onto the table-top. 'That's it.'

Suruk pulled a machete from his belt in a smooth hiss of steel.

Smith glanced at Carveth: she was watching the pair of them with huge, wide eyes, as if she had never seen creatures like Suruk and Smith before.

'Easy, old man,' Smith said.

'What're you going to do?' Carveth said, and she put a hand over her mouth, as if it had slipped out by mistake.

Suruk picked up his battered cod. His knife flashed: one cut opened the backbone and the second lopped off the tail. He tore it open and bit it in two. 'First, I finish my dinner,' he said. 'Then, the show begins.'

Smith was picking fluff off his red fleet jacket when Carveth knocked on the cabin door and came in. 'How do I look?'

Smith tugged at his cuffs. His jacket felt very tight across the shoulders since had sent it to be cleaned.

Admittedly, there had been a lot of alien blood to get out, but a couple more trips to the dry cleaners and it would be the size of a robin's brassiere.

Carveth had not fared much better. She wore her favourite dress, which was blue and from different angles made her look like Alice in Wonderland, a Victorian maid and some sort of nautical road cone. 'You look fine,' he said. 'Heard anything from Suruk?'

She shook her head. 'He's got the door shut and he's playing music.'

'Music? It's not Minnie Ripperton, is it?'

'Yes, actually.'

Smith grimaced. 'Not – *Les Fleurs?*'

'Yeah – how'd you know?'

'Painful experience. Look Carveth, be careful with Suruk, would you? This is a bad time for him.'

'Greetings!' Suruk said from the door.

They glanced round.

'Guilty faces, humans? Do I interrupt the bonky dance?'

'No!' they said.

Suruk stepped into the room. He wore a white dress-shirt with a high collar and a black tails jacket. 'Perhaps you should. Your floaty seer is elsewhere, Mazuran, and the miserable android Dreckitt is off doing other things. Is he still spawning with you?'

Carveth shrugged. 'It's tricky with Rick. It's all a bit touch and go.'

'You touched, he went,' Suruk said. 'So often the way. What do you make of my attire?'

'I think you should turn back into Doctor Jeckyll,' Carveth said.

'At least you humans no longer need that paper bag.' Suruk chuckled and Smith winced at the memory. In those days aliens had been rare in human territory, and Suruk had been obliged to hide his face for fear of causing women to faint. He had drawn a smiley face on the bag to reassure passers-by, but it had still attracted attention. At Cromwell Station a youth had stolen the bag, and a crowd had mistaken Suruk for a horrible monster – if that was a mistake. Smith had been forced to fight through the howling mob to reach Suruk and rescue it from him.

'Memories, eh?' Suruk said thoughtfully. 'Urchin tastes like rat.'

The doorbell sounded, jolting Suruk from his reverie.

'Wonder who that is?' Carveth said, and she stepped into the corridor. A weird sense of foreboding made her shiver. She peered at the filthy window, saw movement behind it, shrugged, spun the wheel and pulled the door open. 'I should have known,' she sighed.

Rhianna was on the doorstep. Her hair was not in dreadlocks any more: it fell around her head like a black cloud, remarkably un-lank. To Carveth's surprise she was not wearing anything tied-dyed: she had on a long, shapeless white dress, like a nightie or an elongated smock. There was some dark stuff around her eyes, which made her look a bit mad. The overall impression was of a minor romantic poet who had woken up craving laudanum, or someone confused into thinking she was an elf.

'Hi,' Rhianna said.

Carveth looked round: Smith stood behind her. 'It's Rhianna's ghost,' she explained.

'Oh,' said Smith. 'Um, hello.'

'Hey, guys.' Rhianna had a soft New Francisco accent, at once dreamy and sincere.

'Hello,' Smith replied, warily.

'Yeah, hi,' said Carveth.

'Can I come in?' Rhianna asked. 'The rain's kind of puddling in my flip-flops.'

There was a moment's pause. 'Of course,' Smith said, stepping back, and Rhianna entered in a swish of damp, voluminous cloth.

'Wow,' she said. 'Are you guys going somewhere?'

'To a show,' Carveth replied. 'Why're you here?'

'Well,' Rhianna said, slipping off her sandals, 'it's really strange. I was working last night, helping with – well, you know, research – and I had this amazing premonition that I'd find you here. And then they gave me a tube map.'

'So you had a premonition that you were going to use the tube?'

'Yes.' She looked a bit crestfallen, and added, 'But it was really spiritual.'

'Why did they send you here?' Smith asked.

Rhianna sighed and stretched, and for a moment the damp dress clung to her taut body. She stopped stretching, and she was back to normal – but that image of her lingered, seared into Smith's mind. He'd slept beside her, once.

'I don't really know,' she said. 'They said we were being briefed tomorrow?'

'Well, welcome back,' Smith said. 'We're all very happy to see you. Aren't we?'

'Oh yeah.' Carveth nodded. 'Look really close and you'll see me jump for joy.' Smith nudged her, and she added, 'Nice to see you. Your room's still as you left it. I've watered your pot plant, although a few of the leaves fell off. And got smoked.'

'Cool,' Rhianna said. 'I'll only stay here tonight, if that's ok. I didn't bring a change of clothes.'

'Never stopped you before.'

'So, what kind of show is it?'

Carveth shrugged. 'It's a variety show. Old tradition of the native indigenous tribesmen of Britain. There's dancing from other cultures, called the Can-Can, and then there's some old general talking about bringing culture to the spiritual alien folk.'

'That sounds fascinating,' Rhianna said. 'Will there be poetry?'

'Does *Roll out the Barrel* count?'

In the dark of the auditorium, Smith felt alone. They sat in a box, looking across the tatty magnificence of the red and gilt hall to the stage and its faded curtains. The hall seemed to exude friendliness, as if its air was thicker and softer than outside.

The show opened with mechanical cherubs descending from the roof and playing a fanfare. Then Lily Tuppence came on and praised the soldiers of the 112th Army for their victory over the lemming men. Once the cheering had died down she sang a song about moonlight, accompanied by holographic birds.

Smith could imagine Rhianna singing to holographic birds, although probably as a result of self-medication, and hopefully not in front of anyone he knew.

The main act came on: two sprightly young women in army jackets who sang witty songs. They were both pretty, and started off with a routine about a novice soldier learning army ways. They were joined by a man with a large, extrovert moustache, and all three broke into song:

'I couldn't get my pole to stand, so I asked a lady friend
And she worked it back and forward until it was up on
end
I asked her 'What's your secret?' and this was her reply,
'You've got to get the flagpole standing if you want the
flag to fly!'

Smith glanced to his right. Rhianna was at the end of the row, legs crossed, watching the performance with intense, scholarly interest. In the dim light of the auditorium she looked almost luminous. Her skirt had ridden up, showing an interesting expanse of ankle and calf. That looked delightful, thought Smith, and immediately there came the stinging knowledge that her delights were no longer his.

The flagpole song reached its climax, and one of the girls sat on the man's lap and jumped back up, to cheers from the audience. They looked like a fine pair, those girls, thought Smith, no doubt up for a bit of manly hi-jinks. He took out his rifle-sight, which he'd brought to get a good view of the stage. He looked left a bit, toward the audience – and a man stared right back.

He was in a box nearer the exit: a tall man in black, with heavy eyebrows and the sort of moustache favoured by villains in silent films. He was holding opera glasses and as soon as Smith saw him he slipped them into his jacket and Smith spotted a flash of steel under his left arm.

A gun. This armed man had been watching them. For a moment Smith thought of telling the others, of clearing the hall, perhaps, and realised what chaos that would cause. No: he'd have to take this fellow alone. The man stood up, realising he'd been seen, and Smith turned to slip out of the box into the corridor.

'And now before the interval, Ladies and Gentlemen, be upstanding for *Land of Hope and Glory*,' a voice cried from the stage.

As one the audience stood. The armed man froze, his escape blocked by standing bodies. Smith froze too, torn between the need to pursue this villain and the duty to sing the Imperial anthem. Music started, and Smith shuffled sideways as he sang, past a baffled Carveth, into the aisle and back towards the doors. The man in the box was doing likewise, as if reeled out on a fishing line.

'Maketheemightieryet!' Smith garbled, and he turned and rushed out of the hall, into the sudden light of the corridor. A dark figure scurried down the steps and out of view. Smith bounded down the stairs after him and burst into the foyer.

'You!' he demanded, turning to the nearest wallahbot. 'Did you see a man come through here?'

'Ices?' it replied, and behind it the front door swung closed. Smith cursed, crossed to the telephone on the wall and dialled up the number for W. He left a message and trudged up to the bar. He'd lost his prey.

Five hours later, Carveth opened the door, tripped on the

lintel and stumbled inside. A light blinked into life above her head, and she opened her arms and greeted the ship with a verse from *Do I Have To Get My Bits Out to Take the Turing Test?*

'Goodness,' Rhianna said behind her. 'I never knew British culture was so. . . vibrant.'

'I'm drunk,' Carveth said. 'I need another drink.' She stumbled off down the corridor as if on a listing boat. Smith closed the door and watched Rhianna stroll towards the lounge.

Smith did not know what you said to a girl who'd slept with you and then left. He had a strong suspicion that one was supposed to say nothing, and with that came the grim, sad certainty that whatever he said would be wrong. He entered the living room and made himself busy by putting the kettle on.

'It's very sad about those indigenous people,' Rhianna said from the doorway. 'Evicted from their homeland, forced to dress up like that. . . did the British annex the Pearly King's home planet?'

Suruk loomed up behind her. 'That was interesting,' he said. 'I got Lily Tuppence's autograph, and she got to keep her skull.' His mouth unfolded and he yawned. 'Now, I must retire, or else I shall be all weary and enraged in the morning. Sleep well, puny humans.'

'Me too,' Rhianna said. 'I need to meditate. Blessed be, everyone.'

Carveth watched them disappear into their rooms. She closed the sitting room door behind Rhianna. 'Blethed be,' she said in a falsetto, adopting the expression of a bad statue of the Virgin Mary. 'If that woman gets any more on my tits she'll start to graze my chin.'

'Really?' Smith felt a sudden burst of liking for Carveth. It was good of her to stick up for him: good of her to take his point of view, to see that Rhianna was lucky to be let back on board after dumping him.

'Of course,' she said. 'Getting all sniffy just because I sold her grass. Oh, and she let you down. You ought to get yourself someone better.'

'Maybe,' Smith said. 'But where?' He sat down on one of the dining chairs, feeling saggy and old. 'I hate to say it, but I could do without Rhianna being here right now.'

'I know,' Carveth said, removing the ship's Malibu from the drinks cabinet, 'The space ship just got a little more spaced.' Frowning, she filled a glass. 'Come on, boss, perk up. Just because she took your pocket battleship on its maiden voyage doesn't make her the only woman in the world. With a smart uniform like that you're sure to find some strumpets.' She took a swig. 'Suruk's on the warpath.'

'Less of a path than a motorway,' Smith said. 'He'll be civil enough – probably stay quite quiet, to be honest – but God help the lemming that gets in his way. How's Dreckitt these days?' he added, weary and keen to change the subject.

'Me and Rick?' Carveth took a huge breath and sighed heavily. 'Well, I don't know. We met, we loved, and we passed, like two really dirty ships in the night. But the funny thing is, I miss him. I mean, I'm programmed to be promiscuous, and yet... Relationships aren't easy, even when you are. Malibu, boss?'

In his room Suruk crouched on his stool in

61

near-darkness, the dim light glowing on the polished skulls of his enemies. He was alone with the spirits.

The House of Urgar is few now, oh ancestors, he thought. Our once-mighty clan has been thinned by war, feud, battle and, in the case of several of its more irritating members, me. I have seen many of my clan die. Helped, on occasion. Now, we are but two: Suruk the Slayer and Morgar the Trendy Architect. One of us must avenge you, my Father, and it will not be the one with the set square.

I disappointed you, Father. I did not become what you hoped. I grew to be a warrior, but you wanted a doctor, or a lawyer or something. I brought honour to our house, when you wanted cheap legal advice and perhaps some stolen medicine.

Suruk snarled. Agshad had been murdered in cold blood. That sort of underhanded viciousness could only be expected from the Yull. Yes, he would have to find this Colonel Vock and settle the score with him in some appropriate manner. Death was too good: rolling Vock in the litter tray would be a step in the right direction. He would think of something suitable. And then, once the Colonel was destroyed forever and the blood of the Yull ran like water, he might even enrol at law school.

The next morning, a man came to collect them with a password and a car. He was a small, nondescript creature, and had he not been in the doorway it would have been easy to forget that he was there.

He stood in the airlock and declared, 'My aubergine is prickly.'

Smith consulted a scrap of paper glued to the underside

of his chair. 'Birds fly south in the winter,' he replied.

'The car's outside,' said the man. 'I'll have my people watch your ship.'

Paragon was coming to life. The roads were full of cars and autocabs: little trains crawled between great buildings on rails like stitches across the sky. A thousand chimney-stacks were belching smoke as they drove by.

'Magnificent,' Smith said.

As they rounded the corner, a row of warbots strode past, all racing green and polished brass, dwarfing the cheering citizens around them. 'Siege units,' the driver grunted. 'Heading to the spaceport. Grand things.'

'Worthy enemies,' Suruk said, his tusks bumping gently against the window. Ponderous and vast, the Empire was going to war.

The car drew up in front of the Great Museum. It was the size of a cathedral, studded with pterodactyls instead of gargoyles. The statue of a bearded man stood over the entrance, gazing across the mighty city from the fortress of learning: it could have been Darwin or God, Smith thought, or perhaps W.G. Grace.

Their guide flipped a switch and the car doors opened. 'Go on in,' he said. 'Your contact's waiting in the reading rooms.'

The museum was cavernous: its entrance hall could have housed a battleship. They bought tickets and ices from a bored man in a box like an oversized Punch-and-Judy stall, and strolled through the vast hall, licking their ice creams.

The reading rooms were at the rear of the building: to reach them, they had to pass through British Natural

History, British Military History, British Social History, and Abroad. Natural History was full of dinosaur skeletons – some of the biggest dinosaurs came from Woking, Smith was pleased to note – and led up to a mural carved into the wall six times man-height. It showed an ancient warship ramming an Aresian death-walker on one side of the doors, and on the other, great figures of history being told about the Empire by a Common Man.

The historical section showed how great citizens had helped lead humanity forward. Here was a section on Henry V and his peasant archers, there Cromwell and Disraeli.

'I don't know about all these exhibits,' Rhianna said. 'All history seems to be about Britain.' She peered through the glass at a robotic model of Francis Drake, busy playing bowls against other robots. 'I don't think it's right somehow.'

At her side, Suruk nodded. 'I agree. They should let him out for food.'

'That's not what I meant, Suruk. It's not the real Francis Drake.'

Suruk looked shocked. 'Do his captors know?' He pointed. 'Look, Mazuran!'

The alien stepped over to a large glass case, and as one they gazed upon the portly, striped-suited man inside. He stood behind a desk, a map of Europe spread before him, his face a mask of determination, a cigar jammed between his teeth.

'The greatest warlord of the First Empire,' Suruk said, awed. 'The mighty Alfred Hitchcock.'

'I think you'll find that's Churchill, actually,' Smith said.

Suruk nodded. 'He looks rather fat to have fought in so many different places,' he said. 'Did they carry him from the beaches to the landing grounds?'

Smith glanced at Suruk, annoyed. The alien was spoiling the atmosphere: the presence of such noble history, along with Rhianna in that white dress, was making him feel rather keen. He felt like blasting hell out of a bunch of filthy Ghasts, then getting Rhianna to dress up as one of the Bronte sisters and giving her a damned good—

Someone coughed, and he looked round and returned to reality. Rhianna wasn't his, there were no Gertie within range, and a tall, thin man with a teacup in one hand was smiling at him. 'Ah, Smith,' W said. 'Come to look at the exhibits?' He stepped forward and shook hands with them. 'Rather pleasant here, for a city. Come along. We've got a lot to do.'

They followed him through the last hall to the reading rooms. Statues of great authors lined the way: Shakespeare, Milton, W.E. Johns. They passed through the main reading room, past shelves and computer screens displaying images of shelves, to a small door at the back marked 'Warning: raw sewage – danger of drowning'. 'Helps put people off,' W explained, and he opened the door.

He ushered them into a cupboard. There was a coat hanging from a peg in the wall: W pushed it aside to reveal a lens. He put his eye against the lens and the room shuddered and sank into the ground.

The spy turned to face them, which was difficult in such a small room. 'What you are about to see is absolutely secret,' he rasped. 'You must never, ever, tell anyone about this. Were information to be leaked about this facility we would have to kill you. I can't even tell you why it would be necessary to kill you, but even if I did tell you why it was necessary to kill you it would then be necessary to kill you just because I had told you it was necessary. So keep it under your hat, alright?'

'Righto,' said Smith.

The lift hit the bottom with a rough clang. W nodded, and Smith pulled back the mesh door and they stepped into a dark industrial corridor. The air smelt of grease and burning. Something whirred and hummed behind the walls.

There were windows leading off the corridor, and as they passed them, Smith caught glimpses of the rooms behind. One showed a plush little study: in a leather chair sat a suited man, his head swathed in bandages. In the next, two scientists were connecting sensors to a wardrobe.

As they reached the end of the corridor there came an odd rushing, roaring sound, and a shimmering white balloon bigger than a man rolled past, chased by three scientists. 'Heel!' one of them called, but the thing rolled on, and they were lost to view.

'Up here,' said W. He opened a door and led them into a cluttered office. A full-length picture of the king and queen with their pet lion hung behind a messy desk, at which sat a fat man doing a crossword. As they entered he stood up and put out a podgy hand.

'Good to see you!' he said. 'Very glad you could make it, gentlemen.' He wore a dark coat and striped trousers, like an undertaker. 'Please, do take seats. Not that one,' he added, indicating a curious armchair on the far side of the room, festooned with dials and quartz rods.

W sat down and folded his arms and legs as if he were made of hinges. 'This is Isambard Smith and his crew: Polly Carveth; Suruk the Slayer; and this is Rhianna Mitchell, of whom I'm sure you'll know much already.'

'Hello all,' the fat man said. 'Gary Sheldon, pleased to meet you. I'm head cogitator here, which means that I run the Empire's department of Psycho-futuro-neuro-history.'

Smith and his crew exchanged glances.

'It's the science of telling people what they've just done just before they're about to go and do it, enabling us to predict what large numbers of foreigners will do at the whim of their tyrannical masters. Here, we use all manner of science and trickery to stay one step ahead of Gertie Ghast and predict his every black and sordid deed, enabling our plucky chaps to confound the ant-man's crooked schemes before they even come to pass. We also deal with telephone queries.'

'Look,' said Smith, 'that's all very well, but what's this all about, eh? If I'm going to help you, I could do with this business being a little less cloak-and-dagger. You could tell us what's going on.'

'Unless you have to kill us afterwards,' Carveth said.

'Feel free to try,' Suruk added helpfully.

W exchanged a look with Sheldon. 'Gentlemen, we have uncovered perhaps the most serious threat to the human race since the beginning of this war. The file you recovered during Operation Bargepole proves what we've suspected for some time – that the Ghast Empire intends to make its soldiers invincible.'

Smith shrugged. 'They said that about Urn. The only Ghast that got to stay on Urn was the one we used as a hatstand.'

'True,' W said. 'But they have been planning something different – something especially evil.'

'Really?'

'Oh yes. The file you found lists a number of experimental procedures for splicing non-Ghast DNA into the dirty double-helix of our enemies. The Ghasts mean to cross their own troopers with the Vorl.' His dark eyes flicked from face to face. 'The Vorl are undoubtedly deadly opponents, if somewhat secretive. The only contact with the Vorl we know of tends to end in people having their heads popped by psychic force. A crossbreed would have the mental powers and gaseous form of a Vorl and the ruthless lust for power of a Ghast. Such a creature would be almost impossible to defeat.'

'Then we must stop them,' Smith said.

'Absolutely. But that will be no easy task: the Ghasts have their best ants working on it. The last time they tried to kidnap Miss Mitchell: this time they mean to use a pure Vorl. We know the Vorl can interbreed with other races, Miss Mitchell here is an example.'

'Hi,' Rhianna said.

'She has the human form of her mother, and some of the powers of her Vorlian father. This file suggests that the Ghasts intend something similar – but as the culmination of precise gene-splicing, rather than the result of a pot-addled shag. The papers you captured suggest that the Ghasts have all the machinery they need to carry out the genetic manipulation. All they need is a Vorl – and it is vital that we get to the Vorl and warn them before the Ghasts can carry out their evil plan.'

'Then we know what we must do!' Smith exclaimed. 'This vile scheme must be stopped. The safety of Britain and therefore the entire human race rests on thwarting this alien plot. With me, crew!' he cried, leaping to his feet. 'Let's load up the ship, fly out to wherever the Vorl are, get them on board, go and find Gertie and kick the floor with him and wipe his arse!' There was a moment's pause. He looked around the room. 'That sort of thing,' he said, sitting back down.

Carveth raised a hand. 'Um, not wanting to fart in anyone's lunchbox here, but where *are* the Vorl, exactly?'

The two spies exchanged another look.

'Thomas and Alan?' said Sheldon.

W nodded.

The cogitator stood up from the desk, reached to the painting of the King and Queen and pulled the side. It swung open like a door. 'Please,' he said, gesturing for them to go through.

W stood up. 'That's the problem,' he said. 'We can't figure out where the Vorl are. But we can ask someone who can.'

It was as though they had stepped into the workings of a gigantic clock. They were in a hall thirty yards wide, the ceiling impossibly high. Vast cogs with teeth the size of doors broke the floor, rotating slowly. The walls were Racing Green, the machinery polished brass. The air was full of the whirr and clank of distant belts, the stink of oil and the rattle of paper spooling from slots mounted in the wall. Above them, electricity crackled and pulsed.

Goggled engineers hurried between banks of levers and dials, white coats flapping. 'Ruddy 'ell, Barry!' one woman called. 'Gearing's all out on t'mechanical brain!'

'What *is* this?' Carveth whispered.

'Miss,' Sheldon replied, 'this is science.'

A great chain clattered down from the distant roof and deposited a tray of bacon sandwiches on the ground. The workers snatched at them, munching as they studied the machinery, racked levers back and forth and shouted into pneumatic speaking-tubes.

Sheldon checked his pocket watch. 'Prepare to consult!' he yelled into a tube, and the workers became frantic, throwing switches, tuning knobs, flicking fingers against dials. Pistons hammered back and forth, fans whirled, the whole room shuddered.

With a grinding roar two colossal doors swung open at the far end of the room. Steam blasted from vents. Two great machines rumbled into the chamber on rails set into the floor. They were bigger than juggernauts, armoured in black steel, shaped like loaves of bread. Sheldon turned to his audience.

'Gentlemen, you are about to witness the brain of the Imperial war machine: Psycho-futuro-neuro-history at its finest. If Gertie comes up with a scheme, we have a scheme and a wheeze to stop him.'

The armour slid back from the front of the machines. Behind it they saw gears, spinning wheels and hammering pistons of brass and, in the centre of each machine where the face of a clock would be, a human face with eyes and mouth, a great grey smiling disc.

'Ladies and gentlemen!' Sheldon cried. 'I give you the finest computer in the galaxy – Thomas, the Difference Engine!'

'Hello, fat cogitator,' Thomas the Difference Engine said.

'And Alan, the Analytical Engine!'

'Hello,' said Alan the Analytical Engine.

'Hello,' said Smith and the others.

'Hello, Space Captain Smith,' the computers said. 'How are you?'

Smith realised that he was addressing the finest minds in the known universe. 'Not bad,' he said. 'And you?'

'Mustn't grumble,' Alan said.

'Pretty good, thanks,' Thomas said.

It went quiet.

'We need to find an alien race known as the Vorl,' Smith announced. 'They are semi-gaseous, psychic beings of immense power. The Ghast Empire wants to harness their strength for the evil end of galactic domination. The British Empire needs to harness their strength for the good end of civilising the galaxy.'

Thomas' eyes moved left, then right, like those of a haunted picture. 'Gosh, that's difficult,' he said. 'The Vorl are extremely elusive. Almost no confirmed sightings exist: everything known is through secondary evidence.'

'Having had a shufty at the papers,' Alan put in, 'your best bet is to track former human attempts to contact them. There are legends, of course, stories that the Vorl have made contact with secret societies, but. . . well, they're nonsense, really.'

'Go on,' Smith said.

The eyes of both engines swung towards each other. 'Well, you asked for it,' Thomas said, and he simulated taking a deep breath. 'The Vorl are rumoured to have made contact with a medieval guild of brewers called the Holy Legion of Hospitable Tipplers. In 1320 on the out-skirts of York, they reported mass visions of a ghostly being that struck them with terrible head pains and vomiting, shortly after the three-day feast of Saint Armand. The Tipplers passed the secret of alien contact down through the ages in mystic ceremonies involving Morris dancing, and are rumoured to have included Pitt the Younger, Buddy Holly and the Montgolfier brothers among their number, although that may just be hot air. It is thought that the handkerchiefs of modern Morris dancers symbolise the wafting bodies of the Vorl.'

'What utter toss!' Carveth exclaimed, and she clamped a hand over her mouth. 'Sorry, I meant to think that, not say it. But I mean, that's daft. Next thing you'll say they built the pyramids.'

'Actually, they didn't,' Alan replied. 'The Egyptians did that, then someone's alien ancestors forged poor-quality evidence of themselves building the pyramids, for a laugh. Not naming any names, Suruk the Slayer.'

Suruk chuckled. 'Indeed.'

'I remember when they discovered it,' Smith said. 'The greatest hoax since the Nazca Indians faked Erik von Danniken.'

Carveth looked at the others. 'Not convinced,' she said.

'There is one more thing,' W said. 'I never realised what this meant before, but. . . well, we keep records on the larger corporations, in case they turn against the interests of the Empire. It didn't seem like much at the time, but Lloyd Leighton, the co-founder of Leighton-Wakazashi – was a Morris dancer. Oh, and he also spent billions looking for the Vorl so he could turn them into a bioweapon.'

'Wait a moment!' cried Smith, clicking his fingers. 'The documents in that Ghast lab had a symbol on the top – Leighton-Wakazashi's headed paper!'

W nodded. 'There is possibly a link between Leighton-Wakazashi and the Vorl – and when I say *possibly*, I mean *definitely*. It is up to you to find out what it is. We will have to infiltrate the company, discover their plans and find out what they know about the Hospitable Tipplers and the Vorl. And when I say *we*, I mean *you*.'

'Infiltrate Leighton-Wakazashi?' Carveth said. 'How? They have some of the smartest people in the galaxy working for them. No offence or anything, but the only one of us with any sort of university qualification has a degree in Creative Dance.'

'Interpretative Dance,' Rhianna said.

'Right. So if none of us can work there, we're stuffed, right?'

Smith had been thinking, slowly rubbing his chin. 'Not exactly,' he replied. 'Even if none of us can be workers, there's one of us who can be a product, isn't there?'

Slowly they turned to look at Carveth, like the turrets of a dreadnought lining up to civilise a hostile spaceport. She sighed, well aware that there was no getting out of this. 'For the record,' she said, 'Bugger.'

'You make the tea,' Carveth said. 'I'll be in the cockpit having a sulk.'

Smith was just stirring the pot when she called down the corridor.

'Boss! Come and have a look at this!'

He put down the spoon and hurried to the front of the ship. Suruk slipped out of his room and joined him. 'Listen,' Carveth said, toggling the radio.

'You have – one – saved message,' the data recorder said, 'left – today – at ten thirty-six a.m., Greenwich Standard Galactic time. Message is as follows.'

The voice was cultivated and hard, infused with a sneer. 'So, the great Captain Smith, eh? No doubt you're feeling very chipper after your little soiree at the theatre last night. Well, the hand of the Ghast Empire reaches even to this pint-sized paradise! We, the Legion of Ghastists, have captured a certain lady of the stage, and I can assure you that if you and Miss Rhianna Mitchell are not at the Municipal Freight Depot at midnight tonight, the next train she takes will have a permanent sleeper car! And bring none of your freakish allies. It'll take more than your pet monkey-frog to get you out of this!'

The radio went dead. 'Scum!' Suruk growled. 'How dare he call Carveth a monkey-frog? Only I may do that!'

'Um. . . do we know this guy?' Rhianna said.

'Know him?' Smith replied. 'Not personally, but I know his type well enough. . . a Ghastist: a traitor not just to mankind but to the British Space Empire, a person willing to kiss the stercorium of Number One in exchange for the chance to bully his fellow man. The Ghasts are filthy enough, but a man who'd willingly do their dirty work is beyond despicable. I'd gladly shoot the bugger myself – but he has a woman captive and we must rescue her. *Then* we can fix him, good and proper.'

'Call me a cynic, but does this look like an obvious trap?' Carveth said.

Smith opened the weapons locker and took out his Civiliser. 'It may be, but ask yourself this: can we leave a woman to die at the hands of Ghastist thugs?'

'Maybe?' Carveth said. 'Just a thought.'

Smith passed her a pistol. 'Let's go.'

It was raining heavily. Rhianna put her umbrella up. Behind them, the city smoked and steamed.

Carveth looked up at the gates. 'Well, I'll stay here then, shall I? You might need a rear guard.'

'And I shall wait with you, Piglet,' Suruk said. 'To make sure the rear guard does something other than guarding its rear. Ten minutes and I will advance from the road. I shall be taking heads.'

Smith and Rhianna passed under open gates, into a compound. The automated station stretched away from them, its greenhouse roof disappearing down the tracks. The night turned its windows black, winking like polished steel where the moonlight caught them.

'Well,' Smith said, 'we have to go inside.' He looked at Rhianna and felt tenderness towards her, which irritated him. 'Be careful,' he said.

'Okay,' Rhianna said, and Smith opened the door and they walked in.

The roof was made of glass panels: the moon caught the frame and threw slanting bars across the floor. They stood on the platform, in the pitch dark just outside the moonlight. Wallahbots rested against the walls. In daylight they would load pallets onto the trains, their boilers and cogs polished and gleaming – now they looked thuggish and hunched.

A locomotive waited at the platform. It was only the engine, but even that was huge: three times man-height, its funnel the size of a castle tower, a monocorn-catcher jutting chin-like from the front. It looked like the helmet of a gigantic knight.

Rhianna ran to the edge of the platform, skirt flapping, and pointed. On the tracks in front of the train was a figure, unconscious and bound.

'Look!' she gasped. 'There's a woman tied to the train tracks! That's terrible – oppressive gender stereotyping at its worst!'

'It's Lily Tuppence, the Nightingale of Mars!' said Smith, and a light flicked on before them.

There was a bridge across the train line, and on it stood a man in black. His hair was harshly parted and gelled down flat: he had a hard jaw and a devious moustache. It was the man from the music hall.

'Ah, Captain Smith!' he cried, and he flung out his arms as if about to introduce a show. He turned to Rhianna. 'And our new ally, the lovely lady.'

'She's not your ally and she's not lovely!' Smith barked back, immediately regretting it.

The man laughed. 'I am Egbert Tench, supreme leader of the League of Ghastists and future Dictator of Earth.'

'You'll let that woman go, or there'll be trouble,' Smith said.

Tench tutted and raised his hand: he held a small metal box. 'I have only to press this button and the engine springs to life. Of course, I'd rather not see blood spilled. I happen to be vegetarian, you know. All the best dictators are.'

Rhianna was glaring at Tench, quietly boiling with righteous fury. As Smith was opened his mouth to reply, she called out, 'Vegetarian? I'm a vegan and I love nature, so up yours, buddy!' She raised a finger at Tench.

'Rhianna!' Smith exclaimed, a little shocked. 'I'll deal with this: now shush–'

'Don't you shush me, Isambard! I will not be silenced—'

'No! Look around.'

Rhianna glanced left and right. Men had crept out: stubble-haired thugs with beer bellies and braces, with faces like uncooked pastry draped over knobbly meat. They held crowbars and rounders bats. A tall hard-faced woman in shiny black gear struggled to hold a bull-terrier on a length of chain.

'Now then,' Tench began, clearing his throat, 'No doubt you are wondering what I want. I shall tell you! I want only to help the British people. For too long aliens have been taking what's ours by right. Do you know, eighty percent of low-paid menial jobs have been stolen from us by colonials? Aliens have robbed the British people of almost all work in the sewer industry! It's time for a change, time to throw off the shackles of democracy and frolic joyfully in the sunlit pastures of an unceasing, brutal dictatorship. It is time that the British people learned to stand up, to speak for themselves, to have their own say, which is why I've been given an important message by the Ghasts for you.'

'Look, Tench,' Smith replied, 'I've heard enough of your Gertie-talk. You said you have a message. What is it?'

'Ah yes. Here we are.' The Ghastist waved his hand and a light flickered in the roof. Smith glanced up and saw a holographic lantern mounted there.

The word 'Pantechnical' appeared about a metre from the ground. It played a little tune. 'It's just warming up,' Tench said. 'It does that.'

The image faded and a ghost appeared in front of them.

They could see the wall through the shimmering apparition, but its outline was clear: a huge red insect in a black trenchcoat, like an ant rearing up. The neck was scrawny, the head bulbous and heavy-brained, marrow shaped. Antennae protruded from holes in the helmet: under the brim was a scarred, narrow face. One of its eyes was a lens.

'We meet again,' said 462. He took a step forwards: his arms were behind his back, all four of them, the manipulating limbs and the great mantis-claws that rose from his back like broken wings. But Smith was used to that. What surprised him was the creature's lurching gait, dragging the right leg behind him.

'It is a pity we met so briefly on Urn,' said the Ghast. His mechanical eye glinted as he smiled. 'We had so little time to talk before you so brusquely knocked me off that Martian war machine. So little time for us to discuss the small matter of my missing eye.

'Were I more expendable, I would have been pulped for my injuries and fed to the praetorians by now. However, I have become a commander of stature. I have, shall we say, considerable weight behind me these days.'

'That'll be your big red arse,' said Smith. 'I believe we've discussed this before.'

'Yes, yes, have your little English joke. I think we have conversed on my stercorium for the last time, Captain Smith. I do not think you will make so many jokes when we next meet, when you will sorely regret making me limp!'

'I made you permanently limp?'

'You certainly di—' The Ghast's small, yellow eye narrowed. 'Oh, how amusing. You think to use my limpness to make some wordplay about puny human reproductive organs, eh? No, I do not think I will give you the pleasure of making a play on my genitals. Thanks to you I now suffer from uncontrollable stiffness in my lower regions. But enough! In time you will pay, Smith. And besides, it is not you I am here to speak with. You are too far gone to be reasoned with.

'You, Rhianna Mitchell! Yes, you. The British Government seeks to use you as a tool for its warmongering. You could be so much more than that. You know, as I do, that your powers are too great a gift to squander on these weaklings. You know, as I do, that direct action is the only way to change the galaxy! Join us, and I will give you the power to set the world to rights! With the Ghast Empire by your side, you can force the galaxy to accept peace and love, marching at the head of an indestructible legion of storm-hippies! Your enemies will be crushed under your plastic sandal! With us, you would no longer be a child of the Earth, but its queen!'

'That's not true,' Rhianna said. 'Gaia created us all equ—'

'Oh no.' 462 shook his head. 'I think not. You know what a lie that is. Look deep inside yourself. Tell me, all the times that you've tutted at people who read tabloids, shaken your head sadly at those who eat steaks rare, lifted your nose at people who prefer electric guitars to acoustic ones – did you really think you were created equal then?'

'I don't know,' said Rhianna. 'You represent a vicious tyranny – but then Dylan did totally sell out when he went electric. . .'

'And you get a trenchcoat,' 462 added.

'No. It's wrong.' Rhianna shook her head as if to clear it. 'It's wrong. I don't wear leather.'

'She's her own woman and she's not interested!' Smith snapped.

'Think about it.' The projection shrugged and turned. 'Tench? Remove these idiots!'

It vanished, and for a moment there was an awkward silence.

'Well? Get 'em!' Tench yelled, and his men ran in, cursing and bellowing. Smith drew his gun and let a shot off at Tench, who was prodding the controls to activate the train, then ducked as a thug tried to break his head with a crowbar. Rhianna jumped down and started to untie the woman on the tracks. Tench ran over the bridge, towards the doors. Smith shot the man with the crowbar and drew his sword.

Glass shattered above – a skylight hung down like a broken jaw – and Suruk dropped onto the platform, cuffed Tench across the head and flung himself onto a Ghastist armed with a rounders bat.

Lights boomed into life along the train. Tench

scrambled upright, holding a Stanford gun. 'Good God!' Smith cried, seeing the would-be Dictator of Earth about to spray them. Rhianna took a deep breath and closed her eyes, exhaled and made a humming sound. Bullets tore the air but none of them found their mark. Suruk's spear flashed, there was a howl of pain and blood sprayed the wall.

Blue light pulsed into the station and a great metal figure clanked onto the platform, steam pouring from chimneys on its back. A lamp spun on its armoured head.

'Dead or alive, you're all nicked, sunshine!' it declared, and it pulled a truncheon out of a compartment in its leg and piled into the fight.

'Eat lead, copperbot!' Tench yelled, loosing half a dozen shells into the front of the thing, and in a flurry of sparks the machine lumbered forward and bashed the gun from his hand.

And then, suddenly, that was that. A body fell in the corner and Suruk stood up, looking quietly satisfied. One of the thugs dropped a cleaver and raised his hands.

The police robot chuffed towards the doors, pushing a handcuffed Tench before it. 'Evening all,' it intoned. 'Move along now.' At the bottom of the stairs it turned to Smith. 'I need you all to come down to the station, sir. Suspicion of assault.'

'Gladly,' said Smith. 'That man's a bloody traitor.'

'I was referring to you, sir.'

'Me?' Smith demanded. He was still panting. 'These are dangerous criminals!'

'You can tell me at the station,' the robot said in a weary monotone. 'If you would, sir. And the Morlock.'

'Well, there's a surprise,' Rhianna said, jabbing the machine's chestplate with her finger. 'The police oppressing an alien minority. What're you going to get him on, suspicion of being green?'

'Actually, madam,' the robot replied, 'possession of three severed heads and a Ghurka knife.'

'Why don't you arrest some real criminals, fuzz?'

Smith grimaced. 'Rhianna, please. This isn't helping.'

'I deny everything,' Suruk added. 'I was not here.'

Rhianna scowled as the police robot handcuffed the surviving thugs. 'I smell mechanical bacon,' she said, too loudly for Smith's tastes.

The automatic PC turned on the spot. 'That's enough, madam.' With a soft whine, it puffed out its chestplate. 'I ham arresting you on suspicion of conspiracy to commit a disorderly act with this here gentleman in the red jacket.'

If only, Smith thought.

'Let us be having you,' the robot said, and nodded at the police car outside.

It took three hours to get released. Smith called Carveth, who by then had given up and returned to the ship, from which she anxiously called up W. W promptly visited the station and told the duty officer that he was a secret agent. 'Secret agent are we, sir?' the duty officer said. W informed him that the liberty of the crew was vital to the safety of the human race. 'Human race is it, sir?' the duty officer retorted, raising one tired eyebrow. W inquired whether the officer was always a sarcastic bastard, and the officer got no further than 'Sarcastic bastard, am I–' when W hurdled the counter and ran into the superintendent's office. Here he received a more friendly reception, as well as a ten pound fine for hurdling the counter.

Outside the station, Smith turned to Carveth. 'Was it you that called the police?'

'Ah, no,' Suruk said. 'I called them. Well, not so much 'called' as 'was pursued by'. I required the toilet while you were in there, so I found a blue cubicle by the roadside. I was just coughing up a pellet in there – surprisingly roomy – when some fool in a long scarf telephoned the police. I thought that I might as well lead them to the battle, for entertainment. Perhaps I should have told them on which side to fight.'

Carveth scowled at the traffic. 'Let's just go. Were it not for Dickhead of Dock Green back there, we'd be in space by now.'

The spaceport was very busy, so the *John Pym* joined an orderly queue and the crew drank overpriced tea in the lounge as they waited for their number to be called.

Around them, shuttles and gunships rose from their landing pads like angered wasps, heading back into orbit to re-equip the Empire's ironclads. The 15th Fleet would be on its way soon, pressing deeper into Yullian space, breaking up the Greater Galactic Happiness, Friendship and Co-operation Collective one vicious planet at a time.

At the landing pad, W beckoned Smith back. The two men watched the others enter the *John Pym*, heard the engines stutter and fire up. W's thick hair rippled in the air as the ship purged its vents.

'This is a race against the Ghasts,' W said, lighting a cigarette. 'The first one to find the Vorl wins – perhaps the whole galaxy.' He held out a battered leather satchel. 'Here, take this: it's got information on Leighton-Wakazashi. Our man inside can brief your android once she's in place. Let me know if the company has any information on the Vorl.'

'Will do. What'll happen about Tench and his men?'

'I'm sure we've seen the last of him. If I'm not mistaken, the boys in blue will have given him a damn good cautioning by now.' He glanced up at the *Pym*, from which steam had started to pour. 'Be careful out there. We're up against it, Smith.'

'I know. 462 tried to persuade Rhianna to join him.'

'I thought he might.' The spy frowned, another line in the network of creases that constituted his face. 'Watch her, Smith. I know there's history there, but you must make sure they don't capture her. Should they get hold of her—'

'I'll do everything I can to take her back. Don't worry.'

'Good fellow. I know it seems unlikely, but she matters a lot to my organisation. Personally, I've always thought of her as a sandal-wearing, fruit-juice-swilling, tree-pestering nuisance, but each to their own, eh?'

'Quite,' said Smith.

W coughed. 'Good luck, Smith.'

'Thanks.' Frowning, Smith climbed up the steps and entered the ship. He slammed the door shut behind him. The *John Pym* creaked, hummed and rose into the air, climbing steadily.

Back in business, Smith thought, settling into the captain's chair. Every time he took the seat there was a new adventure to be had, a new danger to be faced. Even the control panels looked unfamiliar. Spires and chimneys sank away as the ship lifted into the atmosphere. A mighty clock-face dropped off the bottom of the windscreen as they rose over it. Airships parted, lazy as clouds, and the *John Pym* left the planet of Albion Prime behind.

3

A Hostile Takeover

Colonel Vock's homecoming was something of a disappointment. Despite all predictions the Divine Army had taken a fearful mauling: thrown back, harried and battered into almost nothing by creatures that the Yull despised. Vock brought no victory and worse than that, no offworlders to beat up. He was jeered at in the street. A peasant, who he would normally have been allowed to kill merely to test the sharpness of his axe, threw a melon at his head. Vock had failed.

The groundcar dumped him at the edge of his estate and he trudged up the drive to his treehouse. As he approached he saw a heap of objects in the front garden, piled up as if ready to burn: pieces of his second-best armour, his favourite glockenspiel, even his beloved easel.

Vock stormed up the front steps and thumped on the door. 'Wife! What is the meaning of this disgraceful behaviour? Open up!'

A window opened above and Mrs Vock stepped onto the balcony. 'And what kind of homecoming do you call this?' she demanded.

'I have returned,' said Vock, puffing out his chest. 'I led our army in sacred battle against the offworld weaklings—'

'And they kicked your furry arse!' Mrs Vock shouted back. 'I've heard the news – you're a disgrace! All the neighbours are talking about it. The other children laugh at Plig and Vom because of you.'

Vock put his hands on his hips, puffed out his chest and declared, '*Harrumph!* Lies! With my consecrated axe I charged at the cowardly enemy—'

'Blah blah blah!' Mrs Vock yelled. 'Always the same with you, big words and no triumph. You said you'd bring back ten thousand sacrifices. The children are crying, because Daddy promised them a British to torture and what have they got? Nothing! You've not even captured a regimental mascot!'

Vock stared at her. Could she have been the rodent he had married, all those years ago? He remembered a beautiful lemming, not this shrew. Any more saggy and her cheek pouches will hang around her knees, he thought bitterly. 'Where is my servant Hephuc?'

Hephuc stepped onto the balcony, behind Mrs Vock. 'Er, hello,' he said, a little sheepishly. 'I've been, um, looking after your property.'

'Good,' Vock said. 'At least you have protected my wife's honour in my absence.' He turned to his wife. 'Look, Spem—'

'Don't you Spem me!' Mrs Vock snapped. 'You're not fit to wear armour. You're a disgrace! Our noble house has lost respect. Peasants laugh at our army. Even your concubines have sodded off. You're not setting foot in this house until you've gone down to the temple, said sorry and committed ritual suicide. Not a foot!'

Vock thought about breaking in and killing her, but she

had a point. After all, he *had* failed. There was nothing for it but to seek mercy from the high priests – which, knowing Yullian society, was extremely unlikely to be forthcoming.

The Great Temple of Hapiclapu was the finest example of ancient Yullian architecture this side of the Holy Homeworld. It was a huge ziggurat, built on the bones of a thousand slaves, rising eighty feet above the tallest tree-houses. Across the front a mural depicted one of the gentler scenes from Yullian myth: Popacapinyo, the war god, standing over the body of the thief Picapocetortu, holding his enemy's heart and kicking his severed head.

A sort of diving-board stuck out from the summit of the temple, like a plank protruding from a pirate ship. As Vock ascended, a thin scream came from above and a lemming man sailed out from the board, flew overhead and disappeared with a leafy thud into the foliage at the bottom. The gods did not want apologies; they preferred a leap of faith.

It was a hot day, and the climb to the shine of the war-god seemed endless. All around him groups of worshippers whispered and stared. Even the sacrificial squol lowed with contempt.

The High Priest waited for him on the roof. 'Great one,' said Vock, 'forgive me. I have failed.'

The priest pulled back his hood. He was half-blind, and his whiskers were thin and grey.

'Yes,' he wheezed, 'you *have* failed. You promised ten thousand sacrifices, and yet you bring back none.'

'I know,' Vock replied. Guilt was rising in him like a tide: he felt as if he were drowning in the stuff. 'I don't know what happened. The offworlders were berserk: they fought like ten devils each! They left a champion on the bridge—'

'Ten devils – pah!' said the priest. 'Everyone knows offworlders are feeble and cowardly.' He turned and pointed to the scowling idol behind him, thirty feet high and flecked with gore. 'Hear me now! The war god has been cheated!' He looked back, his voice lower, but still grim. 'Now, what will you do to put it right?'

'Say sorry?' Vock suggested.

'*Hwot?* You – you – dickhead!' The priest's thin arm flicked out and cuffed Vock across the ear. 'You are no better than a mangy offworlder! If Popacapinyo is not to see the head of the British general kicked off the temple roof, then something else must fly through the air!'

Vock swallowed hard.

'Now, give me your axe and jump over the edge!'

Vock found himself wishing that his people had chosen a more forgiving god. But worship of the nature goddess had been banned for ten years, and the priests of Popiananetl were all dead – all except the wise and venerable Milf, who still wandered the forests, disgusted by his kin.

Numbly, Vock lined himself up with the plank. It wasn't my fault, he thought. It was the conniving offworlders – most of all, that frog-faced M'Lak who held the bridge. Curse him and his line! What I would do to take revenge on his clan! If only—

'Ahem,' said the priest.

Vock braced his legs like a sprinter in the blocks. '*Yullai!*' he screamed, and he raced towards the plank. The ground disappeared under his feet—

And something hit him across the chest. He thumped down onto his back, winded, thrashing around in rage. What new insult was this? Was he so shameful that he was being prevented even from suicide? A cruel punishment indeed, so cruel that it could only come from another Yull.

Vock turned his head and looked into the scarred, joyless, one-eyed face of a Ghast officer.

'Mimco Csinty Huphepuet Vock,' it said.

'Let me die!' he cried. 'I have no name!'

'Silence! You are addressing Attack-ship Commander 462 of the Ghast Empire. I have orders to collect you for intelligence purposes. Get up. You are still of use.'

Vock sat up. Two huge praetorians flanked the officer, sneering at the inferior architecture around them. 'Of use? To the Yull?'

'We have a mutual interest. You require Suruk the Slayer destroyed. I wish for his comrades to die. In return for your assistance, your name will be restored.'

'But – how?'

'We have ways.' Behind them, a third praetorian staggered along the diving-board, the priest thrashing in its arms. It dropped the priest off the edge. A shriek rose out of the abyss. 'So, you will work with us?'

'Well, I – Yes, on my battleaxe!'

'Excellent. Now,' said 462, watching a group of mendicants climb the temple steps, 'I think it would be wise to have any potential witnesses removed.' One of the praetorians held out Vock's axe. 'Please, feel free.'

Leighton-Wakazashi's headquarters were on YP278, a small planetoid at the far end of the system from Albion

Prime. It was a frozen, inhospitable wasteland: the company had chosen it to exploit a taxation loophole on uninhabitable planets and for the great skiing potential it offered the senior executives. The corporation ran the place, governed by British law. In the chaos and disruption of galactic war, it was hard for the *Pax Britaniccus Interstella* to be enforced as keenly as Parliament would have liked.

The *John Pym* had touched down for five minutes before it had its own icicles. A fine film of snow swished across the landing pad and was promptly swept away by automated ploughs.

'I don't see why I have to do this,' Carveth said.

Smith fastened his coat and wrapped a scarf around his neck. 'Because you're the only one of us connected to the company. You've got a reason to be in there.'

She shrugged. 'All they did was design my basic DNA. They didn't even make me: I'm a custom job. The only link I've had with the company since then is that I play their computer games.' She fastened her flying jacket and put on her hat. 'Can't you go? You could pretend to be a robot and we could wrap you in foil or something—'

'No,' said Smith. 'Remember, Colonial Intelligence has an agent here already. You'll be given false ID and shown how to get inside. After that, all you need to do is access the main data array and send us anything that links the company to the Ghast Empire and the Vorl. Alright?'

'Huh. Alright.'

Rhianna wandered into the sitting room. She was wearing heavy boots, a jacket and gloves. 'I don't think

I'm going to like it here. It seems so. . . I don't know, *capitalist*.'

'Well, it *is* the HQ of a major corporation,' Carveth said. 'Where's Suruk?'

'I'll find him,' Smith said, suddenly a little worried, and he left the room. He knocked on Suruk's door and went in.

The alien stood by the shelves, admiring his skull collection. 'I have made a decision,' he said. 'When this mission is done, I will go to find Colonel Vock.'

'Are you sure?'

'I am certain.'

Smith nodded. 'I'd rather you stayed, Suruk.'

'You think Vock will defeat me?'

'No, I'd just rather – well, you know, I prefer having you around.'

'And you also, Mazuran. You have been a good friend, and a great source of wisdom and bail money. But honour calls – and I shall of course return.'

'I understand. Just - look after yourself, Suruk. And make sure you give him a good smack in the chops from me. Anyway,' he added, forcing himself to brighten up, 'we'd best get going. We'll discuss Vock later.'

'Indeed,' said Suruk, 'Now, let us slay some yuppies!'

They hurried across the cold landing pad, into a smart terminal where a monorail picked them up. The carriage was empty except for a high-ranking executive: the shoulders of his suit were padded, and he gabbled into a mobile comlink the size of a housebrick: 'Buy it out at thirty percent, ditch the workforce and sell the gardens for scrap. What say we meet at Bernie's wine bar, seven of the clock, bring your wad?'

Rhianna scowled. If ever she was going to use her powers to pop someone's head, Smith thought, it would probably be now. Suruk leaned across and whispered to her, 'He is a capitalist and I am an indigenous tribesman. Could it be wrong to detach his head?'

Rhianna grimaced and looked away.

Smith glanced at Carveth. She was putting her mittens on, and she looked small and worried. 'You'll be alright,' he said. 'All you've got to do is talk to our agent, get this info and report back. Simple, eh?'

'Yeah, right,' she said. 'This must be our worst plan since you let Suruk go carol singing on that bullion train.'

'Nobody holds out on the Baby Jesus,' Suruk growled.

'I tell you, as soon as we're done I'm coming straight back. No screwing around.'

The monorail slid to a halt at the main terminal.

There was a logo on the wall outside: a heraldic lion holding up a sword. Beneath the sign an unshaven man was finishing a cigarette.

'Rick?' Carveth gasped, squashing her nose against the window. 'Rick Dreckitt?'

'God,' Smith muttered. 'Not him.'

The doors slid open, pushing Carveth aside. Dreckitt looked inside the carriage.

'Hey, sister,' Dreckitt said. He had a gravelly, slightly melancholic voice. 'How's business?'

She prised her nose from the window before it could get frozen there. 'Brilliant!' she said, beaming at him. 'How're you?'

'Still alive.' Dreckitt smiled, reluctantly.

Carveth waved at the others from the carriage door. 'See you in a few days!' she called, and she skipped away. 'Let's get down to business, Rick!'

Suruk looked at Smith. 'No screwing around, then?'

'So,' said Dreckitt, 'they want me to put the squeeze on you too, huh?'

'Yes please!' Carveth said, trotting along at his side. They were walking through the monorail terminal. It was white and sleek, dotted with odd chrome sculptures like twisted bumpers. Low-ranking Leighton-Wakazashi staff – which Carveth and Dreckitt resembled – hurried past them in work gear. Every so often they would spot an executive from the higher floors, telling someone loudly about his car over the comlink.

'It's a tough draw,' Dreckitt said. 'If you ask me, the company stinks like they pulled it out the bay after a week in a lead vest.'

Carveth was not quite sure what Dreckitt was talking about. His slang originated from Carver's Rock, a very tough colony in the United Free States where he had worked as a bounty hunter. Apparently it was quite common for a man to wear a concrete overcoat out there despite his Chicago typewriter, which just went to show how different things were abroad. Whatever he was on about, it always sounded very exciting.

'Gosh,' Carveth said, 'it is funny us meeting, isn't it? I mean, after Urn and everything.'

Dreckitt frowned, perhaps recalling their last meeting, where Carveth had had her way with him in the *John*

Pym. He had been very drunk. 'Yep,' he said. 'We'll always have the kitchen table.'

'We could always have it again.' Dreckitt said nothing, so she added, 'Tell me what we'll be doing.'

'Okay.' Dreckitt shoved his hands in his pockets. 'Leighton-Wakazashi makes high-grade computers, right? Now, the cutting edge of that is simulants: flesh and semi-blood, cultured in a tank. The brains of the Empire – you and me, sister, you and me.'

She nodded, rapt. 'So we're at it – where it's at, I mean?'

'Exactly. We've been checking L-W for a while, making sure that they don't start doing things they shouldn't – building custom jobs for the wrong reasons, selling andies off to private clients, and so on.'

He fell silent as a woman strode past in a bright red suit, leafing through a personal organiser. They turned into a smaller corridor. 'Beneath here is where the data-bases are,' Dreckitt said. 'I don't have clearance: we can figure out how to get it later. But I warn you: the data's guarded by the most hardcore techs around. They won't be happy about a dame nosing through their business – assuming they know what a dame is.'

Carveth nodded and they walked on. 'Look,' she said, pointing. A cardboard cut-out was propped against the wall: a woman in a steel bikini, six feet tall, wielding a sword. She had huge, pointed ears. '*Galaxy of Battle.*'

The bounty hunter scowled. 'Yep,' he said. 'L-W hold the rights. Most addictive thing in the universe.'

'Don't I know,' Carveth said. Fifty years ago, Leighton-Wakazashi had bought a moribund tool for sharing pornography called the internet. It was now used to support the company's virtual world, a place considered by its inhabitants to be significantly better than the real one. 'I used to play it,' Carveth said. 'I bought my own castle and everything. I wanted my own palace, but the captain made me spend it on a new autopilot for the ship. I suppose on balance he was right.'

'Listen, we need to talk about where you fit into this.'

'I'm all yours.'

'Good. Let's go somewhere private,' Dreckitt said, and he opened the door of the ladies' toilet.

Inside a cubicle, Dreckitt said, 'Here's the deal. It's wartime, and sims are getting requisitioned for logistics work left right and centre. The company knows it can't send andies out untrained. So, it calls them back in and gets them battlefield-ready – and that's where you come in. You're training them.'

'What? I can't do that! I don't know how to fight, let alone how to teach other people.'

'It's a breeze, sister. The real trainer's been delayed: Intelligence gave her ship a Mickey Finn. You're down to do it in her place. There's a neural link in your room: all you have to do is download this.'

He reached into his coat and took out a programme box. On the front was a photograph of a red-faced man, squinting belligerently as if regarding an enemy through a telescope. The title read: *The Davies-McLaglen Complete Sergeant Major Simulator*.

'These broads are all androids,' Dreckitt explained. 'Tell 'em to stand up straight and it's a done deal.'

The man on the box glowered out at Carveth, his chin protruding like a cowcatcher. She sighed. 'Rick, do you remember when you and I went out on that date?'

'When I was hired to kill you?'

'Yes. Do you think that could ever happen again?'

'Depends whether you cross me or not. Listen, kid,' said Dreckitt, 'I get your drift. But this is a job. Maybe sometime we can get together and sink some rye, but for now, Dreckitt's on a case, and there's no getting him off it.'

'Well then, we're partners! We'll sort it all out, and then we can get some time together. I can be on your case too.'

'You already are,' Dreckitt said. He looked glum for a moment, then sighed and added, 'I shouldn't be hard on you. You're okay. Don't look so shook up, kid. You look like you're expecting to get the bum's rush.'

Carveth was not sure whether this was a disease or an unnatural act. 'You wish,' she said, and she opened the cubicle door.

Back in the living room of the *John Pym*, Smith was consulting their library. This consisted of about fifty books, roughly divided between military history, spacecraft recognition guides, battlefield manuals and stories about young women looking for Mr Right.

'Hey, Isambard.'

Smith glanced up. It was warm inside the ship, and the heat made him feel a little drowsy. Rhianna had taken off her coat and boots and, by the looks of it, a good deal else: her t-shirt and skirt seemed only attached to her by accident. Her casual sexiness made him interested, then resentful, then wary.

'Just looking in my books,' he said. 'I wondered if there might be anything useful about the Vorl in them.'

'*The Boys' Book of Uplifting Adventure*,' Rhianna said, picking up one of the titles. 'I doubt it. . .'

Smith frowned. 'I hope Carveth's all right. I never trusted that Rick Dreckitt fellow. Shady type, that.'

'You worry about Polly, don't you?'

'Sometimes. Especially when she puts her arms out and goes *Neeeeeeeyow!* Bad form in a pilot.' He shrugged. 'She's not a bad sort, deep down.'

'I think that's very kind,' Rhianna said. 'It's good that you care so much.'

Smith lifted a volume of *Jane's Fighting Spacecraft* and scowled behind it in the direction of Rhianna's lithe body. He crossed his legs and tried to think about something else, noticing that the old radio mast was getting ready to transmit its message of love.

'How's Suruk?' Rhianna asked.

'He's in the hold, practising. He means to go after this Colonel Vock as soon as he gets the chance.'

Rhianna shook her head, genuinely sad. 'War just breeds war,' she said.

'They don't think like that. To Suruk, the cycle of violence is a bike with scythes. Still, if this Vock fellow is anything like the rest of the Furries, he'll have earned it.' He felt tired and sour. 'How's about a drink?' he suggested.

'Cool.'

Smith got up and opened the fridge. A stop at the company shop on the way back from the terminal had secured them a useful supply of beer. He pulled out a few and set them on the table. 'Here we go.'

Rhianna always seemed to find it hard to sit on a chair properly for any length of time. She pulled her feet up under her and ran a hand through her hair. She looked deliciously scruffy.

Smith opened the hold door. Inside, Suruk was practising fighting with his spear, calling out the names of the strikes as he jabbed and sliced the air: 'Leaping Dog style! Monkey Threatens Biscuit! Solitude Standing!'

'Pint?' Smith asked, making the universal tipping gesture. Suruk nodded.

'You know,' Smith said as he returned to the table, 'I don't trust Leighton-Wakazashi. They're too interested in making a profit and not enough in the galaxy as a whole.'

'Really, Isambard?' She sounded pleased. He realised he had said something right.

'Absolutely. Leighton-Wakazashi exploit the galaxy terribly. Not like our East Empire Company. They know how to exploit the galaxy *properly*.'

Rhianna frowned. 'Soon enough,' she said as Suruk strolled into the room, 'Leighton-Wakazashi's greed will turn against it. It's karma. Karma is inside everything.'

Suruk started rooting about in one of the cupboards. 'Not in here,' he said. 'I think I ate it.'

'That's korma,' Smith said. 'Another beer, anyone?'

The Leighton-Wakazashi buildings were soulless, even to an android. Carveth did not like her small, white, allotted room: the chrome and digital clocks unsettled her. Already she missed the *John Pym*, with its dials, gears and inexplicable pinging sounds. Sitting up in bed, she reflected on the grim task that was to come. She'd registered, claiming that she was here to train the lady androids in basic combat drill, and been given a list of trainees and a programme of activities to run through with them, as well as a uniform in a box.

The list of names sounded reasonable: ten simulants of varying nationality, with the initial R or K in the middle of each name, for Robot or Karakuri depending on the planet of manufacture. The training schedule was less promising, though. There was a cursory bit about tactics and rifle handling, along with longer sections about close-quarter wrestling/hair pulling, beach volleyball and hazardous environment training (mud, custard). Each day was rounded off with a sing-song and disciplining of recruits ('preferably over the knee', someone had written in biro on the timetable. 'Tolerate no naughtiness'). This looked bad.

'Dirty old buggers!' she said. Stuff this, she decided. If she was going to run this show, she'd run it properly, not for the amusement of a bunch of dirty old executives. There was no way that she was going to roll around in mud dressed in anything but tough, sensible clothes. She might perhaps pay Rick Dreckitt a visit in less sensible clothes later, but that was her own business. After all, you had to have some sort of life outside work, didn't you?

There was a neural shunt and a player on the wall. She wired up the basic training disc, plugged it in and went to sleep.

'So,' said Smith, finishing his fourth can, 'Shipping command came to the conclusion that there was probably a connection between Binky landing the ship the wrong side up and the disappearance of half the shipment of Scotch. They accused him of being a drunkard.'

Rhianna nodded keenly. 'How did he get his pilot's licence back?'

'He threw a party for the top brass and paid for the bar.' Smith sighed. 'Good old Binky. I think he captains a dreadnought now. How about you? Any good stories?' He opened another beer.

Rhianna peered into her own can and shrugged. 'Well, I don't know. I've not really had as many adventures as you. We had some pretty crazy times, back in the day, though. There were nine of us in this modern dance group called Starship Troupers – doing spoken poetry, movement, kind of a holistic thing. We used to play whale music in the interval, until they translated whale song. We put our stuff through a translator: it turned out to be a sea shanty called *Right Up the Blowhole*.' Rhianna burst into laughter. 'You should have heard it!' she exclaimed, and she coughed and spilt her beer in a frothy mess.

At the far end of the table, Suruk said 'Holistic!' and chuckled to himself.

Rhianna had the giggles. Smith watched her, intrigued. Suddenly she slipped off her chair, landed awkwardly on one foot and then fell onto him.

He caught her instinctively, and she lay there across his lap for a moment, grinning. He smiled back at her. Their eyes met. Rhianna stopped smiling and hauled herself upright. 'I ought to get to bed,' she said.

'Oh,' said Smith. The spell was broken, if ever it had been there. 'Well then – are you alright to walk?'

'I'm fine.' She rubbed her head. 'Fine. Night, everyone. Nod bless.' She padded out of the room, a little more uneven than usual. Smith heard the door to her room close.

'Bollocks,' said Smith. He looked at the far wall, feeling empty. 'Suruk?' he said after a while. 'How're you going to find Colonel Vock?'

'I will manage,' Suruk said.

'You'll need someone to fly you to wherever he is.'

The alien shrugged. 'I will seek passage with other M'Lak. Much as I like this craft, I miss the ships of my people. They have their own ambience... and aroma.' He opened another can. 'Fear not. I will bring you back a postcard.'

'Thanks,' said Smith.

'She makes you sad,' Suruk remarked. He had mastered the art of using his mandibles to hold his can, freeing his hands to gesticulate. 'You are angry that your end has not got away with the magic woman. You wish to donate her one, and it grieves you that you cannot.'

Smith nodded. He felt defeated. 'Yes,' he said.

'We should find you another with which to spawn. I have an idea! We will advertise, placing cards in telephone boxes. I have seen it done.'

'I don't—'

'Then, we could interview those seeking to apply. And if they are not good enough, they will die by my hand! This will discourage time-wasters.'

'Thanks, old chap.' He sighed. 'I wish it were that easy, Suruk, I really do. Nice of you to try to help.'

'I enjoy a challenge.'

Smith sighed and stood up. It was time to feed the hamster and go to sleep. 'Goodnight, Suruk,' he said.

'Goodnight,' the alien replied.

Smith put on his pyjamas and brushed his teeth. At the door to his room he switched off the corridor lights. The living room was empty, and in the hold, Suruk was practising his martial arts again.

Smith watched the alien leap, duck, cut and roll. He could not help but be impressed, and in an odd way envious. How much easier life would be without the curse of a sex drive, where the solution to any problem was decapitation! There was an elegant lack of complexity, a simple precision to the M'Lak mind that humans lacked. He would never admit it, but sometimes Smith wondered if mankind could learn from the M'Lak. Something crashed in the hold, followed by wild laughter. Maybe not.

It was snowing outside. Around them, Leighton-Wakazashi was keeping its secrets. And further away were Colonel Vock and 462, plotting their evil against Earth. An onslaught against mankind on two fronts. Without help from the rest of the galaxy, the other empires would soon collapse under such an assault. Even Britain might find winning a bit tricky. Troubled, Smith went to bed.

Carveth woke early and prepared for command. She zipped up her utility waistcoat, pulled her hair back into a functional ponytail and looked at herself in the mirror. ''Ow the 'ell am I going to do this?' she asked her reflection. Then, ''*Ow? 'Ell?* When did I stop saying haitch?'

She realised that the programme was running. She hadn't the faintest idea what she needed to do but, in her subconscious, she was a sergeant major.

On the way she bought a company newspaper and rolled it into a narrow tube. With one end jammed under her arm, her hand on the other, she strode onto the training ground.

The androids were chatting, waiting for the course to begin. They were a mixed bunch, from a variety of lines: in once glance Carveth saw a prim, dark-haired girl in a thick fur coat, an acrobat with a stripe of makeup across her eyes, an artificial company wife in a flowery dress and floppy hat, muttering something about a recipe – even an ancient Metropole-class, gold-finished and expressionless. They looked quite reasonable from here, she thought, but the training programme thought otherwise.

'Hatten-shun!' she bellowed. 'Get in a line! Now!'

The androids shuffled into a row. Slightly astonished, and already slightly hoarse, Carveth glanced around the room. The training area doubled as a sports centre for the company executives and the lady androids stood along the baseline of a badminton court.

'Right then!' Carveth said, approaching the end of the line. She dipped her head slightly, shoved her jaw out, narrowed one eye and widened the other. 'You 'orrible crew,' she began. 'You 'orrible bunch of mummies' bots, fresh out the server room.' She took the paper from under her arm and prodded the first android in the chest with it. 'You! What's your name?'

'My name is Emily Hallsworth,' the android said. She was wearing a long dress and a bonnet. 'I am pleased to make your aquain—'

'I didn't ask for the bleedin' Doomsday Book! What's that on your 'ed?'

'It is known as a bonnet,' Emily replied. 'All ladies of—'

'Where're you from?'

'I have of late been residing at the Jane Austen Experience, on New Bath. My calling is to entertain the visitors with polite discourse and the pianoforte.'

Carveth was finding that being in charge of an infantry unit was actually quite easy, once you got into the swing of it. 'Ooh, New Bath, is it? La dee bleedin' dah. Well, this is basic training now, girl. Get that bloody radar dish off your 'ed! Nah then,' she muttered, moving on, 'let's see what else they've given me – oh my God, what's wrong with your eyes?'

The next android in the line wore a white shirt, pleated skirt and long socks, which was odd enough, but her features were even more bizarre. She had a tiny mouth and nose, and vast, round, watery eyes like something that had evolved in a cave. They stared at Carveth for a moment, and the girl gave an idiotic giggle. 'Hi!' she said, 'I'm Robot Pilot Yoshimi! Let's have fun!'

Thrown, Carveth stared back. Yoshimi certainly didn't look like any android she'd ever met – or indeed any person at all. Emily leaned over and whispered disapprovingly, 'Manga specifications, I believe.'

The program recovered Carveth's composure. 'What the bloody 'ell are you on about? Don't give me this *fun* bollocks, my girl!'

Yoshimi looked dismayed. Her huge eyes blinked. She sniffed.

'Don't get soft with me!' Carveth bellowed. 'What are you, a bloody schoolgirl?'

'Yes!' Yoshimi said, and she burst into tears.

'Oh. Sorry,' Carveth said. 'Look, I didn't mean to make you cry.' Feeling that this was all going wrong, she stepped away and surveyed her charges. 'Now, listen. My name is Polly and I will be equipping you to deal with the modern battlefield. The world out there is a tough, dangerous place. You may not like that. You may want to duck out, to run back to your motherboards. Well, there'll be none of that here! You must learn to be as tough and dangerous as anything it can throw at you if you want to survive, understand? – Can somebody give her a tissue, please? – I said, *Do you understand?*'

There was a mumble of assent.

'What was that?' she barked.

'Yes, Polly!'

'That's more like it!' She strolled down the line, and since there were only ten of them, soon strolled back. 'Right, you lot! Hatten-shun!' She jammed the newspaper under her arm and squinted. 'Now, listen! It's a hard world out there, and if you want to survive, you'll 'ave to get wise! And Polly will make you wise! Now, first up, I've made a couple of little changes to your training programme. Today's mud wrestling is off. Instead, we will be learning about the Ensign rapid-fire laser rifle, following which I will be continuing your moral education down the pub. But first, which one of you babies knows anything about Von Clausewitz's dialectical approach to military analysis?'

'The Chairman will see you now,' the intercom said, and the Deputy Director opened the office door and stepped inside.

Chairman Brett Gecko was at his desk, adjusting his braces. *Club Tropicana* was playing on the stereo: as the Deputy Director entered, the music stopped.

'Tell me Patrick,' the Chairman asked, 'have you ever

considered the profundity of the early works of Wham?'
He put his feet up on the desk and pointed at his minion
with both hands, the thumbs cocked up like gun
hammers. 'I'm a busy man, so shoot.'

'You wanted to talk to me about the robot girls, sir. Is
there a problem?'

'Course not. Problems are for wimps. There's no such
thing as problems in this company, only solutions to problems. Who solves problems? *Tigers* solve problems. And
at Leighton-Wakazashi, we separate the tigers from the
boys. Yes, Patrick, there's a problem.'

'Really, Sir? You need me to—'

The Chairman scowled. 'Hold that thought – call com-
ing in.' He lifted the phone and barked into it, 'Hey,
Carter, how's the space-haulage game? An entire ship?
Only one survivor? A woman, you say? That's terrible.
Can we get hold of a specimen for the science division?'
He put the comlink down. 'Now, Patrick, do you
remember Paul Devrin?'

'He was your predecessor, until his C5 transport unit
exploded. . .'

'Damn right. He had a sexbot built, a custom job. I
happened to be watching the girl androids doing their
physical training today, by coincidence, and I noticed
there are. . . similarities between her and the new trainer.'

'They may just be built to the same basic pattern, sir.'

'Get with the programme, Patrick, because this train
waits for nobody! This smells like trouble to me. You
know we don't need any trouble now, what with our grey-
market sales at Tranquility Falls. The ants pay well for
info, and the last thing the company needs is some

renegade custom-job getting in the way. I'm making an informal executive order here: wait a moment. . .'

The Chairman leaned over and spun the needle on his executive toy. It teetered on *Play a round of golf*, rocked, and stopped at *Order an assassination*. He sat up, tightened his red braces and squared his padded shoulders. 'Put the sleeper on standby,' he said.

The Deputy Chairman swallowed. 'Sir, isn't that a bit, well, excessive?'

'This *is* the age of excess!' the Director barked. 'Get wise, Patrick. Out there, it's a jungle, a corporate jungle full of fat cats and wolves in suits. And you know what sort animals rule the jungle? Damn right you do. *Sharks*. You've got to be a shark – a tiger shark – to ride this train. That's why I'm sitting here, swimming in my own jungle, and you're standing in front of that desk, whining like a little girl. Hey, am I right or am I right?'

'Yes sir.'

He clicked his fingers. 'I like the way you think, Patrick. You'll go far. But you can't win the rat race if you can't walk the walk – because it's a dog-eat-dog world out there, and if you can't stand eating dogs, it's time to get back in the kitchen. Understand?'

'Right,' said the Deputy Director.

'Watch this new trainer to the max. Watch her like a hawk, and if she starts poking her nose around – freeze her assets for good.' He leaned back and put his feet back up. 'Later. *Ciao*.'

4

Sin and Synthetics

'Then,' Emily said, delicately sipping her drink, 'Lord Hampton looked down and said, "Madam, I said that the Honourable Member needed the persuasion of a lady to stand at *election*." Most embarrassing, I can assure you.'

'What did you do?' Carveth asked.

'Do? I merely rose from my knees and vacated the drawing room. One has to keep some dignity.'

They sat around a table in one of the company bars. This one was for lower-ranking workers, non-executives, and was called Norm's. It had wooden fittings and stools – unlike Spritzers, the choice for more important company men, which had no seats and served only wine.

'Well,' said the artificial wife, 'it is a woman's purpose to make her husband happy, after all.'

'*No*,' Carveth replied firmly, raising a finger. All thought of being a sergeant-major had vanished now: her mind was too busy concentrating on staying upright. Her finger meandered in her vision, and she tracked it with an effort. 'No,' she reasserted. 'You do not have to do anything unless you want to. You get him to do it instead. That's exactly what I'm talking about. You've got to listen,' she added, her voice rising, 'because this is feminism, right? You have a duty to great feminists like Emily Pankhurst and, um. . . Gloria Gaynor to get ahead. Because if a woman's place is in the kitchen, a man's place is on the kitchen table – on his back. I speak from experience here.'

'It is a truth universally acknowledged,' Emily added, 'that all men are bastards.' She paused and finished her Tia Maria and coke. 'Would anyone care for a choral interlude?'

Carveth looked over her shoulder at the small stage at the back of the bar where Yoshimi was belting out 'Carwash' on the singalongatron. 'Job well done,' Carveth said to the bottles on the tabletop.

'So,' she added, sitting up, 'I hope you've learned something today, because I intend to teach you useful stuff for the real world. You there, Rachel! What've you learned today?'

'How to operate a laser rifle and how not to whore myself to just anyone who walks past.'

'Good! And with that thought I will leave you,' Carveth added, lurching to her feet. 'Tomorrow, we will learn some other stuff about guns and drill and all that. Goodnight, ladies: it's been a pleasure.'

She turned and walked out, a feeling of contentment swelling within her. I trained them well, she thought. My robot sisters.

The door to the bar swung shut behind her. Overhead the neon sign flickered and buzzed. She sniffed and fished a map out of her pocket. Time to go to work.

Carveth took a left, meandered down the corridor and found a door marked 'Authorised staff only'. For a moment she wondered if this sort of work might be better done whilst entirely sober. Ah, but wasn't that exactly the sort of thing that the company would expect? Her drinking spree was therefore a cunning ruse to fool them into thinking she was drunk, which admittedly she was, which was in turn a double bluff – or something. . . She slipped the keycard out of her thigh pocket and ran it through the lock. Apparently she was authorised.

Carveth slipped through and closed the door behind her.

She crept down the corridor, the carpet tiles muffling her boots. There were framed pictures on the walls: a motivational poster, a pin-up elf from *Galaxy of Battles*, a girl in leather smalls draped over some circuitry. The air was stale. She was in the computer department.

As if to confirm this, voices burst out from an office to the left: two technicians, shouting over one another. One started laughing at his colleague's stupidity as Carveth ducked down and crept under the window. She grinned at her own cleverness.

Standing up again, she felt less clever. Her brain swayed worryingly inside her skull, slopping about in Bacardi like a picked frog in ethanol. She reached the lift, pressed the button and watched the big red digital display count up to her floor.

From one of the offices a voice broke out in a snarl. 'Liar, wicked liar! Computers don't break, you fool! *You* broke it!' The door rolled open and she slipped inside, remembered Dreckitt's instructions and keyed in 'sub-basement four'. The lift sank. Pan-pipes started playing *The Safety Dance*.

Dreckitt sat back in his chair and poured himself a shot of rye. He stared into the glass, reflecting how much whisky looked like the urine sample of a habitual whisky drinker. He took a sip and pulled the face he tended to pull when drinking. No matter how many times you swirled it round the bottom of the glass, Famous Teacher still tasted like tractor fuel.

He got up and walked to the little window. It was snowing outside, pitch-black except for the lights on the landing strip. He wondered what was going on in Smith's spaceship. Probably something cheerful. He grimaced and took another sip.

The company radio stations played power ballads and synthesiser pop, so Dreckitt had brought his own records. At the moment, a warbling crooner was telling him that this was not goodbye, but *au revoir*. Dreckitt didn't believe a word of it.

Looking into the black, he suddenly realised that he was lonely. Carveth made him feel uneasy, as well as making him wince, but he didn't feel quite so miserable when she was around. Even the perpetual rain and flickering neon of his homeworld would have been bearable with her. I ought to tell her that, he thought. Let her know she's a doll. Maybe not: *doll* was probably the wrong word for a reprogrammed sexbot.

Someone knocked on the door. Dreckitt opened it.

A sour-faced security officer stood outside. 'Company business,' he said. 'Step aside.'

'I'm stepping,' Dreckitt replied.

'I'm here to search the room,' the officer said, walking in. 'Just a routine check.' He took a scanner from his belt and ran it up and down the curtains.

'Sure, it's routine,' Dreckitt said. 'It's routine, just like a kangaroo practising law. It's routine as a two-bit grifter getting three aces against Nick the Greek.'

The security man frowned, struggling to comprehend. 'So, um, not routine, then?'

'Damn right. Take the breeze, pal. Scram.'

The man's face hardened. 'No deal,' he said, and he reached for his gun. Dreckitt whirled, grabbed at the table and as the gun appeared he smashed the whisky bottle over the agent's head.

The security man crumpled like a sack full of old clothes. The smell of whisky was overpowering. Dreckitt lifted his pillow and took his pistol from underneath. 'Too bad you wouldn't leave,' he said. 'But then again, who does?'

The lift stopped and the piped music cut. As the door opened, light jazz began to play.

'Bloody hell,' Carveth said.

She was looking across a marble hall at a bronze torso, ten feet high. It was stylised: the lack of detail made it eerie. The muscles of the chest were smooth slabs, the face featureless except for a stern brow and a bland horizontal stripe of mouth. On the statue's plinth was one word: COMMERCE.

Awed, she stepped into the hall. Her soles squeaked on the floor. Walnut panels stretched up the walls. Marble women stood on tiptoe at the edges of the room, holding up glowing balls. Everything was sleek.

Carveth felt uneasy, watched.

There was a picture on the wall beside the statue. She closed one eye to stabilise her vision. The picture showed a man in a double-breasted suit, big and healthy, staring into the camera with an expression that was at once jocular and threatening. He had a pencil moustache like W's, but neater hair, and he looked much less ill.

'Lloyd Leighton,' said a voice.

Carveth spun around. Emily crossed the hall in a soft hiss of skirt, her bootheels clicking on the marble.

'The former owner of the Blue Moon Corporation, co-founder of Leighton-Wakazashi. He used to be the richest man in the galaxy,' she explained. 'Until he disappeared.'

'I, um, I just needed some air.'

'Of course. A fundamentally vulgar business, commerce,' she observed. 'Nobody of any real worth *makes* money. One either marries or inherits it. Lloyd Leighton made roller-coasters.'

Carveth peered at the picture: Leighton looked like a tyrant on his day off. 'Roller-coasters?'

'Gaudy, nasty things,' Emily said. 'Not like the sort of entertainments we have at Mansfield Theme Park. We offer lawn croquet and then a little sit-down. But Leighton felt he could make money that way. He went missing at the start of the war, after Leighton-Wakazashi took over Blue Moon.' She looked down at Carveth, frowned and said, 'You seem somewhat lost.'

'Yes,' Carveth said. 'I took a wrong turn somewhere – all a bit much. . .'

'I agree. It's all so crass and cheap-looking. Terribly vulgar.' Emily sighed. 'Would you care to join me for a stroll?'

'I'm alright, thanks.'

'Then goodnight. My constitution demands that I

retire.' Emily smiled, turned, and disappeared down the corridor, her skirts whispering around her.

Carveth watched her go and exhaled. She glanced at the map. Nearly there. The bronze statue glowered at her as she left the room.

Smith answered the doorbell with a pistol in the pocket of his dressing gown. 'Dreckitt?'

The android stumbled in and slammed the airlock behind him. Suruk, who had been hiding behind the door with a machete, waved.

'We've got a problem,' Dreckitt said.

'What is it?'

'My cover's blown,' Dreckitt said. He was shivering, Smith saw: he wore his raincoat over a shirt, hardly sufficient for the cold outside. 'They sent some gunsel to check out my room. He drew on me and I knocked him cold.'

'Dammit,' Smith exclaimed. 'Are you sure?'

'If I'm not sure, I just wasted good hooch on some guy's head. We've gotta go. If they've found me, they'll find Polly.'

'Right,' said Smith. 'I'll radio in to HQ.'

'That's really bad!' They looked round: Rhianna stood in the corridor, wearing a kaftan. 'This is an act of corporate oppression, not to mention attempted murder! We should picket their offices at once!'

Dreckitt turned back to Smith. 'Why the hell are you packing a rod in your pyjamas?'

Smith took the Civiliser out of his pocket. 'For close encounters.'

Dreckitt shook his head. 'This whole place's gone crazy.'

'Nonsense,' Suruk said. 'It has become good!' He disappeared into his room and returned a moment later, spear in hand. 'I have never taken the skull of a yuppie,' he said, 'but I understand that they often have a bull and a bear in their market. It should be an interesting fight.'

The basement was deserted. Carveth crept through a little communal mess-room, down a narrow corridor and reached the main data archive. A sealed glass door blocked the way. She pushed her keycard into a slot in the wall and the main lights flickered into life. The computer made a set of staccato mechanical barks and the door slid back.

The data archive consisted of one seat and a terminal. Diodes flashed on the walls like Christmas lights. She had no idea what they did.

Carveth lowered herself into the seat and turned on the monitor. She wiggled her fingers, ready to go to work.

Lines ran up and down the screen. It emitted a stuttering rattle, as if its gears were not quite meshed, and then the screen flashed white, black, and white again. In the upper left corner of the screen was the message: *Go to Line 10.*

She put her keycard into the memory slot and words clattered across the screen: *How can I help you today?*

Carveth closed her eyes, the world wobbling a little behind them, and remembered her mission. 'Show me all files relating to selling things to the Ghasts,' she said.

Sorry! the computer replied. *Those files are encrypted. Special company order.*

'Can't I just copy them?'

Sure! You just won't be able to read them, that's all. Copying right now.

Bloody computers, Carveth thought. It wasn't like this in the Empire. Proper computers had cogs and paper spools.

'Just out of interest,' she said, eyes fixed on the screen, 'who encrypted the files?'

There is no name on file, the computer replied. *It's credited to 'a lady'.*

'A lady?' Carveth said.

She flopped back in the seat. 'A lady'. Who the hell would call themselves that, except—

A sense of leaden horror dropped over her, like a curtain coming down. 'Oh, hell,' she said.

Words scrolled across the screen. *Download complete.*

She reached forward and pulled out the keycard. As the screen went black she saw Emily's face reflected in it, like a ghost.

'It would be only understandable for one to expect an explanation.' A blank, meaningless smirk spread across the lady android's face. 'One half of the world cannot understand the pleasures of the other,' she observed. 'But it can never resist sticking its nose in to have a look around, can it now?'

Carveth started to rise.

'Not so hasty,' Emily said. 'I believe we have a little unfinished business to discuss. Tell me, did it not occur to you that the company might have the gumption to install a sleeper in the ranks, as the common people put it? Someone to keep an eye on proceedings, to guard the data files, to keep our papers safe from a dirty little back-stairs menial like you?'

Carveth leaped out of the seat. Emily made a grab for her, Carveth ducked, and in a moment they faced one another, the armchair between them. 'Now look,' Carveth said, 'let's be reasonable here, right?'

'One does not reason with the likes of you!' Emily snarled. 'A thief, a spy, and. . . and a *social climber*!' She lunged around the chair. Carveth darted left, spun the chair and ran. She thumped the panel and sprang through the airlock as it slid open. She tore down the corridor, stumbled, glanced back and saw Emily rushing after her, filling the passage with skirts that hissed against the wall, a tidal wave of silk. Emily's legs were longer – and as Carveth reached the mess-room Emily grabbed her pony-tail, yanked her back and tossed Carveth across the room.

She hit the floor. Like a mad bride Emily stood in the centre of the mess, looking round. Her hands shook as she slid a fountain pen from her decolletage.

Carveth pulled herself onto her hands and knees. Emily's twitchy fingers started to dismantle the pen, turning it into some kind of weapon.

'Time,' she said, 'for this pen of mine to dwell on guilt and misery. Yours.'

Carveth jumped up. Emily jabbed, but missed, and Carveth fell across the mess table. Emily sprang onto her, pen raised to stab, and Carveth's hand closed around a bottle on the tabletop. Emily lunged and Carveth twisted round and smashed the bottle over the lady android's head.

Emily fell in an explosion of sauce. Carveth stumbled back and Emily rose from the floor. Her scalp was covered in salad cream. She looked as if she had been standing under an albatross.

A droplet of salad cream trickled down Emily's forehead. She sniggered.

Carveth ran.

In the wrong direction.

Suruk lead the way, Dreckitt following. Smith was next: he kept glancing back to make sure that Rhianna was still with them. Nobody tried to stop them: tough executives turned and fled rather than confront them, three-wheeled scooters rattled away from the sound of their boots.

'Down here,' Dreckitt said, and they hurried into the stairwell. 'We don't have long.'

Suruk raised a hand. 'I smell something. It is like. . . fizzy drink and food that is taken away. I smell men.'

'Food?' Smith said. 'Carveth may be nearby. She's like a dustbin sometimes.'

'No,' said Suruk. 'I mean *men*.'

'We must be in the computing section.' Dreckitt cocked his huge automatic. 'Not far now. We just need to—'

A door dropped out of the ceiling behind them, cutting them off like a portcullis. Smith glanced round, and with a crash a second door fell at the far end of the passage, sealing them in.

Dreckitt drew his pistol. 'Trapped! Those cheap punks've scammed us!'

Smith frowned. 'In which case,' he said, 'follow me.' He threw open one of the doors leading off the passage and stormed in. 'Hands up, everybody!'

In the light of a dozen computer screens, two men raised their hands.

'You there, computer people,' Smith said, nodding at the nearer and fatter of the two. 'I need your help. This is a matter of extreme importance to the security of the British

Empire. As employees of the Leighton-Wakazashi Company, which is subject to British law, I am commandeering you to – what're you looking at?' he glanced to his right. 'Ah, yes. This is my colleague, Suruk the Slayer, a Morlock. He is a noted warrior and decent fellow and—'

'It's a girl!' said the fat man.

His friend, still sitting at his desk, nodded. 'A real one,' he whispered. 'With – you know—' He made a gesture in front of his chest.

'Quiet!' Smith barked. 'Now listen closely. We need those security doors outside lifted. We are on a mission of utmost urgency.'

'Yeah, as if,' said the thin man. Now that the shock of their arrival had passed, his voice had become tired and slightly contemptuous. 'Can't do it. Those are director-controlled only. Even if you did bypass the anti-hack firewall without neural blowout – which you couldn't do —– the grid it's running on's parallel, so you can't jump from one to the other. I programmed that,' he added to Rhianna. 'I could show you how it works sometime.'

Smith glanced at Dreckitt. 'You're an android – did you understand any of that?'

Dreckitt nodded. 'Sure. In layman's terms, he's saying that if you want the little dame busted out it's nix but an inside job. The joint's sewn up tighter than a Bay City caboose.'

Puzzled, Smith looked to Rhianna.

'It's all about the flow of negative energy—' she began.

'Not so!' Suruk put in. 'Mazuran, imagine the fierce beasts of two hunting packs, bound together in a network of blood—'

'Everyone, please!'

They fell silent, waiting for Smith to speak.

'Our friend is trapped in the data library, deep below here. We have to talk to her – urgently. Do you know how to do that?'

The thin man's fingers clattered over the keyboard. 'Nope, can't do it, line's down. Place is sealed up. There's two life forms in there, but the door's jammed from the looks of it.'

Suruk was leaning against the wall, arms folded. 'Perhaps this man could help us.' The M'Lak pointed to a picture on the wall. It showed a pixie holding a massive blunderbuss. 'He could burst the door with his hackbut.'

'That's not a real person,' Smith said. 'It's some character from *Galaxy of Battles*, a computer game. It's only a pretend hackbut.' Something touched Smith's arm and he glanced round. 'What is it, Dreckitt?'

'Wait,' Dreckitt said. The dim glow of screens gave his face an unhealthy, sepulchral look. 'There is something. Polly told me she had an account. All the machines here are wired to *Galaxy of Battles*. I'll guard the doors, and you could. . . enter the matrix.'

'Sorry?' Smith said. 'It sounds unnatural.'

Suruk's eyes widened slightly. 'I have heard of such things. Computers linked for the sharing of images of nude human females. We can turn this evil to our own ends! Quick, let us don the helms of virtuality – and rescue Piglet!'

Rhianna folded her arms and peered at the pictures on the wall. 'It looks kind've. . . puerile. All the women have really demeaning outfits. Can't I help Polly without having to look like some kind of teenage fantasy-figure?'

'Carveth needs us,' Smith replied. 'We must all make sacrifices, Rhianna. If Suruk and I are willing to expose ourselves to death and danger, you must be willing to expose yourself to. . . um. . . us. Dreckitt, watch the doors. Suruk – fetch the hats!'

Smith opened the door of his level-one hovel and stepped into the sunlight. Rhianna was waiting for him.

They stood on the edge of a forest. Ahead, the fields rolled away to a rather-too-perfect sunset. Something large and multi-winged flapped its way across the sky.

The dusk made Smith's armour glow. *Galaxy of Battles* had analysed his brain activity, giving him an appearance suited to his personality: he wore a breast-plate, mail shirt and leggings and there was a sword at his waist. Smith thought that he looked rather dashing.

Rhianna crossed her arms and huffed. It was surprising how much decoration they could fit on so small a metal bathing suit, Smith reflected. She sported a staff, a kind of tea-towel that hung between her legs and a look of deep annoyance.

'Hello there,' Smith said.

'I feel totally objectivised,' Rhianna said. 'I wanted to be a druid. Druids don't dress like this.'

'You've got leaves in your hair.'

'That is not druidism, Isambard! Druidism is an authentic pre-Christian religion. This is me, cold, in a metal bikini. If I'd have wanted a piece of chain up my ass I'd have sat on a bathplug. I only hope Polly has not been put through this indignity.'

Smith felt that he ought to calm the situation. 'You do look jolly nice, though,' he suggested.

'Huh!' Rhianna snorted and turned her back. On the minus side, he seemed to be in her bad books again. On the plus side, she had been absolutely right about the underwear. Fantastic. Why did women have to be so difficult?

'Right then,' he declared. 'Time to find Carveth. Any thoughts?'

Suruk stepped out of the trees. The programme had given Suruk a savage appearance: he wore a dented patchwork of armour, and his exposed skin was a lattice of scars. Bones and trophies hung from his belt; knives were strapped to every available surface of his body. He looked much the same as usual. 'Behold!' he declared.

They turned: behind the hovel was a very large white castle. Unicorns grazed on its lawns, minded by strapping young grooms. Flashing lights stretched between the gaudy turrets. They spelt out the words: *Princess Polly's Magic Castle*.

Suruk pointed. 'There, perhaps?'

Carveth was back in the data library, looking for a weapon. The only thing that could have worked was a screwdriver, now wedged into the door controls to stop Emily getting in. Even that would not hold for long. Croquet and vigorous social dancing had left her cunning and tough.

'Open the door this minute, young lady! I will not hesitate in inflicting crippling malfunctions!'

'Shove it up your crinoline!' Carveth shouted back.

Emily paused. 'I have food out here,' she called. 'A most

diverting rack of lamb. I could have Cook save you some, if you agree to come out. . .'

'Jump in a lake!'

'Venture out, you pint-sized slattern, or I'll fix it so you never waltz again!'

With a calmness that surprised her, Carveth looked through the door at the refined, furious face pressed against the glass. 'I will,' she said. 'But only if you tell me what's on those files.'

'You perused the files,' Emily retorted. 'I thought it was obvious.'

'I didn't see them.'

'Sales,' Emily said. 'Commerce. Nasty things like that. Selling things to some dreary moon-people for some war or other.'

'What things?'

'Oh, information. Some piffle about Lloyd Leighton. Goodness knows. Anyway,' she added, cheering up, 'enough chatter.'

She had been fiddling with the controls, Carveth realised. The door shook but did not open, but whatever Emily was doing to it she was not far from gaining access. 'I've rewired the door panel, Polly. It would be far easier for both of us if you'd let me in.'

'Stick—' the screen flickered at the corner of her eye. A picture was forming there, a dragon, and above it a message: *Captain Smith and Rhianna are online.* Carveth grabbed the controls.

Smith's feet were silent on the thick red carpet. In the castle foyer, a baby dragon fluttered between the chandeliers, trailing sparkling dust like radioactive farts.

'So this is where the ship's computer budget went,' he said.

Suruk growled. 'Hear me, Mazuran,' he said. 'I have fought in foul places, on a hundred worlds, but never have I been anywhere that grieved me as much as the inside of the little woman's head. How can there be so many ponies and so little dung? This is the Abyss.'

'Carveth designed it,' Smith said. 'We can only hope she realises that we're here.' Before I go completely mad, he thought.

At the far end of the hall the carpet rose over a set of steps. At the top of the steps was a thick curtain.

Smith reached for his sword. Suruk made his purring, croaking sound.

Beside him, Rhianna said, 'It's. . . um. . . kind of tacky, isn't it?'

Lights flared up around the steps. The great curtains rolled back to reveal a small figure in a ballgown and a tiara slightly smaller than a radio mast. Princess Polly hovered a few inches from the ground: she floated towards them down the stairs.

'Hello Boss,' said Carveth. 'Welcome to my. . . uh. . . castle.' She glanced around, a little embarrassed, and fluttered her fairy wings. 'Look, I'm stuck in this little room and there's this crazy android who thinks she's Jane Austen trying to kill me with a biro – I know this sounds strange–'

'Not here it doesn't. Listen, Carveth,' Smith said. 'We're coming to get you out. But we need the information you downloaded. Can you pass it to us here?'

She glanced around. 'Well, alright. Here you go.'

Carveth reached to her side and took out a magic wand. She pressed a button, and the star on the end flashed into life. 'I give you data,' she said, tapping Smith on the head with it. 'You'd better work quick. If you've got a gun I could borrow. . .'

Smith glanced down. 'I've got a sword,' he said. 'But I don't think it'll work in real life.'

'*I* know!' Rhianna exclaimed. 'Polly, true empowerment comes from *knowledge*, not weapons.' She raised her hand: the palm glowed with green light. Rhianna touched Carveth's shoulder. 'The Ancient Arts of the East,' Rhianna said.

'Thanks,' Carveth replied. 'I'd better go. Wish me luck!'

The screen went dead. Carveth's eyes flicked open. She disconnected the terminal and looked around the archive room.

'I know Feng Shui,' she said. 'Well, that's just *great*.'

Smith took off the helmet and turned to the programmers. 'You there: send that data to our ship on the landing pad and copy it to the Imperial Navy. Tell them to send a dreadnought at once.'

'Or I splice your mainframe,' Suruk added, eyeing the computers. They typed.

Smith stepped into the corridor. 'How's things, Dreckitt?'

The bounty hunter stood by the pressure door at the end of the passage, trying to pick the lock. 'Almost done. . .That's it!' Dreckitt exclaimed and the pressure door slid open. 'Let's go!'

Smith ushered Rhianna in. An alarm sounded from

outside. Smith slipped into the door after the others. Dreckitt jabbed at the controls and the door slammed shut behind them. Smith blasted the lock.

'Now then,' he said, 'let's find Carveth.'

Carveth dropped onto her hands and knees and crawled under the console. She felt terribly vulnerable: Emily could be in at any moment, wielding her fountain pen, and if that happened, Carveth knew she would fare better without her backside in the air.

Carveth's hands found what she was looking for: the plug. She yanked it out of the wall and the computer and the winking lights went off. In the dark, she could hear the fans powering down as if she stood in a huge, disconnected amplifier.

Quickly, she wheeled the chair to where it would be guaranteed to create negative vibes and laid it on its side. Then, she picked up the bible-sized *Galaxy of Battles* instruction manual.

The door shot open like a greyhound trap and Emily rushed into the room and fell over Carveth's chair. Carveth heard a prim voice cry 'Shite!' and she raised the manual and brought it down hard on Emily's bonnet.

Emily made a garbled malfunctioning noise, tried to rise, and Carveth hit her again. 'Read this, Regency bitch!'

Emily froze, stiffened and said, 'A remarkable prize bullock—' and dropped onto the floor like a landed fish. Carveth stared down at her, panting.

The loudspeaker crackled into life in the corridor outside. 'This is HMS *Hampson*, dreadnought of the British Space Empire. You are to drop your weapons and surrender or we will commence orbital diplomacy. You will cease your nonsense at once. I repeat: *at once*.'

Carveth glanced round and saw Smith in the doorway, pistol in hand. 'Are you alright?' he called.

'I'm fine,' Carveth replied. 'I knocked her out cold. Actually,' she added as Dreckitt entered the little room, 'I'm not fine at all. Swooning!'

She collapsed. Dreckitt was left with no choice but to catch her. 'Easy, lady,' Dreckitt said. 'Let's get you upright – hey, hands, hands!'

Dreckitt holstered his pistol and rubbed his backside. His arm around the unsteady Carveth, he helped her from the room. They stepped past Smith and Rhianna and started down the corridor. Carveth looked back and gave the others a broad, wide-awake grin.

'Poor old Dreckitt,' Smith said.

'I think it's kind've sweet,' Rhianna said.

Smith looked at her. He realised that he didn't know what she meant. Was this an insinuation? Was Rhianna saying that she missed him? That she wanted someone else? He felt a sudden rush of anger and, with it, despair. Damn her and the whole bloody woman business! The sooner he was back in space and fighting in proper company the better, drinking gin and blasting holes in Gertie, with Wainscott on one side and—

Suruk strolled into the corridor, mandibles open, beaming. His spear was in one hand, and something football-sized and gory was in the other. 'Greetings! Look what I acquired!'

'Oh Buddha,' Rhianna groaned.

'All is well, floaty woman. This enemy executive was

calling reinforcements on his mobile telephone when he was cut off. Or at least his head was.' He sighed, deeply contented. 'I could get used to corporate headhunting.'

'I don't see what good this is supposed to do,' Carveth said, unfastening Emily's bonnet. 'She's a complete nutcase.'

They stood in the sitting room of the *John Pym*: Emily had been laid out on the dinner table. Outside, policemen in long blue coats were carrying boxes and personnel out of the company buildings. The Empire had the evidence it needed.

'She may have information vital to our cause,' Smith explained. 'The company has been trading information to the Ghasts. We just need to know how. Initiate her startup sequence.'

Carveth picked up a mug of water and tipped it over Emily's head.

Emily awoke with a start, twitched, coughed and sat up. 'I seem to have fainted.' She looked around, alarmed. 'What manner of iniquity is this? Unhand me at once!'

'It's alright,' said Smith. 'You're quite safe.'

'Who are you dreadful people?'

Suruk stepped closer: Emily recoiled. 'Suruk the Slayer, trophy displayer,' he announced.

'Polly Carveth. You tried to murder me with a pen.'

'Ah yes,' Emily said. 'I do seem to recall your face. No hard feelings?'

'No, *you tried to murder me with a pen.*'

'Well, you broke a bottle of salad cream over my head. Do you have any notion how long that will take to wash out?'

Rhianna smiled and said, 'Rhianna Mitchell. *Namaste.*'

'*You* clearly wouldn't,' Emily said, peering at Rhianna.

'Talking to you about washing would be as worthwhile as trying to explain "exciting" to a Belgian. Well, if you want me to talk, you can forget it. As if I would spill the beans to a stumpy android, an unwashed colonial and an alien! I can assure you that I shall inform you of absolutely nothing.' She folded her arms and cocked her head back as if preparing to fire something out of her nose.

Dreckitt was sitting on the other side of the room. 'Reckon you'd better sing, Florence Nightingale. Squeak like a rusty mouse.'

'Now look here,' said Smith, stepping closer to the table. 'You are under arrest for facilitating the diversion of materiel to the enemy. You're in a tight spot and no mistake.'

'Well!' said Emily. 'And who are you to say so?'

'I am an officer in His Majesty's merchant space fleet,' said Smith. He opened his coat, revealing his red jacket and insignia.

'Oh I *say*,' Emily said. Her eyes widened, and to Smith's surprise there was a smile forming on her prim features: a rather large smile, similar to the one Suruk made in times of war. 'Well, that is a smart uniform. A real fleet officer?'

'Yes,' said Smith.

Her voice was a little breathless. 'Good gracious. Well now, I think I might be able to divest myself for a smart fellow like you. I've always loved to hear about dashing young men in uniform.' She turned to him and leaned forward, displaying her décolletage. 'So tell me, Captain Smith: do you enjoy *Hornblower*?'

Twenty frightening minutes later, Smith knew all he needed to know, and more. In four hours, an unmarked company ship would deliver information and technology to the enemy. They would meet at the high-altitude research platform Tranquility Falls, a known rendezvous for pirates and criminals.

Smith sat in the cockpit, drinking tea. Carveth was making some last-minute checks on the ship before they left. Smith suspected that this involved counting the number of engines to make sure none had fallen off. Dreckitt stood outside, smoking. Rhianna was guarding Emily in the sitting room.

Carveth strolled into the room and dropped into the pilot's seat. 'So, if you don't mind me asking, what's it like turning down a shag?'

'Sorry?'

'Austen-bot back there. She couldn't get more eager unless she stuffed you up her petticoats. With us, she was all "Ooh, I'm too much of a lady", but as soon as she sees you, there's more snow-white frontage on view than a Harrods Christmas display. Her bosom really heaved.'

'So did my stomach. She's patently insane –' he began, and Dreckitt wandered in.

'Looks like we've enough dirt to kick the Leighton-Wakazashi highbinders in the can,' he declared. 'You'd better haul this boiler to Tranquility as soon as you're able. I've got the co-ordinates,' he added, passing Carveth a scrap of paper. 'Me, I'm staying put till the boss man can get a shuttle down from the fleet.'

Smith nodded. 'Righto.'

'You're not coming, then?' Carveth said.

'Nix,' Dreckitt said from the door. 'So long, lady. But I'll be back.'

Smith stood up. 'Will you be taking Emily?'

'Yeah. The company boys programmed her to go section eight. Once we've sorted her noodle she'll be on the square again.' He looked at Smith and grinned. 'She wants to say goodbye.'

Smith strolled down the corridor, past the cabins, to the lounge door. Behind the glass, Emily and Rhianna were engaged in animated conversation. He put his head round the doorframe.

'Then more fool you,' Emily said, jabbing a finger at Rhianna. 'You'll get to thirty-five, and then what? Darning, crochet and endless misery!'

'It's not like that!' Rhianna retorted. 'It's not practical – oh, hi, Isambard. We were just talking about... um... the notion of marriage as fundamentally gender-oppressive.'

'You've got a point,' said Smith. 'There're some dreadful old girls out there.'

Emily was sitting at the table now, instead of lying on it. There was a mug of some herbal-smelling stuff in front of her. 'We were discussing the possibility of one of us netting her man before she gets left on the shelf.'

'I'm sure you'll find somebody, Emily. No need to be downhearted. Now, we need to get moving. Would you mind joining the others at the airlock?'

In a rustle of skirt, Emily stood up. 'Of course,' she said, shaking her bodice into place. 'You just can't talk sense to some people,' she added, and she stalked out of the room. Smith heard the others leave, and the door clang shut behind them.

'What was all that about?' Smith asked.

'Nothing.' Rhianna sighed and pinched her brow. 'Nothing.'

Dreckitt closed the airlock behind him and pushed his hat down low against the wind. Up ahead, Emily was making her way towards the rail terminal, assisted by a police-man. Two officers helped Chairman Gecko into a blue police shuttle, his braces drooping in disgrace.

Dreckitt was halfway down the steps when Carveth caught up with him.

'Hey!' she called. 'Aren't you going to say goodbye?'

He turned. 'Sister, I *said* goodbye.'

'Then say it again,' Carveth said, 'and this time, take your cigarette out.' She kissed him. 'And no messing with Emily's noodle, alright? You let the science people do that.'

'Sure. Damn, it's too cold out here to pitch woo. Here,' he said, and he passed her his hip flask. 'Look after it.' Dreckitt pulled up the collar of his trenchcoat, turned to Carveth and looked into her eyes. 'Now get on the damn ship, Polly. If you don't go now you'll regret it. Maybe not today, maybe not tomorrow, but – hands! Easy with the hands!'

5

Tranquility Falls . . . screaming

'It should be straight ahead.' Carveth consulted the controls. 'Looks like the atmosphere thins out about half a mile up from here. Wait a moment. . . there it is!'

Smith took out the binoculars and peered through them. In the centre of the chilly-blue sky, a speck was taking shape. There it was indeed: a cross between an oil-rig and a zeppelin, a flat platform hanging under half a dozen immense balloons. Small spacecraft clustered around Tranquility, moored in tiers to its sides. As he watched, a new ship docked with the platform and another balloon blossomed out of the rigging to compensate for the shuttle's weight.

Smith looked at Dreckitt's scribbled notes.

'*Tranquility Falls metrological research station,*' he read out. '*Operating staff of a hundred and twelve. Technically abandoned.*'

'It doesn't look very abandoned from here,' Carveth said. 'Looks like it's full of crims.'

Smith nodded. 'No doubt Leighton-Wakazashi use it to further their less legitimate ends. They could finance a place like this, yet disown it if they needed to. Take us in, Carveth. Dock us on the third tier down, out of the way.'

'Aye aye,' she replied, a little grimly. With a minimum of creaking, the *Pym* swung into the final approach. 'What're those ships with all the red paint?'

'M'Lak,' Suruk said from the back of the room. Smith glanced around: both Suruk and Rhianna were watching. He had not heard either of them enter the room. Both were good at moving quietly: Suruk from hunting; Rhianna from a lack of shoes. 'Warriors like myself, perhaps. Or worse.'

'Worse?' The bad lighting made Carveth look severe. 'How?'

Suruk frowned behind his mandibles. 'Sometimes M'Lak go bad. They take up the human's vices: gambling, using guns, drinking carbonated drinks. It is very rare, but. . . I have said enough. We shall have to go carefully.'

'That goes for everyone,' Smith added. 'Carveth, bring us in. If they ask, we're civilian. I'll get the guns.'

The *John Pym* was smaller than most of the other ships, but otherwise it was in good, battered, rusty company. It docked with the side of Tranquility, above a M'Lak ship festooned with skeletons and under an anonymous lump that might have been a cargo box before someone stuck an engine up its back end. In the next berth men in furs shambled out of a gunship bearing the double eagle of the mad Czar of Russia: the Russian navy had gone entirely renegade at the start of the war and was currently busy fighting itself.

'Mercenaries,' Smith said, looking out the windscreen. 'Hired dross.' He slung his rifle over his shoulder and fastened his coat. 'Everyone stay close and be careful. Suruk, if there's any trouble—'

135

'There will not be,' Suruk said, slipping another knife into his belt. 'Not for long.'

Smith turned to Rhianna. 'Tell me if you. . . er. . . sense anything.'

She nodded. 'Okay. I can do that.'

Carveth checked her revolver and tightened the strap that held the *Pym*'s shotgun across her back. 'Can't I stay here? I could lock myself in the loo—'

'No,' said Smith. 'Now, come along. Stick close, and let me do the talking.'

He turned the wheel and pulled the airlock open. They walked out onto a gantry of perforated steel and creaking wires. Wind threw Smith's coat against his legs and set Rhianna's skirt flapping like a pennant. Smith glanced down: under the metal lattice of the walkway there was sky and cloud. He suppressed a shiver and pulled his scarf tight around his neck.

The platform was eighty yards square and buildings were dotted around its edges. Between the buildings stood stalls, kiosks and animal-pens, big upright cages and machines. People moved between the stands; rogues, mercenaries and traders from a dozen empires come to buy and sell. Everyone was armed.

Massive ropes rose from the platform like the trunks of twisted trees. At the top of the ropes were the great balloons that kept Tranquility in the sky, shifting in the wind like tethered clouds.

A thug in overalls watched the four newcomers, tapping a wrench against his palm. He was leaning on a sign that said: *Tranquility Falls*. Under it, someone had written: *Or was it pushed?*

'Well, here we are,' Smith said. 'Let's have a look around, shall we? Where shall we start?'

'Anywhere warm,' Carveth replied, wishing that she had not left Dreckitt's hip flask in the ship. 'It's freezing!'

'Indeed,' Suruk said. 'Monkeys of brass.' He reached into his thigh pocket and pulled out a small bottle. 'Here. This will lessen the chill.'

'Thanks!' she said. '*Royal Lady?* Hey, this is mine! And it's perfume!'

The bazaar smelt of smoke and greasy meat. A tired-looking man was testing the weight of a shotgun at one stall. '*Achetez!*' a vendor cried, brandishing a kebab that looked much like mud on a stick. Smith advanced with the calm, alert expression of an explorer pushing through undergrowth. Behind him came Rhianna, intrigued by the local customs, then Carveth, her face a mask of trepidation, and Suruk – biding his time.

Something grabbed Smith's elbow: he looked down and saw Carveth, her eyes bulging, her free hand pointing to a building on the far side of the platform. 'Look! Look!'

'What is it?' Smith's hand flicked to his Civiliser.

'There's a sale on!'

Smith gazed across the square. Carveth was pointing to a squat, long-fronted building like an army surplus store. Grinding music seeped from the doors, and the sign over them read CRAZY SHANE MAXWELL'S. With the seductive grace of the contractually obliged, a girl twirled in the window in camouflage hotpants – not British army issue, those, Smith noted.

A loudspeaker squelched and squealed from the shop roof. An Australian voice called: 'Are you a smart man?

Then you'd better be a quick man too, and get down to Crazy Shane's Outland Emporium as fast as your ute'll take you! Twenty percent off all clothes, goggles and tyre irons. You'd be a flamin' galah to miss it!'

'Come on, boss,' Carveth said. 'Sales save us money.'

'Certainly not. We have a job to do.'

'He's right, Polly,' Rhianna said gently. 'It's just cheap indulgence. Real meaning comes from. . .' She made a vague gesture at her midriff. '. . .within.'

Carveth raised her hands. 'When've I indulged cheaply? Besides, you can come with me. It's alternative clothes. They'll have things made of hemp and all.'

At the word *hemp* a sort of light flared up in Rhianna's eyes. 'Well, if it's really alternative I guess it can't do any harm, right?'

Smith looked at his watch: an hour to go. Bloody ridiculous. Typical women, turning his stake-out into a shopping trip. No sense of purpose. He decided to go to the pub.

'Suruk,' he said, 'would you mind accompanying Rhianna and Carveth? This place is full of disreputable men.'

'I shall protect them from her,' Suruk promised. 'Perhaps I shall pick up some fishnets in the process.'

'You've got half an hour, alright? And I mean it. I'll be in there,' he added, pointing to the pub beside Crazy Shane's. It had once been the main office of the research platform. On the door was a sign: *The Villainous Hive welcomes you. No flamethrowers, automatic weapons or dogs. Except guide dogs.*

Smith took a deep breath and stepped inside.

A warm wave of smoke, argument and staleness hit his face. He walked down a dingy set of stairs, stepped over what was either a draft excluder or a severed arm and looked around the room.

About fifty people were packed into the bar: the low ceiling made it seem as if there were many more. A free-lancer captain in a long coat was arm-wrestling a man in biker leathers whose jacket was missing a sleeve. In one corner, a brutal-looking trio were banging out jazz on clarinets that had clearly been used to break heads. Three shabby M'Lak were swilling Irn Bru and guffawing madly, addicts of the pink man's fizzwater.

Smith took a step forward and a muscled man with a goatee loomed out of the shadows. 'Not so fast, friend. You looking for something?'

'A drink?' Smith said.

The man snorted. 'You don't look like – hey, I'd know that coat anywhere! You were at the Battle of Barbour Ridge! C'mon in, pal!'

'Battle? Er, yes, so I was,' Smith said, wondering what this might be. Something between the United Free States irregulars and the Republic of Eden? 'Of course. Battle. I always find it interesting to note that we, er. . .'

'Interesting? Terrible, more like! Worst damn tragedy there's ever been!'

'Lost. Shame that. Listen, old chap, do you know anything about Leighton-Wakazashi being here? On the. . . ah, sly. . . so to speak?'

'I ain't the man to ask,' said the bouncer, and he leaned back into the dark. 'But there's plenty who would. Lot of these guys run stuff on the quiet for the Company. Maybe if you buy a few drinks, people'll start talking. Understand?' He patted Smith on the back. 'Drink one for me, pal.'

'I certainly shall,' said Smith, and, pleased by his cunning but a little ashamed for stealing someone else's credit, he walked to the bar.

'. . .but they both loved their old mum,' said the aging barmaid, and she turned to Smith. ''Allo luv, what can I get yer?'

'Pint, please,' he said, and he glanced around as she poured it. An old man was staring at him from the corner of the room. He seemed to be wearing a dressing gown and a bowler hat. Smith looked away. Now, he thought, what next? From the bouncer's comments, it sounded as if some of these rogues would be open to bribery. Quite where to start was another matter. He would need tact and subtlety—

'Hello boss!' Carveth called.

'Good Lord,' he replied.

With a creak of leather she walked into the room, the buckles on her boots clattering. Scarred, bearded heads turned. She wore armoured trousers and a red bodice under a jacket with metal shoulder-plates. Overall, he reflected, she looked like the cycle courier of the living dead.

'Hi there,' she said, joining him.

'Why on Earth are you dressed like that?'

'It was a sale,' she explained. 'Besides, when in Rome. . .'

Smith shook his head. Behind Carveth, the others had entered. Rhianna had acquired a new shapeless cardigan: this one, unusually, was able to cover both of her shoulders at once. Suruk might have obtained new clothes; it was quite hard to tell. Smith looked back to Carveth who was fiddling with the metal plate down the front of her left boot. 'You look like Suruk's wife,' he said.

'Bleargh!' Suruk observed.

'Besides, I hope you've got a receipt for all that. We need cash. If we're going to get any information here, we're going to have to buy it.'

Carveth took a step back. 'Oh no. This stuff stays. After all the effort I spent cramming myself into this corset top, I am not going back just to take it off again. In fact, I may never be able to take it off at all.'

'I would not worry,' Suruk said. 'You are already half out of it now –'

'That's as maybe,' said Smith, wishing that Suruk had not made him aware of Carveth's frightening, prow-like décolletage, 'but we still need money. Pool resources, men.'

They opened their pockets.

'Two Ollies and a George,' said Carveth. 'Twenty-five quid. It might buy us directions to the exit door, but otherwise we're stuffed.'

'Bugger!' Smith looked around. The band launched into a jaunty cover of 'Hello Mabel'. He scratched his head, lowered his arm, and his elbow nudged something.

A hand grabbed his upper arm. He looked round: a small man stood beside him holding a shotgun sawn down to pistol size. He had a sour, crinkled face, as if someone had sewn weights into a prune, dragging its creases towards the floor. 'Oi! Don't you elbow me in my manor! Who the hell're you?'

'I'm Isambard Smith. Pleased to—'

'I'm 'Arry the 'Ammer McAdam, that's what they used to call me. And I've got no time for Space Fleet ponces what mess around in my gaff. I'm drinking 'ere, and I don't like you. Naff off!'

'One moment, if you would,' Suruk said. 'Perhaps I may assist.' Smith shot him a look. Suruk leaned close. 'Fear not, Mazuran. I understand his type. I am wise in the ways of the Ancient East End.'

'And who're you? What's your game, you green slag?'

Suruk threw open his arms. 'I am Henry the Eighth, I am, son of my old man, who is a dustbin! Slayer of wives, King of Pearly, lover of a duck! My crew are deadly warriors, yet nice boys what would not hurt a fly. Be afeared, or I shall slay any man that regards my pint within the sound of Bow Bells!'

Harry the Hammer looked back with eyes like scraps of coal. 'Are you telling me,' he said slowly, 'that you're some kind of Cockney?'

Suruk looked down at his legs. 'No,' he decided. 'That is just the way my trousers hang. They are cor blimey trousers, you see.'

'Oh, I see alright,' said the wrinkled face. Smith's hand moved to his waist, where the Civiliser waited. Suruk smiled. As the band began *The Watermelon Song*, Harry McAdam cocked his gun.

Carveth had wandered off, drink in hand, followed by Rhianna. She looked the part. Her leather jacket would keep her warm and her boots, solid and flat-soled, would be ideal for running away from danger shortly after kicking it in the shin.

Rhianna took a rolled cigarette. 'At least no-one here will hassle me for lighting up.'

'We need cash,' Carveth said. 'How about we sell some of your grass?'

'No!' Rhianna froze mid-toke, horrified. 'That would be immoral. Maybe we could bet on something.'

Carveth nodded at a table against the wall. Two men sat on battered chairs surrounded by empty glasses and creased, filthy notes. Seven or eight others stood around the drinkers, encouraging them and throwing money onto the table. Slowly one of the contestants, a huge bearded fellow, rolled back his eyes, dropped his half empty glass and slid under the table, comatose. His opponent started to gather up the money.

'That's two hundred pound you owe me,' the winner said. A horrible gargling sound came from under the table. 'And a pair of new boots.'

'I've got a plan,' Carveth said. 'Stay back; it might get messy.'

Rhianna took a deep drag on her rollup. 'I'm not sure you've got the karma for gambling, Polly. Maybe I should—'

But she was too late. Carveth strode to the table and tossed twenty pounds onto the chipped formica. 'Any of you boys want to make a bet?'

The bouncer from the door had wandered over to watch. 'What's the game?'

Carveth put her hands on her hips and scowled. 'It's a drinking game.' She looked from one tough face to another. 'I'll challenge any man to match me.'

'You're on,' the man at the table said. 'Hell, I've got money to spare.'

Carveth nodded. 'Good. It's a simple game. It's called 'Downing a pint'.'

There were chuckles around the table. 'Go on, luv,' someone called. 'Tell us the rules!'

'Very well. You drink a pint of beer in one sip. No breaths. If you can beat me, there's twenty pounds in it for you. And a spaceship. And this dancing girl.'

The joint fell out of Rhianna's mouth.

'So, who'll take me on?'

Rhianna tugged at Carveth's sleeve. 'Polly, this is getting really heavy! If you lose –'

'I won't. I was built for a purpose, remember.'

A lank-haired thug like a grubby Viking thumped two pints of lager down on the table. 'You're on,' he said. 'I could drink twice that much without taking a breath.'

'Excellent,' Carveth said. 'I'll go first. Place your bets.' She reached to her back pocket. 'One breath. The whole pint downed.'

'Yeah, yeah. Get on with it.'

'Of course.' She took two long, thin objects from her pocket and dropped one into each drink. 'One breath, one pint.'

'The hell's that supposed to be?' her opponent growled.

'A straw.'

'Perhaps it would be better if you put that down.'

It was a rich voice, smooth and dignified. Smith looked round, and saw the small man in the dressing gown who had been watching him.

McAdam snorted. 'Yeah. Perhaps it would be better if I

put it down.' He laid the shotgun on the bartop and the barmaid broke it open, took out the cartridges and removed the gun from view. 'Erm, I think I was gonna. . . spill some claret, or something?'

'You were going to *order* some claret,' the little man said. As McAdam turned to the barmaid, he put out a hand. 'Captain Smith, I believe?'

'Yes. And you are?'

'George. George Benson. I have, shall we say, interests similar to your own. I believe we share an acquaintance in intelligence circles.'

Smith looked at the place on the bar where the gun had been. 'I saw what you did there,' he said. 'You made him put that gun away. You have the Bearing.'

Benson chuckled. 'Oh, surely not. I'm just an old fellow, pottering through life with the help of his psychic powers.'

'So,' Smith said, 'you know the Shau Teng trick too.'

'Trick? One should not treat such powers lightly. Half of mild, please,' he added to the barmaid. 'Why don't you just put it on the tab?'

'Why don't I just put it on the tab, dear?' she replied, pushing the glass across.

Suruk had been staring across the bar, watching Carveth drink. Smith leaned over to him. 'Everything alright, Suruk?'

'I think so. The little woman is drinking a pint of beer through a straw. She has powerful lungs, Mazuran; no doubt she would be well suited to playing the euphemism.'

'You mean euphonium.'

'I am not sure I do,' Suruk said.

Benson leaned closer. 'I know that you seek the Vorl, and I know that the Ghasts do too. If you wish, we can pool our resources. My knowledge and your urgent need for more knowledge. How does that sound?'

Smith glanced at Suruk. The alien nodded. In Asur'a he said, 'He seems truthful, Mazuran.'

'Indeed,' Smith replied. 'He will assist us.' He turned to Benson and said in English he said, 'My friend likes you. I like you too. It's a deal.'

Carveth's eyes had become huge, her cheeks close to meeting in the middle of her face. The straw suddenly sucked on air, and she let go, panting. Slowly she turned the pint glass upside down. 'Anyone?'

Uproar at the table. Palms slapped the formica, and men laughed and argued as they snatched up their winnings. The man opposite snorted and shoved a pile of money to Carveth. She reached over and picked the pile up as coolly as she could.

The bouncer had watched the contest, scowling in concentration as she put the straw away. 'Now that ain't natural,' he growled. 'You doin' anything on Friday night?'

Carveth's opponent turned away, muttering.

The man whose leather jacket was missing a sleeve pushed the onlookers back. He had made money on the bet; suddenly he was Carveth's friend. 'Easy, mates!' he called. 'Give the lady space! Life's too short to argue, right?' He clapped Carveth on the back. 'Ignore them, miss. There's too much intolerance and bigotry in the world as it is. I blame the dirty Swiss for that,' he added, and he held out his glass to her. 'Have a drink.'

Carveth reached out and the man in the leather jacket froze, grunted and flopped across the table. For a moment she saw the skull painted on the back of his jacket split in two by a throwing-axe, and then the table tipped up and he pitched onto the floor, beer and ashtrays fell after him.

She whipped around. In the doorway stood the first Yull she had seen close-up: slightly bigger than a man, wearing a breastplate and huge shoulder-plates, holding a two-handed axe. She had expected a monstrous rat, but it was no beast: the head was blunter than she had thought, the eyes big and round, the teeth more like incisors than yellow fangs, the whiskers starched into a moustache. It's almost cute, she thought, and then the Yull buried its axe in the bouncer's chest and screamed 'Now you die, offworlders, nice and slow!'

'Eat lead, squeaky!'

Carveth looked round. Smith stood against the bar, pistol aimed.

The pistol roared and the lemming man stumbled into the back wall. It slid down the wall, clawing at the picture of dogs playing poker. For a moment Carveth stood frozen, and then a scream came from outside.

Rhianna grabbed her by the shoulder. 'Come on!'

The patrons rushed for the exit. People struggled past each other towards the door. Guards and customers drew guns and ran up the stairs. Smith forced his way through the crowd, wading against the current of panic, Benson and Suruk behind him.

'It's a raid!' Smith yelled over the chaos. 'We've got to go!'

'Wait,' Benson said. 'There's a back way.'

Smith shoved through to Rhianna and Carveth. 'Are you alright?'

'We're okay,' Rhianna said. Carveth nodded.

Benson gave them a deep nod, almost a bow. 'Miss Carveth, Miss Mitchell. Pleased to meet you. We had best leave.' He looked frail and pink, like something prised from its shell. 'Shall we?'

Smith booted open the back door of the bar and they were on the edge of the platform, the wind howling round them. Smith slipped and Suruk pulled him upright. 'Thanks, old chap,' he said. 'Follow me, everyone. Stick close.'

The market was full of running, shouting bodies: some scattering to their ships, others snatching up goods too precious to be left behind, others loading weapons and taking up positions.

'Someone at the company must've put out a message,' Smith said. 'They must've been waiting for—'

Shrieks in the crowd ahead: people scattered like startled fish. A drumming sound over the voices – disruptor fire. And then, between the fleeing traders, Smith glimpsed a wide-eyed monster with an axe in its hand, snarling as it hurdled one of the stalls.

'Lemmings!' he cried, pulling his rifle into his hands.

A hatch had opened on the far side of the platform and they were swarming out of it like a tide of fur, howling their battle-cry.

Smith raised his rifle and a grinning Yull appeared in the sights, its jaw flecked with froth. He fired and saw the thing fall: 'This way, men!' he called, and they ducked behind a row of market stalls.

Behind the Yull came Ghasts, as coldly ruthless as their allies were berserk. A praetorian kicked down the door to the manager's office and tossed in a bio-grenade. Another picked up a mercenary and pitched him over the side.

Stray bullets hit one of the support balloons and it started to deflate. Tranquility shuddered.

Smith led the others down a narrow corridor of battered stalls and scattering outlaws. One of the stalls fell apart with a splintering crash as a Ghast overturned it, sending sizzling meat hissing across the ground. Smith shot the thing with his rifle and it dropped onto the barbecued food like a giant prawn. Rhianna called out 'Over here!' and as Smith spotted the ramp that lead to the ships, Suruk took hold of his arm.

'How long will it take to ready the craft, Mazuran?'

'A couple of minutes. Are you alright, old chap?'

'I am very well.' The alien looked calm, oddly detached from the anarchy around them. 'I will return presently.'

Smith stopped and looked hard at Suruk. His friend smiled gently, as if he had realised the answer to a question that had been troubling him. 'Make sure you do, alright?' Smith said.

Carveth realised what was happening. 'Are you bloody mad? We have to get out of here!'

'We will,' Smith replied. 'Let's go.'

Suruk vaulted one of the stalls and ran into the crowd, slipping between the panicking outlaws like a wolf through a stampeding herd. 'Come along!' Smith called, and he motioned towards the stairs. 'Quick!'

Their boots clanged on the rungs. The platform groaned and shook. Wind whipped around them. A red glow stretched around the edge of Tranquility; it had caught fire.

'There it is!' Carveth said, pointing to the *Pym*. 'We made—'

A lemming man stepped out in front of them, a grenade smoking in its hand.

'You there!' Smith called, settling his voice in the stern tones of the Shau Teng style, the mystic Bearing of Command. 'Step aside!'

The Yull chuckled. 'No ordering me around, off-worlders. I take divine orders from Popacapinyo!' It held up the grenade and smirked. 'No pin. See? I let go and *boom!* You kill me and I let go and still *boom!* Win-win for the war god!'

'Umm. . .' Rhianna hummed, readying her powers like an orchestra tuning up.

'No tricks, witch lady!' the Yull yelled.

Smith tensed his muscles, ready to shoot.

'Wait.' Benson took a step forward. 'I wouldn't do that,' the spy purred. 'It'd be a waste to blow yourself up, surely, after coming so far. All this way up off the ground. So *very* high off the ground. *Higher than a cliff. A nice, big, tall cliff—*'

'Cliff!' the Yull shouted, and it turned, sprang to the edge and swarmed up the railings. 'Goodbye, stupid offworlders!' it yelled, and it reverted to instinct and leaped into the void. '*Yullaiiii. . .*'

Far below, the Yull exploded.

'Well done sir!' Smith exclaimed. 'Now, to the ship!'

They ran to the airlock, tore it open and raced inside. Smith slammed the door behind them and spun the wheel. 'But Suruk!' Carveth said, surprised by the worry in her voice. 'He—'

'He'll come back,' Smith replied. 'Start the engines.'

6

Vock runs amok

Suruk ducked under a fallen sign, slipped past a thug with a shotgun who seemed to be firing at anything that moved and was suddenly in the centre of the market. The floor shook beneath him, a girder moaned as it stretched. Tranquility was breaking apart.

A group of Yull were looting an overturned stall, stuffing bottles of dandelion wine into a sack. An officer watched approvingly, barking orders and occasionally whacking his soldiers with his stick. Suruk know him at once: partly from his appearance and partly from the aura of arrogance that surrounded him like mist.

'Vock!'

Colonel Vock looked around and saw Suruk. Vock wore a polished red breastplate and his fur was flecked with blood. There was an axe in his hand. 'Too stupid to run, M'Lak scum?'

Quietly, Suruk said, 'I am Suruk the Slayer, son of Agshad Nine-Swords, whom you murdered at the River Tam. My father sends me to do justice unto you. Or at least parts of you. Be afraid, soft furry one, for I shall rip your kapok out.'

'*Hwot?* You insult me, savage!'

'You seek a fight, Vock? Then you must fight me. We shall see then whether you are man or mouse – or some unnatural offspring of the two.'

Vock snarled. 'How dare you! By Tictocikloc, your time has come! Yullai!' he shrieked, and charged.

Vock was so quick that Suruk only just blocked his swing in time. Then the lemming was leaping and slicing, springing forward, every step accompanied with a neat, vicious slash.

Suruk ducked, knocked Vock's legs out with the butt of the spear and swung the point down at him. Vock rolled aside and came up cutting. Suruk sprang back, heard the *vwum* of the axe as it whipped past his mandibles. Vock screamed something and Suruk jumped onto a poultry stall to dodge his next blow, sprang off and the axe smashed the stall apart like a bomb.

Splinters, dirt and frightened chickens flew into the air. Vock stood in the debris in a fighting stance, listening for footsteps above the sounds of panic and destruction. His nose twitched as he sniffed: the M'Lak was gone. The flat-faced savage had fled.

'Pah!' he said, and he spat on the ground, and the spear-blade whipped past his muzzle and sliced several of his whiskers off. He dived headlong, heard the blade hit the ground where he had just been and swiped with his axe from the floor. The M'Lak jumped back, a sort of reverse pounce, and Vock felt his axe cut through something thicker than mere air.

Suruk crouched ten yards away. His spear was in his right hand. His left was pressed to a dripping wound in his thigh. Vock grinned.

Colonel Vock took a step forward and raised the axe above his head.

'So, frog-scum,' he said, 'you are weak too. None can stand before the blade of Mimco Vock. Now I kill you in the ancient way of our people: *very slowly*.'

Vock ran forward, calling to Popacapinyo, and Suruk stepped off the platform.

Vock walked to the edge. The wind howled around his fur, and he felt the inevitable temptation to jump after his foe. Not today, he thought. 'So, you died properly,' he said into the wind. 'Send my regards to your father.'

Ships pulled away from the platform down below. Vock watched as a dark-blue shuttle struggled to break free, the crew wrestling with a broken docking clamp. He smiled at their panic. Stupid offworlders, too weak to welcome the drop into infinity.

Suruk stepped out from behind the ship's main radar dish and gave the Yull a cheery wave. Vock tensed his legs, roared and sprang down onto the ship.

The crewmen scattered as Vock thumped onto the hull. He ignored them and charged at Suruk. The M'Lak side-stepped and flicked one of the radio antennae with his spear – the aerial whacked Vock across the muzzle and he stumbled back, rubbing his throbbing snout. Suruk jabbed and Vock blocked him with an inch to spare. The lemming man jumped aside, remembered he was on the back of a shuttle and dropped off. He landed on the wing and Suruk leaped after him and, the wind tearing at their bodies, they fought on.

Carveth dropped into the pilot's seat and flipped up half a

dozen switches. Smith ran in behind her. Around them, the *John Pym* was coming to life: needles quivered in dials, light flickered from a hundred diodes. The walls and floor rattled and a steady bass hum rose up, spluttered and rose again. 'Check the main engines, would you?' Carveth called.

'Main engines, main engines. . .' Smith glanced around his quarter of the cockpit. A note had been sellotaped to one of the consoles. It said: *Main Engine Stuff*. 'One minute to full power!' he called back.

'One minute?' Carveth cried. 'That's ages! And where the hell is Suruk? If that boar-faced git isn't back in ten seconds time, I'll go without him!'

Something on the platform exploded above them. Girders warped and screeched.

'He'll come back,' Smith said.

'Let's just calm down, okay?' Rhianna said from the doorway. 'Deep breath everyone, and. . . calm.' She smiled beatifically. 'There. Isn't that better?'

A figure dropped onto the nose-cone. Carveth yelped and flailed at the controls. Smith gasped. Rhianna said, 'Oh, no!. That's really bad!'

It was Suruk. He was bloody and battered, and falling out of the sky had not helped. Carveth gestured frantically. 'Get in! Get in!'

Misunderstanding, Suruk waved back.

'Go!' Smith said. Carveth pulled away, and fire burst from the side of the platform. The *Pym* shook. A smell of burning filled the cockpit. Smith strode into the corridor.

Benson was in the lounge, engrossed in a paperback. 'Everything alright there?' he inquired as Smith ran into the hold. The ship lurched, one of the cupboards opened and the vacuum cleaner rolled after Smith like a vengeful robot. Smith reached the ladder and clambered onto the balcony that ran around the inside of the hold. He wrenched the roof airlock open and stuck his head into the sky as they tore towards space.

'Suruk?'

'Greetings!' The alien scrambled into view. 'I can see the Ghasts from up here!'

'Get in, dammit!'

Suruk ran over and dropped into the hold. Together they hurried into the living room and slammed the door behind them.

Smith found that he was panting. 'It was Vock, wasn't it?'

'Yes.'

'Did you get him?'

'No, but he is hurt.'

And so was Suruk, Smith saw; his friend was wounded in half a dozen places. 'Are you alright?'

'I need merely rest. Vock escaped me. The ship onto which I sprang moved too fast for him to follow.' He pulled a chair back from the dining room table and hopped up on it. 'I thought a foolish Ghast tried to follow me, but it must have had the sense to flee.' He scowled. 'For now, though, the lemming runs free.'

Rhianna entered the room, carrying a plastic box. 'Okay, Suruk, I've got some things here for your wounds. You've obviously experienced a lot of stress. This,' she said, taking out an ornate bottle, 'is a holistic oil to relieve tension and restore *ki*. You put it in the bath.'

Suruk picked it up, unscrewed the top and took a swig. 'I can bathe later.'

'Oh-kay, this candle here is for your joints, and this *is* a joint. That'll help provide balance and energy. We just put the candle in your ear, like this—'

'Keep away, Hippocratic oaf!' Suruk snarled, and Rhianna flinched and drew back.

'Suruk!' Smith said. 'I know you're injured, but that's a woman you're talking to.'

'Give me only a needle and thread,' Suruk said. 'I have acquired holes.'

Rhianna gave him a sad, remonstrating look. 'Now, Suruk. I appreciate that you have your own tribal culture, which I respect, but don't you think it's a little bit patronising to expect a woman to produce sewing equipment?'

'It *is* the medical kit,' Suruk replied coldly. He sighed. 'I appreciate your attempts to help, but your medicine is weak. I shall be in my room, stitching myself together.' He started to climb down from the chair. Smith moved to help him, but he raised a hand. 'Thank you, Mazuran, I am fine.'

Suruk's door slammed shut. Smith looked at Rhianna.

'Well, I tried,' she began.

'I know you did,' Smith said. 'He's in a bad way. It's best to give him a wide berth for a bit. He won't want to talk about feelings or anything.'

'I know,' she said. 'He's like you.' She caught his eye and added, 'Sorry, I don't mean to hassle you.'

'Oh, that's no problem. I. . . ah. . . dig.' She shook her head, smiling.

She looked best when she laughed, Smith realised. He liked her much less when she was serious, but behind all that disapproval, she was beautiful. 'I miss you,' he said. Suddenly he was aware of the inappropriateness of what he'd just done, as if he'd farted in the Space Fleet lifts.

Rhianna looked at him. The room was full of escaped sincerity. 'I know,' she said.

'Captain Smith?' He glanced around; Benson stood at the door in his coat and bowler hat. 'I'm afraid you're needed in the cockpit.'

Rhianna said, 'Maybe we ought to talk later.'

'Alright,' Smith said, his soul deflating at the thought of it. He ducked under the doorframe and walked up to the cockpit.

'You've met the Cap,' Carveth was saying, 'and in this cage you can see Gerald – at least you could if he'd not been burrowing.'

Benson peered into the hamster cage. 'Gerald is a mole?'

'Hamster. The Space Navy's too cheap to give us a cat.'

'I see. Where are we going, Captain Smith?'

Smith glanced at Carveth. She said, 'Um. . . as far from Tranquility as we can?'

'Wise,' Benson replied. 'More wise than you can imagine. May I?' He pulled down one of the emergency seats and lowered himself into it. Benson took off his glasses and cleaned them on his tie. 'Those were no ordinary praetorians we saw back there. Those were the personal bodyguard of Number Eight, the seventh most powerful Ghast after Number One. Miss Mitchell's talents have attracted some very serious attention.'

Carveth glanced at Smith and raised her eyebrows.

Benson said: 'We believe that your old adversary, 462,

has acquired the patronage of Number Eight. Captain Smith, Eight is unique among the Ghast leadership for not being either physically deformed or extremely fat. He is cunning, powerful and highly ambitious. Eight has initiated a top-secret project that will enable him to harness the power of the Vorl, strengthen his own soldiers and become the new Number Two. From there, his path to control of the entire Ghast Empire will be clear.'

'I see,' said Smith.

'So to sum up,' Carveth said, 'Eight intends to squeeze out Number Two, and once he's pushed Number Two out, the way will be clear for him to pass Number One. Very devious,' she added. 'And no doubt, once he has sat on the throne and seized the chain of command, he'll follow through with a savage purge. But how does this affect us?'

Benson rubbed his glasses on his tie. 'Well, you see, the connecting link to all of this isn't the Ghasts, or the Yull. It's the company. The former director of Leighton-Wakazashi was a man called Lloyd Leighton. He went missing around the start of the war, presumed dead. But we suspect otherwise. It was following up a lead on his disappearance that brought me to Tranquility—'

A light flashed on the dashboard. One of the control panels let out a thin, annoying beep. Smith waited for Carveth to say something; that sort of fine detail was her area.

'We've got a problem with the pressure,' she said. 'Did someone leave the back door open?'

'That must have been when we got Suruk back in,' Smith replied. 'We must have been too concerned about getting him inside.'

'Fair enough,' Carveth said. 'I'll use the emergency switch.' Distantly, from the hold, there came a dull clang. 'Hope Rhianna wasn't having a look out the sunroof,' Carveth added, 'because if she was, I've just chopped her head off. . .'

'I'll be back in a moment,' Benson said, getting up. 'All that excitement back there. . . not good for an old fellow, if you see what I mean.'

He left the room. Smith looked out the window and watched the atmosphere thin into black as the *John Pym* entered space. So, the Ghasts had joined forces with this Colonel Vock, had they? 462 must have gathered his cronies and started working for Number Eight. What an opportunity! If he could stop them, what a blessing for the Empire that would be, and what an excellent set of trophies for the sitting-room!

'Boss?'

He glanced round.

Carveth said, 'I'm picking up a transmission. Says there's fighting going on around Tranquility.'

'The enemy must've had air support to land troops there. Alright. Plot a course back to Paragon on Albion Prime. We'll put Benson's information before Thomas the Difference Engine to find out what he thinks.'

'Will do.'

She began dialling in the co-ordinates. Suddenly, Rhianna ran in. 'I found this in the corridor,' she said, holding out Benson's bowler hat and gown. 'He's. . . dematerialised!'

'He's in the crapper,' Carveth replied, not looking round.

'Oh,' she said, a little disappointed. 'So, what's going on, guys?'

'We're heading back to Albion Prime,' Smith said.

Rhianna nodded. She stood there, eyes half-closed, as if savouring a taste. 'Something's wrong,' she said. 'I can feel it.'

'Are you sure?' Smith replied. This looked like Flighty Woman Stuff. 'It might be the stress of getting out of that Tranquility place. Don't worry yourself about it.'

'No, no. There's something in the ship, Isambard. *Really.*'

'I can't think of what. Maybe you've got a headache, or you ate something funny? Drugs, perhaps?'

'No!'

Smith stared back at her over his shoulder, shocked by the force in her voice. 'I'm telling you, Isambard.'

Carveth said, 'Look, Boss. . .'

Smith got up. 'Alright. Carveth, lock the cockpit door.' He stepped into the corridor, Rhianna following. 'Any idea where this is coming from?'

'No. It's kind of. . .' She made a swirling gesture. '. . .All around, you know?'

'I see.' He knocked on the toilet door. 'Hello? Sorry to interrupt. All right in there?'

Nothing. He looked at Rhianna. Her face was close. He could smell the joss on her.

'Try again,' she said.

'Benson? Are you alright?'

The door flew open and hit him in the nose. Smith stumbled back, cursing, and Benson was thrust into the corridor, his brogues kicking an inch above the ground. As he looked up Smith saw a thick red pincer around Benson's neck. Slowly, a Ghast followed the spy out of the lavatory, its disruptor pressed to the back of Benson's head.

'Hands up,' it rasped, 'or I shoot.'

'Don't listen to him!' Benson gasped. 'You're in trouble, you bloody insect! Strike me down, and I will become more ticked-off than you could ever imagine!'

The praetorian smirked. 'You will surrender at once, or the old man will be shot.'

Smith slid his hand to his holster. The Ghast had the drop on them – but if he could lure its gun away from Benson's head, he would stand a good chance of firing first.

Suruk crept into the corridor.

'You will drop your weapons and pilot this craft to Tranquility orbital platform,' the Ghast continued, rubbing its antennae together. 'And you will bring me the hamster at once. I am hungry.'

The cockpit door burst open. 'Bastard!' Carveth yelled. 'Touch my hamster and I'll rip off your arse!'

Benson struggled in its grip. 'Dammit, Smith, shoot him!'

The Ghast laughed. 'He will not shoot. His puny altruism prevents him.'

Yes I will, Smith thought, just give me the chance. . .

'How feeble your Earth-biology is! I captured this old fool while he was at his weakest. Human bladders are puny and inefficient. We Ghasts are able to store waste for months. My stercorium is a model of genetic perfection. It is much like me—'

'Because it's full of crap?'

'That is enough, scum!' The Ghast tossed Benson into the far wall and whirled at Smith, raising its gun – and Smith shot it in the side. It stumbled and Smith closed one eye, aimed and fired twice more.

The shots rang around the corridor. Smoke rose from torn leather. Smith kicked the Ghast's gun away and hurried to Benson's side.

Rhianna crouched beside the old spy. His glasses were broken and a thin trickle of blood ran from a gash in his forehead. 'He's alive,' she said. 'It knocked him out.'

Carveth glowered at the dead Ghast, screwdriver in hand. 'Nobody eats my hamster,' she said, and she ducked back into the cockpit.

'It is dead,' Suruk said, prodding the corpse.

'Right,' Smith said, getting up, 'Benson's out of the running. Let's get him to the medical bay.'

'We don't have a medical bay,' Rhianna replied. 'We could use the kitchen table, I guess. . .'

'Good plan. We can eat off trays for now. Can you and Suruk get him down to the kitchen?'

'Easily,' Suruk said. 'The seer here can lift his legs and I will take his head. . . not like that.'

'Thanks,' said Smith. 'Good chap. Carveth,' he called, 'set a course for Paragon Docks, Albion Prime.'

The simulant called back, 'No can do, Cap.'

'What? Why not?'

'Well, there's a space battle in the way.'

Smith thought: I am in a nightmare.

'*What?*' he cried, and he ran into the cockpit. Far off, in the very centre of the screen, lights flashed. It looked like a strange mix of neon and flame: lasers and burning ships. Smith dialled up the scanner. 'Bloody hell,' he said. 'Carveth, keep on course. We'll need to help out.'

She whirled around in her seat. 'Are you mad *and* stupid? Boss, we've got no guns! They'll fry us alive!'

Smith frowned. 'I don't care, Carveth; we have to help defend the Empire.'

'But—'

'Now, look: if we're to have any chance of getting out of this mess, I need your complete co-operation. You'll have to forget about your inherent cowardice for a moment. Remember, Carveth, there's no 'I' in teamwork.'

'Yeah, but there's a messed-up "me". Cap, this isn't just stupid, it's – wait a moment, incoming message.'

The radio crackled. 'Smith? That you?'

'W!'

'Where are you, Smith?'

'In orbit. Bloody enemy raided Tranquility. We got out just in time.'

'Did you find Benson?'

'Sir, yes. A dirty Ghast jumped him in the loo.'

W spluttered with fury. 'Bollocks!'

'He's still alive, but out cold. We're headed for Albion Prime right now. If you've got a medical team—'

'Keep away!' W barked. 'For God's sake, Smith, the Ghasts and Yull have raided the system. There must be two dozen warships up against us. Albion Prime is under siege. We're holding them back, but there's no chance of getting anything past them.

'They want you, Smith; they want Rhianna Mitchell! We're holding them as best as we can, but we've lost the

Frobisher and the *Staines*. I don't know how long we can hold them back.'

Fuzz rose up and swallowed W's voice. There was a muffled, distorted explosion on the far end of the line. Voices yelled and screamed; flame roared.

'Sir!' Smith called. 'W! Dammit, man, what's happening? What do you need us to do?'

The voice that came back was little more than a croak, a whisper at the bottom of a well. 'Your ship can still fly, can't it?' W gasped. 'Then fly it, you fools!'

'Of course, you could never understand.' Colonel Vock tightened the bandage on his arm and prodded himself in the chest with a drunken finger. '*I* follow a code, the ancient teachings of the god of war. This gives me dignity.' He took a deep swig from the neck of a bottle of dandelion wine and let out a raucous burp.

'Fascinating.' 462 sat on the other side of the little room, watching as Vock stuffed his cheek pouches with sunflower seeds, storing them for the campaign. Vock's binging disgusted him. Any Ghast soldier doing that would be shot for wasting materiel. 462 thought back to his own diet of pulped minions and Ghastibix and reflected that he could not recall asking for a second helping in his life.

The Yull were quartered in one of the auxiliary holds of the *Systematic Destruction*, 462's own ship. Vock's tastes were frugal: apart from a heap of malodorous sawdust in the corner, his only addition to his room was a painting of one of his illustrious forefathers, standing on a cliff-top and glowering.

'Your problem stems from being descended from insects,' the lemming man explained. 'Ridiculous little animals.' He jabbed a finger at 462. 'And while you are here, I want to make it clear that the conduct of your soldiers is a disgrace. Your refusal to take prisoners is shameful. If you continue with this tactic, I will have no option but to sacrifice my own soldiers to the war god instead. Sacrifices bring us victory!'

'And yet the beast, Suruk, nearly bettered you.' 462 was tired of Vock already. These mouse-men lacked discipline, 462 thought: once Vock was of no further use, he would let the praetorians cook and eat him. Indeed, the colonel's breastplate would make a passable frying pan.

Hephoc, Vock's civilian servant, slipped in and placed some more wine on the table, then scurried away before Vock could steal his spectacles and hit him on the head.

'He did not better me,' Vock said. 'No scum-frog can better a Yull! Victory was stolen from me by chance. The next time we meet, I shall finish him.'

462 grimaced as Vock took a deep swig from the bottle of wine. Drink did not agree with the Yull – it made them lustful and reckless. Recently, General Rimm had been stripped of his honour after the sacking of Neustadt: not for butchering its inhabitants, but for being found nude and bleeding the next morning in Neustadt Zoo, having attempted to perform an act in the beaver enclosure that dared not squeak its name. 462 scowled and flexed his antennae.

'I expect to make the first attack on the offworlders,' Vock said. 'At close quarters none can survive the ferocity of our assault. It will be my pleasure to destroy the offworlder devils where I can see the terror in their eyes.'

'By all means. Your willingness to deplete enemy ammunition supplies is commendable. But you will leave Captain Isambard Smith alive. I will deal with him personally,' 462 added, rising from his seat. He pulled his trenchcoat close around him and limped to the door.

'Remember, Smith is mine!' 462 barked, and he lurched into the corridor.

A Ghast captain waited outside. 'Strength in unity, great one! We have found no trace of the psychic human Rhianna Mitchell among the dead. We believe. . .' It paused nervously, perhaps wondering how the war was going on the M'Lak Front. '. . .that the *John Pym* escaped us.'

462 nodded. 'And the assault fleet?'

'They have made good progress against the British system, but the defences of Albion Prime are holding. There is no possibility of assistance being sent to Isambard Smith. It is regrettable that my minions have not located him yet.'

'So, Smith is alone.' 462 chuckled. 'Excellent! Here is something that will perk up your antennae: before the attack I gave one of the storm teams a suicide order to plant a tracker on the *John Pym*. They appear to have succeeded.'

The captain snarled. 'Then we must strike fast and eliminate them!'

462 smiled around his scars. 'Not yet, Captain. We will bide our time. We shall follow the Earthlanders. They will lead us right to the Vorl and, when the moment comes, we will crush and smash them all!'

'A brilliant plan, great leader!' the captain replied, and they shared a few moments of cackling laughter. 'I must get on,' the captain said. 'Things to do, underlings to slap.'

462 stayed in the corridor, watching the captain's stercorium bobbing as he strode away. He looked at the poster in the passage, one of a series designed to boost productivity. *Denounce a minion and you could win a staff-car!*

462's thin hand closed around the tracking device in the pocket of his trenchcoat. Nobody else could track the *John Pym*, not even Eight. He did not need to win anything. The winning ticket was already in his hand. He had only to cash it in.

'Pay attention, men.' Smith put the teapot down on the table. 'Benson's out of the running and W – well, who knows. To my mind it's down to us four to find the Vorl, defeat the enemy and rescue Earth. I'll be mother,' he added, pouring out the tea.

The old spy lay stretched along the sofa, wrapped in a blanket. The emergency life-support kit was on the floor beside him. Lights flickered on a long, ticking box: slowly, a bellows rose and fell like a plastic gill.

Carveth wandered over from the galley, thoughtfully chewing a biscuit. Suruk crouched on a chair beside the table, waiting. He had mixed up a luminous, evil-looking fluid in his room and used it to seal up the gash in his leg. He always smelt faintly of ammonia; now he smelt of iodine as well. His wounds did not seem to discomfort him.

'Now,' Smith continued, 'Benson had a number of documents on him. I've looked through them, and they all point in one direction.' He took a swig of tea. 'We all know there was a connection between Leighton-Wakazashi and the Vorl. None of us knew what it was until now. The connection is this man: Lloyd Leighton.'

He held up a printout of a photograph, folded in two. It was a group picture, taken at some kind of dance. Healthy faces in evening dress beamed at the camera; a few raised cocktail glasses. The style of the clothes was not Imperial. In the centre of the picture was a big man with a moustache, smiling broadly.

'I know him!' Carveth exclaimed. 'There was a sort of display about him in the company buildings. Emily showed me a bust.'

'I thought it was only Mazuran who witnessed that,' Suruk said.

'He used to own. . . Blue Moon, is it?'

'Blue Moon got bought out by Leighton-Wakazashi,' Rhianna said. 'My modern dance group staged a satirical protest at their board meeting.'

Smith held up a newssheet clipping. It showed a row of demonstrators baring their backsides at a large building. '*Blue Moon face mass-mooning in morning*', he read out. 'Lloyd Leighton was a powerful man: Lloydland, his theme park, made him very wealthy. He had friends in high places – useless riff-raff, by and large.'

Carveth examined the photo. Smith was right: she recognised several of the faces around Leighton from old magazines. Here was Percy II, the chinless predecessor of King Victor, who had been replaced when he started bleating about the need for strong leadership – preferably the sort with antennae. On his left, Parity Wickworth, the noted socialite, who had famously propositioned Ghast Number One and had received the sort of response to be expected from a sexless, human-hating army ant. Or maybe it was a different Wickworth sister: Calamity perhaps, or Indemnity or Janet.

'Parasites, the lot of them,' said Smith. 'Now, open out the picture.'

Carveth did so. At the edge of the party stood Ghast Number Two.

It looked so horrible, she thought, so unnatural and wrong. Here were all these people, dressed beautifully, smiling away – and in the middle of them, heaped with insignia, stood the sworn enemy of the human race. And they were treating him as a guest!

Carveth said, 'So Leighton knew the Ghasts. Did they eat him?'

'No,' said Smith. 'He went missing just before the war. Blue Moon was going downhill, and there were bad rumours about Lloydland. For one thing it was in the wrong place: at the far edge of human space, out of the way. But – pay attention everyone – Benson's file says that just before Leighton went missing he was researching the location of an ancient Morlock artefact which, he believed, would provide the final clue as to the location of the Vorl.'

'I know of this object,' Suruk said. 'It is the Tablet of Aravash. The tablet is thousands of years old and very precious. It is written that the light of the sun must never fall upon the tablet and, that should this happen, the apocalypse will begin.

'The tablet has a long and bloody history. Some years ago, the Edenites tried to bribe our elders into giving it away for fifty thousand Imperial pounds. Bah! Fifty thousand pounds for the writing of the ancients!'

'Terrible,' said Rhianna. 'Imagine putting a price like that on tribal heritage. What did you do?'

'We held out for seventy-five.'

'You *sold* your heritage?' Rhianna gasped. 'For money?'

'The elders are wise. They caused a hatchling to knock up a copy the night before. After all, one picture of stick-warriors looks very much like another to the untrained eye. When the Edenites found out about the forgery, they were enraged and sent soldiers up the Vargan River to steal the tablet. We threw the soldiers back at the water-side. After that, the elders hid the tablet in a dark cellar, deep underground. And thus it is proven that—'

'If you can't take the tablets by water, you should stick them where the sun doesn't shine,' Carveth said.

'Don't mock Suruk's native culture,' Rhianna put in, turning to her. 'What seems primitive and backward to us may mean something very important to more. . . *authentic* peoples. To us, Suruk may appear somewhat—'

'Right,' Smith said, thinking it best to step in before Rhianna's head talked its way onto Suruk's mantelpiece. 'So where is this tablet? Is it still hidden in a cave?'

'Ah, no,' said Suruk. His mandibles parted and he smiled. 'This is where the true wisdom of the ancients can be seen. They placed the tablet in an ancient fortress, known to men as the British Museum.'

There was a pause. Rhianna blinked. 'You gave your most sacred artefacts to the British Museum? Suruk, really! The British Museum represents the most rampant forms of imperialist colonialism!'

'A cunning double-bluff,' said the M'Lak, flicking his tusks casually. 'Now the tablet is safe behind glass. Braves may quest to the museum, behold the stone and devour an ice-cream as they do. Everyone is happy.'

'So after all this time, the clue we've needed is on display, on Earth,' Carveth said. 'Typical – whenever you go looking for something in space, it's always where you started!'

'The British Museum on Dalagar,' Suruk said. 'Not on Earth.'

They finished their tea. Carveth put her mug down and said, 'Well, it looks like it's pretty clear. We head to this Dalagar place, pop down the museum, get a picture of Suruk's holy rock then fly out to wherever they tell us and get chummy with the Vorl. All we need is a weepy speech about how this war affects everyone, even psychic ghost-people, and we're home and dry. Now then, where is Dalagar? Can't say I've heard of it.'

'Dalagar is its Morlock name,' Smith said. 'We call it New Luton.'

'New Luton?' Carveth echoed. 'Then we're dead.'

7

City of the Future!

Six Ghast fighters screamed over the horizon as the last of the transport shuttles came in to land. The AA lasers opened fire and men and aliens ran for cover. To the West an Aresian deathwalker trained its dessicator on a missile battery. Rockets corkscrewed up from the ground and popped against the walker's force-fields, overloading them, and then the seventh rocket slipped through and blew the walker's canopy apart. It staggered into a factory chimney with a yowl of tortured machinery, collapsing in a shower of shattered bricks.

Doors dropped open in the transport shuttles and a horde of beetle-people scurried out. NCOs with loud-hailers awaited them.

'Citizens! The British Space Empire has rescued your species from lives blighted by idleness and free love! This is your chance to pay back that debt! This city was built as a symbol of our future. Today you join the gallant defenders who unite to say: *This is enough! This is where we turn the Ghasts, no matter what the cost!* Bloody hell! *Duck!*'

The *John Pym* touched fifty yards further down the landing pad. A medical team jogged over to collect Benson, pushing a stretcher between them like a battering-ram. The air was thick with the drone of gatling guns.

M'Lak braves strolled out of the next craft down, bundles of weapons under their arms. A M'Lak was waiting for them in a red coat. 'Greetings campers! Welcome to the city of fun!'

'Ah,' Suruk said. 'Package holidays.'

Soldiers were unloading food from the shuttles. Cranes swung out, men shouted to one another over coughing lorry engines. To the right, Smith glimpsed a clanking warbot stride between the shells of two houses, steam pouring from its chimneys.

Smith took a deep breath of the damp night air. It smelt of burning and wet dust.

The four of them hurried from the ship and a ground crew ran in and threw camouflage netting over the *Pym*. Smith glanced back. With the camouflage the *Pym* reminded him of a rusty tin overgrown by weeds.

'Come along, men,' he said, and they jogged through the gates of the landing pad and into the city itself.

New Luton was in ruins. The Western Sector was in enemy hands: between that and the Imperial camp were six miles of broken masonry and wrecked vehicles. This place had once been the City of the Future, and battered statues of heroes still protruded from the chaos as if drowning in a sea of stones.

Suruk stopped and looked into a crater beside the road. He stared at his reflection in the stagnant water, his shrewd eyes a little distant behind the stern complexity of his face.

Beside him Carveth said, 'You alright?'

The alien glanced round. 'Yes, I am fine. I was just thinking. . . one day I shall spawn into a pool like this.'

'Spawn?'

'Create offspring.' Somewhere far off, a shell whined. 'Continue the line of Agshad.'

'You mean – *have babies*?'

'I would merely cough up a special pellet full of spores into the water. In time, some of the spores might become adult M'Lak. Most would not.'

Carveth nodded. 'I can't imagine you bringing up children. Unless you ate them too quickly, that is. But you – a mum!'

'I am not a "mum", nor am I female. We are asexual, but for reasons unknown to me we tend to be described as male. Now, enough of this emotional talk. Let us find some warfare.' Suruk belched and walked on, scratching the place where his backside would have been.

Rhianna was quiet. Smith tried not to mind. He had stopped thinking about the moments that she had seemed to feel something towards him. He had been deluding himself. He stepped over a fallen signpost and glanced back to make sure that Rhianna's insubstantial footwear could deal with it. She smiled and he looked away.

A figure rounded the corner and trotted towards them. It was a M'Lak, even slimmer than usual, in a strange mix of clothes: tough army trousers and boots, traditional M'Lak armour and a roll-neck sweater. Smith watched the alien approach, finding the combination of soldier, savage and jazz fan curiously familiar.

'Morgar?' Suruk said.

'Hello Suruk!' the alien called. 'Captain Smith!'

'It's you!' said Smith. 'Hello there!'

Morgar ran to meet them, putting on his glasses as he approached. 'Welcome everyone! Captain Smith, Miss Mitchell, yes? And Polly Anorak.' He put out a hand and shook with each in turn. 'And, most of all, welcome, Suruk.'

'*Jaizeh*, Morgar,' Suruk said. 'What brings you here, my brother?'

'My architectural experience got me posted here as alien liaison officer with the Royal Offworld Engineers. Their fortifications have a fascinating blocky style – naïve, you might say.' He paused. 'I heard about Father, Suruk.'

'Indeed. We must speak of this,' Suruk said.

'We will. But first, let's get inside. Look, Suruk, clan colours,' he added proudly, pointing to a cloth in his belt. 'I use it to polish my specs.'

The headquarters were underground, in what had once been the spaceport hotel. It pulsed with energy, movement and sound: people hurried back and forth with wads of papers, pointing to screens and relaying orders. Voices – human, M'Lak and even the odd Kaldathrian beetle-person – rang around the halls.

Morgar led them down a great departure lounge. Once it had been luxurious: now the red striped wallpaper was peeling, the carpet ruined by army boots and fallen plaster. But it was still busy, for technicians now worked on the leather settees and the gilt-edged monitors flashed up information about the war outside. It smelt of synthetic bacon and solder. At a table a row of people were assembling small mechanical cats.

'Kitten bombs,' Morgar explained as they passed. 'The bomb has a core of TNT with a sodium fuse. We leave them out next to a bucket of water: the Ghasts can't resist dunking them out of spite. This way, if you would.'

At the rear of the hall was a waiting room equipped with three battered armchairs and a coffee table. The display board said: *All flights delayed owing to leaves on landing pad and galactic war.*

Suruk looked down to the end of the hall at a small group of M'Lak. 'I see that the elders of our tribe are here.'

Morgar grimaced. 'You can *never* get away from the elders,' he said glumly. 'We evacuated the civilians, but unfortunately they count as military personnel.' He brightened up. 'I'll fetch the major for you – back in a mo. Cricic!' he called down the hall, 'could you fetch our guests some drinks?'

A Kaldathrian turned from its work and lumbered over. It was the size of a shire horse and looked like a cross between a stag beetle and the contents of a cutlery drawer. 'Welcome, honoured guests,' it buzzed. 'Please, accept some dung as a token of our hospitality.'

It passed Smith a neat ball about the size of an orange. 'I rolled it myself,' it said, proudly.

Rhianna reached into her satchel. 'Here,' she said, holding out a cigarette. 'I rolled this myself.'

Smith bowed. 'Thank you for the dung, beetle-fellow. I'm afraid we can't return the favour right now, but we'll see if we can turn something out later.'

The Kaldathrian peered at the cigarette. 'Most kind,' it said. 'So. . . who likes lemonade?'

'Haven't you got any tea?' Smith asked.

'Of course. I forgot. Our section commander doesn't drink it.'

'No tea? Is he ill, or just foreign?'

'Depends on how you define "foreign",' said a voice. Smith looked around. A man in battledress and field armour stood at the end of the sofa, helmet in his left hand. 'Gareth Lloyd Jones,' he said. 'Nice to meet you. I'm in charge of this lot.'

Smith stood up. Jones was two inches taller than him and considerably more solid. His head was shaved and, had he not been smiling, he would have looked like a tough customer. 'You're not Jones the Laser, are you?' Smith asked.

'Yep, that's me. Straight out of Cardiff.'

'Cardiff, Wales?' Rhianna exclaimed, slightly awed. 'That must be incredible, living beside Stonehenge.'

'Um, right,' Jones replied. 'Stonehenge is in the county of Wiltshire – in England, see?'

'Oh, okay. So which county is Wales in?'

Jones sighed. 'Walescestershire. Happy?'

'Perhaps I'd better handle this,' said Smith. 'These are my men, Major.' He introduced the crew. 'We're on an important mission and we need all the help we can get.'

Jones nodded. 'So I see. You've already got one man in the sick bay. Alright then, what can I do?'

'Excuse me,' Suruk said. 'My brother calls.'

He stood up and crossed the room. Morgar waited by the wall, under a battered map of the city underground. 'I was sorry to hear about Father, Suruk. He died bravely.'

'Indeed. But he was killed by a trick, struck down from behind. The human master-spy, W, told us this. He

178

was murdered with treachery, not defeated in battle.'

'Murdered?' Appalled, Morgar's eyes widened behind his spectacles. Then his mandibles closed and his brows lowered, as if his features were setting hard. 'Who did this?'

'Mimco Vock, a colonel of the Yull.'

'*Urushet!* Suruk, we must find this furball!'

'Fear not, Morgar. Our quest brings me close to him. If you help me consecrate my spear, we can add Father's skill to the spirits of the ancestors that live within it. Vock will not escape.'

'Consecrate? That old ritual? But Suruk, that's. . . alright, we'll do it. But – oh dammit, here come the elders.'

Three ancient M'Lak approached, veterans of the family homeworld. They were careful and slow, but not weak: any of them would have been a match for a young human. They dressed like Suruk, but carried more trophies. The elders were trainers of the young, advisors to armies and caretakers of the tribe and, from the look of them, they knew it.

'Suruk the Slayer!' the elder with one eye said, pointing at him. 'Is it you?'

'It is, venerable ones. I have come to fight beside my brother here and honour the name of Agshad, son of Urghar. Now, I seek your help in calling on my father to bless my spear.'

The elders nodded thoughtfully. 'Hasn't he grown!' said the second elder. He was missing a tusk. 'How old are you now?'

'One hundred and six.'

179

The elders slowly exchanged a look, then, as one, they turned back to Suruk. 'Suruk,' said one-eye, 'you travel from place to place, making one swift kill after another, always moving on to the next. This is fine in a young warrior, but you are no longer a youth. It is time you stopped slaying around and found yourself an arch enemy, someone with whom you can share a lifetime of mutual hate.'

Behind them, Morgar sighed and shook his head.

'Take your brother Morgar here. He is a successful architect and is well regarded in the British Army. You should get yourself established, like him. But do not worry, Suruk! For we, your elders, are here to help.'

The third elder, who so far had remained silent, took a picture from his pocket and held it up. 'This is Azrogar the Foul. He is from Clan Oreod and he commands many warriors. Were you to choose him as a nemesis, Suruk, our houses would be linked by fifty years of vendetta. Think of the battles we could all have!'

'He is a vile boy,' one-tusk added, nodding.

'No,' Suruk growled, 'I do not want your arranged carnage! No, elders, I have found a nemesis of my own. His name is Colonel Vock, a noble of the Yull.'

There was a pause. 'Isn't he a bit out of your league?' one-tusk said.

'Not so. I will take revenge on Vock for the death of our father, while Morgar here leads our kin to victory on the battlefield. In the meantime, you will assist me in performing the rituals needed to add my father's strength to that of the ancestors already in my spear, and I shall face Vock in the traditional manner of our people.'

The elders frowned and glanced away. Suruk was right: this was a matter of clan honour and they could not avoid their obligation to assist. For a strained moment they did not reply, and then the elder with one eye said, 'Yes, we will help you. In this era of mechanised warfare it is easy to forget the time-honoured beauty of ramming a spear through someone's head.'

Suruk smiled. 'Good! A reckoning with Vock is long due. As they say on Earth: he is cruising for a bruising, if not actually aiming for a maiming. We shall speak later, elders. You too, Morgan.'

He slipped from the conversation and crossed to the settees, where Smith was outlining his plan to Jones.

'So,' said Smith, 'what I would require is guidance to the British Museum, and enough men and equipment to raid it and transport what we need back to our own lines. I expect the mission would take a few hours at most. It would be best done before dawn. What do you say, Major Jones?'

Jones frowned in thought. 'No,' he said.

'No?'

'Yes, no. No as in, *this plan is insane, and you are a special mentalist for suggesting it.* Sorry, but no.'

'Why not?'

Jones shrugged. 'Well, to start with, you've not told me what you're looking for in there. It could be a little piece of paper or some great big statue. You've not told me what it's needed for either. For all I know you could be planning to break in just to do a bit of brass rubbing.'

'Actually—' said Carveth, and Smith nudged her.

Jones said, 'Look, mate, I don't want to come across

181

unfriendly here. But I won't start sending my people off on weird missions that make no sense just because I'm told it's classified. My men are a good bunch. I'm not having them getting shot up for no good reason. Sorry,' he added, getting up, 'but that's how it is. Did you want some lemonade?'

'No,' said Smith. 'Thanks.'

'I'd better get back,' Jones said. 'Got to see a man about a beetle. Good to meet you, and I hope it works out alright.' He shook Smith's hand and gave them a quick, cheery salute, then strode back into the busyness at the far end of the room.

'Well!' said Smith. 'So much for keeping a welcome in the bloody valleys. I can't believe he thought it was a bad idea!'

'I dunno,' Carveth said. 'At least he's looking out for his men. I'd be happy to be under an officer like that. Don't even bother,' she added, as Suruk opened his mouth.

'Perhaps he needs to consult his gods,' Rhianna said. 'They do that in Walescestershire, right?'

Smith got up. 'Excuse me a moment,' he said.

He pulled his coat around him and walked down the hall. Something boomed far away and dust trickled from the roof like thin snow. Towards the rear of the hall a door was open, and inside a small room Jones was conversing with his staff.

'. . .landship brewed up in the North Sector,' a woman was telling him.

'Warn O'Donahue down in Sector Six. Make sure our own chaps are ready.'

'Major Jones? Am I interrupting?'

182

Jones looked round. 'Yes, you are. Hello again, Smith.'

'Look here,' Smith said. 'You're right: you've got a right to know what we're here for.'

'Alright then, what *are* you here for?'

'Well,' said Smith, 'it's quite simple really. The lady back there – the one who smells of joss – is actually descended from a race of mystic ghosts, who taught mankind the art of Morris dancing hundreds of years ago. We have to find them before the enemy does. To do this, we have to study an ancient stone tablet that my alien friend back there donated to the British Museum. Once we have broken into the museum we need to take a brass rubbing of the tablet, which we will then use as a map to locate the Vorl according to the teachings of a secret society of drunkards whose last leader was possibly Lloyd Leighton, who built Lloydland and may well have been giving one to Parity Wickworth. After that, we'll probably go home.'

'I see. I see. . .' Jones rubbed his chin. 'Alright then – that sounds tidy!'

It was dark. Across the city, distant fires burned. The great guns were firing in another sector. As Smith watched, some low building popped in a sudden blossom of flame.

A factory had half-collapsed beside the street, its original function unguessable now. Girders stuck out of the ruins like the stems of dead plants. Crouched on one of them, still as a resting stork, Suruk the Slayer watched the city.

Smith slogged up a pile of rubbish, detritus crackling under his boots. The smell of greasy food filtered up from

183

the camp below and his stomach rumbled. He looked up at his friend.

The alien did not move. He gazed out across the great battlefield of New Luton, once the perfect city, now a place of death. Smith wondered what must be going through his mind as he surveyed the folly of the human race. Did he despair of mankind, fear them, or merely think of them as fools?

'Tell me this, Mazuran,' Suruk said, 'if the Pope's head happened to come off, and someone nearby offered to do the Poping instead, would he become Pope?'

'No,' said Smith.

'Huh.' Suruk hopped down. 'Soon it will be time to perform the Rites of the Blade. I will need Morgar for that.'

'How long will it take?'

'As long as my father's spirit needs. Once we are done, and Agshad's power is added to the spirits within Gan Uteki, I shall be ready to join you.'

'Well, Jones is calling a meeting in two hours' time. You don't have all that long. There's food down here, you know.'

'Thank you, but I will not eat. I need to turn my mind to noble thoughts, in preparation for the ritual I must perform.'

'Of course. I'll leave you to it then, shall I?'

'Thank you.'

Smith turned to leave.

'One thing more, Mazuran. What about the Chief Rabbi?'

'Same thing, I'm afraid,' Smith said. He climbed back down. Across the road a canteen had been set up in the municipal scout hall. Men sat in the ruined gardens, eating out of plastic tubs.

Carveth and Rhianna sat at a bench, prodding their food warily. Smith sat down beside them. Morgar strolled over, tub in hand, smiling. Smith was struck by his similarity to Suruk. Of course, Smith thought, aliens all looked much the same, but there was undoubtedly a family resemblance.

'Hello,' Morgar said. 'You're just in time for food.' He opened his tub and took out a long, brown, dangly steaming thing. 'Homage?'

'Sorry?' said Smith. His stomach twitched at the sight of the item Morgar was holding up; possibly from hunger, but possibly from disgust.

'Homage,' Morgar explained. 'It's a synthetic sausage made from Sham. Surprisingly tasty.'

'I wouldn't risk it,' Carveth said from the bench. 'Bad news.'

Smith frowned. 'I thought you liked Sham, Carveth? You used to swear by it.'

'I used to swear *at* it. Seriously, stick with the artificial bacon.' She held up a sheet of facon, which looked like the insole of a shoe.

Morgar grimaced. 'I'd best be off. Wouldn't want to be late for the spirits. Toodle-oo.' He turned and sauntered across the road. In the broken windows of a tall, narrow building, a coal fire throbbed. As Morgar reached the doorway, Suruk stepped out of the shadows and joined him and the two M'Lak disappeared from view.

'Oh, sod it,' said Smith, reaching for the facon, 'let's give it a go.'

'It works best with brown sauce,' Carveth said, passing him the bottle. 'Practice safe eating – use a condiment.'

She watched as Smith cautiously lowered the facon onto a plate and started to douse its flavour with brown sauce.

'It must be strange to be in a family,' Carveth mused. 'How can two brothers be so different?'

'It's often the way,' Smith said. 'Take the Marx brothers – one a comedian, the other the inventor of Communism. But still family.'

The M'Lak had made the New Luton postal depot into their own private domain. Humans were allowed to visit but they seldom did; the place looked more like a mausoleum than a mess. A fire burned in the centre of the main sorting room, the flames tinted green in the traditional manner. From racks on the walls, the wide sockets of dozens of skulls gaped at the five warriors, as if with awe.

'Now,' declared the one-eyed elder, 'now the stars are right. Now the spirits are aligned. Now the fire burns high, and in its heart past and future meet. Sons of Agshad, call upon your father!'

Suruk drove out his arm and held his spear above the flames. 'This is Gan Uteki, weapon of the ancients! Since Agshad Nine-Swords consecrated this blade with the spirit of his own father, Urgar the Miffed, a thousand foes have fallen to its wrath. And so, as Agshad son of Urgar called upon his father's skill, Suruk son of Agshad calls upon his father's skill. Agshad, honoured warrior, Suruk seeks your blessing on this blade!'

The elders nodded sagely. The flames danced around the tip of Gan Uteki.

'Well spoken, Suruk the Slayer,' said the one-tusked elder. 'Your words are noble.'

The assembled company turned their gaze to Morgar.

'Smashing,' he said. 'Me too, please.' He caught Suruk's eye and added, 'What? I said it was good, didn't I?'

'You are calling on our father's soul,' Suruk said, 'not offering him a biscuit.'

'Oh.' Morgar fiddled with his glasses. 'Right then. Er. . . Dearly beloved, we are gathered here to celebrate the union of our dad Agshad and. . . well. . . this spear. We wish the spear of the ancients all the best. . . and hope that with Agshad's help it brings many years of trouble-free slaughter. Erm. . .'

He looked at Suruk hopefully. Suruk motioned for his brother to continue. Morgar took a deep breath.

'Well, General Vock murdered Agshad, and I guess that's what this is all about. I'm needed here as liaison officer for our clan, and I suppose even if I took Vock on I wouldn't win. But Suruk here's good. He knows his stuff. And if you help him, father, he'll pay Vock back. And to mark that, here's the broom of Pillbox 218, Fort Tambridge.'

He raised an army standard broom and held it aloft above the flames.

'This is the broom with which Agshad struck the first blow in his final battle. So, Dad, help Suruk find the furry bastard and rip his knackers off! How's that?'

Suruk opened his mandibles and smiled. 'And who speaks it?'

'Well, I do, Morgar the Architect – of Doom!' Wind swept into the room. The flames leaped up, roaring around Suruk's spear. Through the fire, Morgar saw Suruk, his face a grin of exhultation. 'A sign!' cried the one-eyed elder, 'Agshad has sent us a sign!'

Awed, Morgar glanced from one M'Lak to the next. Finally, he found his voice. 'Suruk, the broom's on fire! Help, please?'

At one-thirty Jones the Laser called a meeting in the hotel billiard room. Chairs were hauled up in a rough semicircle and Jones waited until the room was full before he began. He nodded to a man standing at the back, and the lights dimmed. Jones reached to his side and held out a box to the front row. 'Tiffin slices. Pass 'em round.

'Right, in the absence of anyone coming up with anything better, here's the plan. Fifty of us – ten Morlocks and forty humans – will be going up in boats along the main canal to Lock Four, here, by Branwell's Tea Shoppe. At the shop, you'll leave the boats and enter the museum by the rear gates. Morgar the Architect will be in charge of the Morlock contingent and the whole force will be lead by Captain Green here.'

A small man with a targeting monocle gave Jones a brisk, causal salute.

'Captain Smith, who you see back there, will be joining the raiding party. He will be able to point us to the artefacts we need to recover.

'Once the Ghasts discover that we're this far forward, they are certain to try to take advantage and cut the raiding party off. So, as soon as you lot let up a flare, I will counter-attack with our Leviathans and provide cover while the raiding group pulls back. Any questions so far?'

A hand rose.

'Vargath?'

A M'Lak stood up. 'You mention the canal. It seems that we would be heading north. That way will lead us into the hunting ground of the great beast.'

Carveth glanced at Smith. 'Great beast?'

'Indeed.' Vargath turned to them both. 'A fell beast guards the river, as fierce as a praetorian and more vicious than any Yull. Not a week passes that it does not feast on the flesh of Ghast, M'Lak or man, dragging them to its watery lair. I know not from whence it comes, but in our speech it is called Tar'khar – in yours, the Death Otter.'

A rumble ran through the room. Men whispered to one another, M'Lak growled and croaked. Cricic's six knees shook.

Jones stood up. 'I'll need the raiding party ready to go at four.' He glanced around the room. 'And about this Death Otter. . . It won't be a problem. Remember, we got our name from taking care of business. Let's get going, men.'

The meeting broke up and the chairs were pushed back, the soldiers suddenly busy and alert.

Carveth said, 'What is their unit's name?'

Smith replied, 'The Shopkeepers.'

'Don't worry, Polly,' Rhianna said. 'I'm sure I can deal with this otter they're talking about. I was fine with the sun dragons back on Urn. Otters are much smaller.'

'Well, just be careful,' Smith replied. 'I wouldn't want you getting hurt, Rhianna. A normal otter can give you a pretty nasty nip, so I dread to think what a Death Otter could dish out—'

'Death?' Carveth suggested, and Smith turned and scowled at her.

Rhianna yawned. 'I need to chill out for a while, guys. I'll see you later, okay?'

They watched her go. Soldiers talked around them, chairs scraping the floor as they were rearranged, and Carveth had to raise her voice a little. 'Look, Boss, I wanted to talk to you.'

'What is it?'

'This might get pretty hairy, from the sounds of it. If – well, if things go wrong or something, I'd like you to have this.' She took a slim book from her thigh pocket.

'What is it?'

'My war diaries. If I ever don't make it, I want you to get it published. With the money from the sales, I'd like a charitable fund to be set up aimed at bringing me back to life.'

Smith looked at the volume. Carveth had drawn a flower on the front, in correcting fluid. The book was entitled 'Adventures in the Pollyverse'. He opened it at random and encountered a picture of a horse executed in biro.

'Don't read it!' Carveth cried.

'Sorry.' He put the diary into his coat. 'Don't worry, Carveth, you'll come back. We all will.'

The *Systematic Destruction* tracked the *John Pym* to New Luton and touched down safely behind Ghast lines. It had not been standing on the landing pad for ten minutes before a hard-faced squad of praetorians arrived to take 462 and Colonel Vock to Number Eight.

Things were grim in Ghast territory. The first wave of attackers had been convinced that they could sweep through New Luton like a hurricane, but their advance had been slowed by ferocious defenders and unpleasant local diseases. Without proper food or medical supplies, the drones had developed a painful condition of the stercorium known as *slaksak*, which was only halted when the praetorians ate them all.

But reinforcements were flooding in and each day more Aresian battle-walkers strode through the wreckage of the city like vast wading birds, plucking men from the streets like herons seizing fish. They disembarked from transport ships by the half-dozen, spindly and strangely coltish as they paced towards the battle-line.

The hovercar stopped before a sleek black ship on the other side of the landing field. An airlock opened with a wet squelch and a lift whisked Vock and 462 into the presence of Number Eight.

Eight stood at a railing, looking down into a pit. He was reading the *Origin of Species* with one hand and beating time to piped Bruckner with the other. As 462 approached he glanced round and smirked.

'All hail, mighty Eight!' 462 cried.

'Hail.' Eight twitched his antennae. 'And this is the Yullian warlord, I assume. Primitive. I am pleased to make your flea-ridden, degenerate acquaintance, Colonel.'

'*Hup-hup*, offworlder coward,' Vock said graciously. 'I am barely ashamed to be in your soul-tainting presence.'

'Good.' Eight put his book down. 'You are no doubt surprised to see me here, 462; I secreted a tracking device in the hold of your ship.'

'Your secretions are always welcome in my hold, great one.' 462 glanced away, making a mental note to have his personal security team investigated by his other personal security team.

Eight continued: 'I intend to be present for the capture of the Vorl. Now, where is this Captain Smith and his associated rabble?'

'On the other side of the city, Eight. We will know if they try to leave the planet.'

Eight nodded and turned to the pit. 'It disgusts me that so few of them could cause us so much trouble. Perhaps this Captain Smith should be thrown to the ant-wolf. Assault Unit One likes mammals, but the all-doberman diet tires him.'

Vock grimaced, although whether he was disgusted by the concept of keeping pets or worried that he might be mistaken for an unusually mobile chew-toy was hard to tell.

'I believe that the value of a culture can be gauged from the size of its attack dogs,' Eight observed. 'Good boy, Assault Unit One.'

462 looked down into the pit. Assault Unit One crouched in a heap of doberman bones, chewing. It spat out a spiked collar.

Vock puffed his chest out. 'I have questions!'

Eight peered down at him and smiled, bearing slightly more fangs than necessary. 'Yes?'

'Why has this planet not been overrun yet? When will we close with the enemy and offer up their hearts? And why have I not been given my own spacecraft?'

Eight scowled and licked his thin lips. 'Simple, my furry

ally. First, this planet has not yet been conquered because of the deranged efforts of the Earth-scum in resisting our inevitable success. Second, we will destroy the enemy when it is most effective to do so, without unnecessary waste. And third, you are travelling on a Ghast ship because if you had your own vessel you would drive it into the ground.'

'Only ground with offworlders on it. Ground occupied by Suruk the Slayer and his disgraceful minions!'

'Precisely why your revenge will have to wait.'

'Wait?' Vock looked around the room and sneered, a gesture 462 was growing to despise. 'And who are you to tell me what to do? Your warriors die without victory. Death is no excuse for failure! You dare tell me to wait, offworlders? Popacapinyo does not wait, insect! You do not speak to Mimco Vock like that! You will show respect, lobster-men!' he yelled, voice rising to a neurotic scream, 'Because I am Yull and I have lots of honour and important and am very very *very* dignity!"

Vock stopped, panting, hand on his axe, his muzzle dripping with froth. The Ghasts studied him with quiet contempt.

Eight sighed. 'You have a choice, rat-thing. You can complete this mission intact, in which case you will have the opportunity to murder your enemies in whichever sick manner your tiny mind prefers, or you can complete it as an amusing novelty rug. Now, I have assumed temporary control of our forces here and have had the previous commander shot. The troops are on high alert: as soon as Smith has completed his orders here – whatever they are – we shall capture and interrogate him and his crew as to the location of the Vorl. Then, and only then, he will be utterly destroyed. I understand 462 will deal with Smith himself. His comrades will be yours to annihilate, Colonel Vock.'

'Yes?'

'Yes, Colonel Vock.'

'Good.' Vock rubbed his paws together. 'Kill all,' he whispered. 'Kill all, nice and slow!'

'We will conquer as one!' 462 cried. 'Surely this brilliant plan calls for laughter, Eight!'

'Yes,' said Eight, 'yes!' He threw his head back and cackled with insane merriment. 462, who had been practising his own laugh, waited politely and then joined in. Vock squealed with evil glee. The guards chuckled and, as if to answer them all, a tight-jawed snigger came from the pit.

8

Hands Off My Culture!

Smith looked down the boat. It slid silently through the canal, passing the buildings on the waterside. The soldiers sat quietly behind; each one a small, hunched shape like a roosting owl. Every few seconds came the soft plop of the paddles as they dipped into the water.

He felt a stab of fierce pride. Only a year ago these people had been civilians; now they were elite. Knobbly faces looked back at him from the boat, different features and colours but all determined and sharp-eyed.

And then there were the M'Lak, Morgar amongst them, mankind's partners in this war. How quickly things could change when survival depended on it! Smith remembered when Suruk had first entered human territory, eager but naïve. Suruk had only ever come to Britain as a tourist, convinced by a misread tabloid editorial that hordes of aliens had already arrived to view Britain's rivers of blood. Smith had helped Suruk out of a nasty altercation in Debenhams, and the two had renewed the friendship they'd forged on Didcot 3, where Suruk had tried to hack him into bits.

The boat rocked and Smith glanced up. Gunfire came from one of the further sectors of the city: it sounded like a football rattle from the canal.

Carveth pointed to Suruk's spear. 'How's Sticky?'

'Benighted midget, my blade bides well,' Suruk said. 'The ritual is done.' He gazed across the black canal, fingering the shaft of his spear. He's looking for the otter, Carveth thought, and she too looked across the wide canal, half expecting the beast to rear up behind them.

The water was full of junk: lumps of masonry, girders, even half a fighter plane, sticking out like the tail of a metal shark. No monsters, though, unless you counted the dead Ghast that bobbed as they slipped past. Its coat hung around it like the wings of a crashed bat. Water slapped gently against the side of the boat.

A chubby woman scanned the banks with thermal binoculars. 'Nothing, Grocer.'

Green raised his hand and made a gesture to the second boat. He turned to Smith. 'No enemy in sight,' he explained. 'So far.'

Smith felt Rhianna turn beside him. 'Look!' she whispered.

Two huge statues appeared like approaching giants, flanking the canal. On the left was King Arthur, his sword raised, a dragon coiling around his armoured feet. On the right, a woman raised a great steel lantern over the water.

'That's the largest statue of Florence Nightingale in the known universe,' Green said softly. 'People used to stand under her lamp for luck.'

As the boat slipped past Carveth looked up at the calm stone faces, pitted with shell-holes. She thought: knowing my luck, if I stood under her lamp it'd drop on my head.

'And to the right,' Green said, 'our destination.'

He pointed and, as if summoned by him, a great white

slab of a building slid out of the dark ahead. Carveth stared. It was bigger than the Parthenon and had more pillars than a wedding cake. Rockets and gunfire had battered and smudged the sides, but it could never have been anything other than the British Museum.

Carveth slipped a hand into her jacket. She had once heard that young conscripts carried ammo while old soldiers carried food. By this logic she was a hard-bitten veteran. She dipped her head and took a large surreptitious swig of whisky from Dreckitt's hip flask. The whisky made her think of Dreckitt going away; it made her feel bad and want to cry, although Dreckitt had said that Famous Teacher did that to everyone.

She glanced over her shoulder as if to take one last look at the world behind. As she did, she noticed something odd: the dead Ghast was sinking. It twitched in the water, snagged on a branch, then shot down out of view as if pulled under by a whirlpool.

Or something else, she thought.

'Bring us in,' Green whispered, and the boat swung towards the shore.

The prow bumped against the side of the canal and at once men and M'Lak sprang onto the towpath and spread out. Beam guns and laser rifles covered the area while men with Stanford guns crept ahead.

Smith climbed out of the boat and, motioning for the others to follow, entered the museum gardens.

It was a tea party in hell. There had once been a neat little lawn here, and there were still wrought-iron tables and chairs, shadowed by tattered umbrellas. Skeletons in fine clothes sat around the lawn like victims of the galaxy's slowest table service. Their clothes were undisturbed; their food lay in front of them.

A little light-headed, Carveth picked up a scone from one of the plates. Its bony owner grinned at her. 'These'll make you fat,' she told the skeleton.

Suruk tapped her on the arm. 'Go quietly. Dead men eat no scones.'

Rhianna leaned close to Smith. 'What happened here?' she whispered.

'Marty,' he replied. 'A walker must have hit them. A low-power dessicator beam could do this.'

Green strode over. 'It's Marty alright. There's ruddy great holes in the car park. You don't want to see it. Half a dozen dead bodies lying there, sticks still in their hands, hankies still in their belts. Bastards must've hit them mid-dance.'

'Morris dancers?' Smith looked at Rhianna; she raised her eyebrows. 'There were Morris men here?'

Green nodded. 'You a Morris dancer, then? You could get a good session going here,' he added. 'Maybe set up a square on this grass here, have some light refreshments over there. . . Gertie don't Morris dance,' he added darkly, and he walked off to join his men.

'Morris men,' Rhianna said. In the dark it was impossible to tell where her hair ended and the night began. She looked as if she had formed out of the air, Smith thought, alluring and otherworldly, like something from folklore. An elf, or a gnome or something. Maybe not a gnome. 'I wonder who they were?'

'The last of the Hospitable Tipplers, perhaps,' Smith said. 'Who knows? Maybe they came here to study the artefacts, just as we mean to. Maybe they got too close to the truth and that drew the enemy here. That and the sound of bells.'

'And for all that they were murdered.' Rhianna looked very sad. 'The last of the Morris people,' she said.

'This senseless violence won't go unpunished,' Smith promised. 'We'll find some aliens and blast the crap out of them.'

Morgar beckoned from further ahead. Smith went first, making sure that Rhianna was close behind. They scurried under a battered sign that read 'Branwell's Tea Shoppe' and reached the door.

Smith turned to Morgar and Green. 'I'll do it,' he said. 'It's my mission, after all.'

He took hold of the door handle and turned it. He pushed gently. It wouldn't budge.

'Locked,' he whispered.

'Pull,' Carveth whispered back.

Smith pulled and the door swung open. He stepped over the threshold, rifle in hand.

He looked into a long corridor, its high ceiling exaggerated by the whiteness of the walls. There was a pedestal on Smith's right, like an empty lectern. On the opposite wall a little brass plaque hung under a big discoloured space. Smith peered down the hall. There were glass cases, racks of leaflets and no exhibits at all.

He took a leaflet from a dispenser and unfolded it as the others followed him in.

'We're in the 20th Century hall, from the looks of it,' Smith said. 'This must be where they kept all the cultural artefacts. . . but it looks like they've gone.'

'Gone?' Carveth turned from one of the brass plaques, appalled. 'Gone? Are you telling me we've gone halfway across the galaxy to find it's all bloody gone?'

'Shush,' Smith replied. 'We're in enemy territory. Come on.'

One of Green's men waited at the end of the corridor. 'You won't like this,' he whispered.

Smith looked around the corner, into the entrance hall. The hall was decaying, but it had once been magnificent. Behind a ticket box, a grand staircase rose to the upper levels of the museum. A ten-foot statue of Saint George dominated the foyer, his uplifted sword almost brushing the chandelier above his head.

The hall had been looted. Ropes and posts had been thrown through the windows of the ticket box. The heads of the two lions that crouched at the bottom of the staircase had been smashed to dust. A sooty mess in one corner showed where a fire had been made from books, leaflets and pieces of broken chair.

But the statue was the worst; that was sacrilege. Someone had drilled two holes into the saint's forehead and thrust bits of metal into them so that they jutted out like antennae. A rope had been tied around his waist, attaching a rusty barrel to his rear so that it stuck out of his backside. They had turned Saint George into a Ghast.

'Bastards!' cried Smith. 'That's Saint George! They've given Saint George a metal arse, the filthy swine!'

A shadow moved on the staircase. '*Ak?*'

Green gave Smith a hard look. 'That's torn it. You've got them going,' he whispered.

'They've got *me* going,' Smith replied. 'How dare they do that!' He reached to his side, for his sword.

'What're you doing?' Green hissed.

'I'm off to get some exhibits for the Dirty Moonman display.' He drew the sabre. 'Get a glass box ready, Green – I'm going to pin some insects.'

Green grabbed him by the shoulder. 'Let me do this,' he said.

Step by step, the Ghast descended into view. It was an early-model drone, Smith saw: brutish and slightly porcine, like a school bully. The thing was cautious. It approached as if on unstable ground, its disruptor gripped firmly in both hands.

Smith slipped the Civiliser out of its holster.

At the bottom of the stairs, the Ghast turned left and Green ducked into the shadow of the statue of Saint George.

The Ghast approached, picking up its feet to avoid making noise. Its coat creaked softly. Green crept out behind it.

Green's hands snapped around its helmet, his leg tripped the Ghast and he yanked its head back and up. Smith heard Green grunt, saw the Ghast kick once, and there was a sound like a branch snapping in cloth. Slowly, Green lowered it to the ground, grabbed its coat and dragged it back into the shadows.

Suruk made his purring, croaking sound. Smith nodded approvingly.

'Ugh,' Carveth said. The whole scene reminded her far too much of a man trying to ravish a lobster.

'Looks like they've sacked the place,' Smith said. 'I suggest we split into teams and see what's left.' He stepped over the dead drone and took a handful of Family Fun Maps from the leaflet rack. 'Here. We'll take the Yothian Cultural Artefacts hall.'

The hall was broad and high, lit by ferroglass panels in the roof. It felt desolate and cold – haunted. Carveth peered into a glass display case, which showed a dummy wearing Yothian formal dress. The Yothians were tall and broadly conical, with little yellow heads. The dummy looked like a huge road cone.

'What an amazing civilisation,' Rhianna said.

'Do you think they stack?' Carveth replied. She squinted at the metal plaque. The light was bad, and it was hard to make out the words.

'Only in the mating season,' Smith said. 'Come along, men.'

They walked on. There was no sign of the tablets, nothing that would indicate where they had gone. This part of the museum had been largely left alone by the Ghasts; it was clear that it would never have housed anything of M'Lak origin.

'Look!' Carveth said, pointing into one of the Yothian display cases. 'That one's pulling a moony!'

'The model's fallen over,' Rhianna explained. 'The Yothians are far too dignified a people to do that.'

Carveth huffed. 'Another "higher" lifeform.'

Rhianna quickened her pace to catch up with Smith and Suruk, her sandals flapping.

Carveth stayed behind, struggling to read the plaque beside the fallen model. She reached out and ran a finger over the embossed words. '*In courtly dress,*' she made out, '*which is*—' Confused, she ran her finger back and forth before realising that she was trying to read the head of a screw. A screw in the dark leads to confusion, she thought, reflecting that this was probably worth remembering.

Behind the plaque, something went *thump*. She sprang back, stared into the gloom and looked down at her hand. The wall had shaken; she'd felt it in her fingers. Surely not. But here was the proof: as if into quicksand, the plaque was sinking into the wall.

'Boss?' she said, much quieter than she had intended. 'Boss!'

Ten yards away, Smith looked round. 'Shush!' he hissed. 'Keep it down, Carveth. Come on.'

'But I—' The wall split open. Air blasted into the hall and light shot around the edges of the glass case with the fallen Yothian as if a door were opening into heaven. The case swung back, and blinding light flooded the hall, turning Carveth into a silhouette. Smith ran to her side, pistol ready. Suruk raised his spear ready to throw.

A figure stood before them in the centre of the light. The rush of air set her skirt and sleeves fluttering. Slowly, gracefully, the woman stepped into view. Wise blue eyes looked them over. She smiled.

'Halloo! Come here for the tour, have you?'

The woman stood at the edge of the doorway. She was attractive, Smith noticed, and vaguely familiar. She was an android, he realised, and a remarkably pretty one.

'Well,' she said, 'welcome to my abode! A lady and gentleman, a Morlock and a fellow simulant. Certainly makes a change from school parties.'

Smith took a step forward. 'Good evening, madam. Do you live here?'

She smiled again. 'Yes, indeed I do! For I am the Archivist, you see. Ah, the Yothian seems to be pulling a moony again. He does that. Very bad. Really must sort that out.'

She led them down a set of steps, spiralling deep into the earth. Smith followed, then the others, and behind them half of Green's men, their boots clanking on the metal stairs. The Archivist glanced over her shoulder. 'Nearly there,' she told Smith.

'What is this place?'

'This? Ah, you'll see. Should be rather interesting, I think.'

The walls were white, as was her dress. It made her seem ethereal. She reminded Smith of the Lady of the Lake, albeit dryer. But she was too smart to be ghostly, too clever and quick. Smith thought it quite appealing.

The stairs ended at an airlock door. The Archivist paused at the lock, ready to dial the entry code. 'Seeing that you're not a school party, I don't think we need to scan for lice,' she said brightly, and her finger flicked around the dial. The airlock slid open and lights boomed and flickered in the cavern beyond.

They stood at the edge of a warehouse the size of a cathedral nave. Rows of packing cases made corridors and partitions in the vast room, interspersed with relics too large to be packed away. Paintings lined the walls.

'Blimey,' Carveth said, which Smith thought was pretty accurate.

Kaldathrian dung-statues stuck their heads above the lines of crates like malodorous giraffes. A Yothian fertility glider hung from cables in the roof, its landing gear dangling lewdly over their heads. Smith recognised a sphere of rock, twenty yards across and etched with symbols: the ball from a game of planet-hockey played by the Voidani space-whales, a sport capable of devastating whole solar systems. Current thinking held that the ancient Voidani had once played this sport near Earth, leading to the extinction of the dinosaurs when the ball went off-side and demolished Central America.

'Behold!' Suruk pointed to a statue of a huge M'Lak, throwing its head back to laugh – unusually, this one was broad as well as tall. 'Brehan the Blessed. We are in the halls of the M'Lak.'

'Amazing,' Smith said to the Archivist. 'You compiled all this yourself?'

'Well,' she said, 'I had a couple of robot forklifts to help, but yes. I'm rather glad you dropped in, to be honest. Terrible conversationalist, your robot forklift.'

'It must have been a lot of work.'

'Not really. I mean, a lot of what there was has been lost. The war does that, of course. The best you can do is keep a few things safe. We all need culture, don't we? Look at that,' she added, pointing to a framed picture on the wall. 'I bet you've never seen one of those before.'

They stopped. Smith peered up at a poster almost as tall as he was. It looked like Ghast propaganda, but although the style was right, the subject was undoubtedly wrong. It showed a Ghast perched on a stool under a spotlight, legs crossed in front of it. Instead of a trenchcoat and helmet, it wore long gloves and a little round hat and was sticking its stercorium out.

'What the devil is that?' Smith said.

'It's an advertisement for some kind of show,' the Archivist replied. 'It's almost two thousand years old, dating just before the first Number One took power. Once, the Ghasts had names, lives, identities of their own. But then they had to take the choice that comes to all sentient life sooner or later: the tough option of individual freedom, or the comfort of collective obedience. Mankind chose freedom, after some indecision. The Morlocks have always chosen freedom. But the Ghasts chose. . . poorly.'

'So they were once proper people,' Smith said. 'Foreigners, of course, but still people. Incredible. But not impossible, I suppose. It just goes to show how far you can fall.'

The Archivist pointed at the picture. 'It may be all the history they have. Once, even the Yull were sane. They had a civilian government, a developing society. . . back then they only jumped off cliffs on special occasions.'

Smith stepped back from the picture, its spell broken. 'It's quite something,' he told the Archivist. 'You've done the Imperial People a great service by keeping all of this safe.'

'Unless anyone actually wanted their ancient artefacts back,' Rhianna observed from behind.

Smith didn't comment: Rhianna had been quiet and a bit sulky ever since they had got here. Her disapproval of the museum had increased greatly since they had met the Archivist, for reasons he could not figure out. Funny bunch, girls. You'd have thought that two intelligent, attractive women would get on very well. He thought about this for a while. Something tugged at his sleeve.

'—think we've found it,' Carveth was saying. 'Come on boss, wakey-wakey.'

Smith followed her past scowling statues of famous M'Lak. At the far end of the corridor stood a slab of stone nearly nine feet high, covered by a tarpaulin. At a nod from the Archivist, one of Green's men pulled the tarpaulin away.

Down one side of the stone were blue characters; down the other, red markings, representing concepts and arguments respectively. There could be no mistake – this had been made by the M'Lak.

'Whoa,' Rhianna said.

'This is ancient indeed,' Suruk declared. 'I can read ideas – notions – but I am shamed to say that the exact meaning is lost to me. It tells of the days before time, that I know, but otherwise it is as clear as a Scotsman's mist.'

'Me too,' said the Archivist. 'Not really my area, I'm afraid.'

'Perhaps I may help.' They looked around: Morgar stood behind them, cleaning his glasses on his clan colours. 'There is one amongst us who understands ancient things. Tormak!' he called. 'Come here a moment, would you?'

From the troops stepped a slight, rather refined-looking warrior. He ran a hand through his thick mane, looked up at the stone and said, 'Ah, yes, well, yes. . . *quite.*'

'This is my old friend Tormak,' Morgar said. 'Listen closely, for he's a clever chap.'

Suruk turned to the newcomer. 'You are a speaker of runes, friend?'

'Fine art and antiquities, actually,' Tormak replied. 'Not really my field, this, but still. . .' For a while he scrutinised the stone. 'Well,' he said, 'this is definitely the Tablet of Aravash. As you no doubt know, it is written that if the Tablet ever sees the light of day, Armageddon will begin. Which *would* be a problem, were Armageddon not going on right now.'

'Oh,' said Morgar, 'I suppose galactic war does rather count. I never thought of it like that. . .'

'So there is nothing to fear from the Tablet,' Suruk observed. 'Let us shed some light upon it.'

Smith turned to the Archivist. 'Could we move the tablet?'

'Oh no,' she replied, 'we can do much better than that.'

She reached up and pulled a cord, and a lamp flicked on above the stone.

'Daylight bulb,' she explained.

With a soft crackle, the tablet began to fall apart. Dust trickled from the blank rock, rolled down the face of the stone, piled itself into a heap at the base. The sand fell in thin sheets over the rock, and where it had been there were little marks, channels cut into the stone. Like the breaking of a mould or the stamping of a coin, images appeared in the smooth face of the tablet.

There were two figures repeated several times on the stone: one could have been Suruk as drawn by a six-year-old, or by Suruk himself. Smith found the other unsettling. It was a M'Lak, no doubt, but a sort of upright shadow with huge holes instead of eyes, leaping over the horizon.

'Shall I read?' Tormak asked.

'Go ahead,' said Smith.

'Proceed,' Suruk replied.

Tormak pointed to the top right of the stone. 'Well, I'd say this stone depicts several scenes involving the afterlife. Up here is a pair of stock figures, you see: a warrior and, next to him, this rather sinister stylised person. He represents death. He is the Dark One, who leads warriors from this life to the next. The pictures show the warrior's journey in a sequence, rather like the *Beano*.'

Tormak moved his hand across the stone.

'In this picture here, the writing reads: *Suddenly, the warrior's bright eyes burn dim. How can this be?* The answer is that the Dark One has come to take him. In this next picture, we see them passing through the Ways of the Dead, until finally they arrive at Ethrethor, the hunting-ground of the dead. The last picture reads *The Dark One leads the warrior to the ancestors. The ancestors hail the noble hunter and they all have a party.*' Tormak stepped back and rubbed his chin. 'Interesting. Now that *is* unusual.'

'Go on,' Smith said.

Tormak indicated a set of runes. 'These are very peculiar. They give a location for Ethrethor. It says: *They shall meet where the day never ends and laughing they shall ride the very lightning.*'

They looked at the stone, staring at the symbols as if the force of their gaze could draw meaning from the rock.

'I know not,' Suruk said.

'It's really interesting,' Rhianna said, 'but no.'

'So we draw a blank,' Smith observed.

'Maybe not.' He looked round. It was Carveth. She glanced nervously from face to face, as if surprised to find that she had spoken. 'Chances are I'm going to regret this for the rest of my life. But that's what the adverts say for Lloydland: *There's so much fun the day never ends.*'

'But what of the lightning?' Rhianna asked. 'Surely that's a reference to the respect for the power of nature held by indigenous peoples.'

'Nah, it's a ride at Lloydland.'

Smith turned from the stone to Carveth. 'How do you know all this?'

The android shrugged. 'They send me offers sometimes. I get discounts from being in the Pony Fan Club.' She folded her arms, suddenly defensive. 'I can join the Pony Fan Club if I want. I'm only two.'

Smith looked back at the tablet. 'So it's some sort of prophesy, you say? I'm not entirely convinced. I've never heard of a prophesy advertising a theme park before.'

'Well, not a prophesy as such. But if Lloyd Leighton owned the land, why not stick a theme park there anyway?'

'Hey, yeah,' Rhianna said. 'And Leighton was well-acquainted with Number Two. Maybe there is more to Lloydland than we thought. . .'

'So Lloydland is where Leighton went to research the Vorl,' Smith said quietly. 'And that's where he disappeared. And, from the looks of it, where we will find the Vorl.'

Carveth nodded. 'And by a happy coincidence, it has rides and ice cream. Everybody wins.'

Boots clanged on the stairs behind them. A soldier jogged into the hall, gun swinging against his hip as he ran. 'Captain Smith? Orders from the Grocer to get you topside, sir. Gertie's here.'

They hurried back up the steps into the museum. Green was waiting for them. At the doors, Smith turned back.

'Thank you, madam,' he said. 'Your assistance has been invaluable. It may have saved the universe.'

'It's always nice to have visitors,' the Archivist replied. 'Toodle-oo. Oh, Captain Smith?'

'Yes?'

She held out her hand. 'Souvenir pencil and eraser. Do come again.'

The door swung shut, and she disappeared back into her realm. The dust settled, and the hall was empty and derelict again, as if she had never been there. 'Most obliged,' Smith said.

Rhianna sighed. 'It's a collection of looted artefacts, taken from helpless—'

Suruk raised a hand. 'Be still. Our foes are close.'

They crept down the hall, weapons ready.

A squad of praetorians was busy in the atrium. Two had pulled down a statue of Athene and were kicking it. Another pair had mistaken the ticket booth for an item of historical significance and were tearing it apart with pincers and teeth. A scrawny lieutenant looked on approvingly.

Smith aimed his rifle at the lieutenant. 'You there! Get your hands off my culture!'

As he said *culture* it reached for its gun. The rifle-shell slammed into its chest and it flopped twitching into the back wall. Smith cranked the handguard and Green's silenced Stanford tore the two praetorians at the ticket booth apart. Frantic movement at the statue. Smith put the crosshairs on one monster, blew its head off, lined up the other as it lifted its disruptor and shot it through the neck.

'And *that's* why they tell you not to touch the exhibits,' he said.

Only gunsmoke moved in the atrium. They advanced, the soldiers spreading out to cover the staircase and doors. Tormak took a fact-sheet from a dispenser and slipped it into his back pocket.

Smith glanced at Suruk. 'Hear anything?'

The alien shook his head. 'Not even a sausage.'

Green motioned to the main doors and his troops took up covering positions. A bearded soldier drew the bolts back and opened the door.

New Luton was silent. The ruins were oddly peaceful, as if the city was still being constructed and the builders had gone home for the night. A fire glowed in the distance, an ember in a scene of grey and blue.

'Looks clear,' Green said. He took a step towards the door. 'Alright, let's go.'

'Wait!' Rhianna hissed. Green looked round as she rubbed her temples. 'Everyone, look out!'

Green said, 'What?' and above them, something creaked.

Spikes drove through the ceiling, twisted into tentacles and ripped the roof away in a scream of girders. Suddenly the cold sky was above them, studded with stars. Lights swung into the aperture and a dreadful howl filled the hall.

'Marty!' Green called. 'Get down!'

A dessicator-beam punched through the roof, turned a joist to rust, clipped a soldier and blasted her to particles. The war-machine honked and whined. A metal tentacle snatched a soldier into the air and squeezed him in two. 'Plasma, now!' Green bellowed.

'Behind us!' Carveth cried.

Smith spun round: a figure ran into the corridor behind them, leather coat flapping, backside bobbing behind it. 'Ghasts!' he called, and he fired from the hip, missed and the Ghast threw itself down, aiming its disruptor. There was a loud flat boom and the alien slumped like a puppet without strings. Carveth stood there, panting, the shotgun smoking in her hands.

Behind it, two more Ghasts ran into view, carrying a heavy disruptor between them. Smith fired again and one collapsed. Suruk hurled a knife into the other's throat. From the hall came the roar of plasma-fire and a sudden glow as if a furnace door had been thrown open. The war-machine bellowed.

'Back!' Green shouted. 'Back to the boats!'

Ghasts poured into the corridor. Disruptor fire rang around the hall.

Rhianna was motionless, eyes closed, concentrating, using her powers to shield herself. All very well, thought Smith, but soon the Ghasts would be within striking range and what good would her skills be then?

He grabbed her arm. 'Rhianna? We have to—'

Something hit him hard, as if God had punched him in the chest. The world swung up and he felt his back strike the floor. A scream, and then voices shouting 'Boss! Boss!' and 'Isambard!'

Hands grabbed him and pulled him up. He was hauled out of the corridor, across the chaos of the atrium, his head spinning. A woman was yelling something. The arm holding him up smelt of ammonia. Suruk, he realised. His crew – where were they?

'Rhianna?' He thought he saw her and reached out.

'No time for love, Captain Smith,' Suruk growled, and he was dragged through the doors, felt the night air on his face and shook his head like a dog shaking water off its chops.

'I need a bit of a sit-down,' he said.

The world was going dim. He slipped out of Suruk's grip and sat down on the museum steps. Men were running around him, shooting and firing. A weird mechanical yodelling was going on nearby. Something like a metal mosquito was striding through the street, bits of the museum roof still clutched in its tentacles. A rocket spiralled through the sky and burst prettily against its shields. Something huge and lithe slipped between two houses on the waterside, half a boat in its mouth.

Carveth hopped from foot to foot, making agitated sounds. 'Get up!' she shouted. 'We have to go!'

'Um,' Smith replied, rubbing his skull. He felt wetness there: blood. 'Bit of an achey head, I'm afraid.'

Rhianna knelt down in front of him. He smiled at her. 'Hullo, girlie.'

She took his hands in hers. 'Isambard? Look at me.'

He lifted his head, aware of how tired he was and how pretty she looked. It would be so easy to close his eyes, to topple forward and bury his head between the soft pillows of her benevolence. He let himself fall, feeling only drowsiness and the softness of her hands – and sound rushed through his brain like a tidal wave. Suddenly he heard gunfire, explosions, shouts and the whine of machinery.

Morgar was in the middle of Green's men, directing

their fire. To the right, Suruk whipped his spear round and sliced a praetorian in half.

Smith scrambled to his feet, sharp pain jabbing at the back of his head.

'We have to go!' Rhianna called. 'Any longer here and we're herstory!'

'Too late!' Carveth yelled. 'Look!'

The war-machine turned and the blinding glare of its spotlights swallowed them up. Their shadows stretched in the light as if trying to pull free from their bodies. The walker hooted in triumph, and as Smith lifted his rifle, it fired its dessicator.

The beam tore open the concrete on which they stood, cracked the pavement apart, turned a tree behind them to confetti. They were silhouettes in the light, statues trapped in a bubble of roaring sound. Carveth was flinching, Suruk hurling his spear. And before Smith, hair streaming around her like a goddess, Rhianna shielded them all.

The beam flicked off. Suruk's spear sailed out and hit a Ghast in the chest. Carveth peeked between her hands. The war machine lifted the dessicator to its main portal and gave the gun a good shake.

Rhianna smiled at them all. In a circle around them, the pavement was unbroken. The crack in the earth stopped just before her sandals.

Carveth turned to Smith. 'I *told* you she was weird.'

The walker took a step towards them and its cockpit exploded, its pilot bursting like a dropped blancmange. The legs buckled and collapsed.

A landship rolled around the corner of the museum, a

clanking, puffing castle on tracks. A great ramp dropped open in its prow. Half a dozen turrets swung to cover the road, and a figure appeared at the battlements on the main tower, waving down to them.

'Mayhem, is it?' Jones the Laser called. 'You'd better get inside. I would let you have your boat, but the death-otter's eaten it, see?'

The landship creaked and shuddered to a halt in the Imperial sector and the soldiers ran out into hard, slanting rain. Smith jogged behind Green's men, wincing as the night air chilled the back of his head. He had spent the last forty minutes in the landship's medical bay, drinking tea and sitting still as a surgical wallahbot stitched his scalp together, and his head was stiff with anaesthetic and surgical Brylcreem.

'A successful mission, I think,' he said, and a bioshell exploded twenty yards away.

The compound was under siege. Ghasts lay around the perimeter in heaps. Soldiers manned the concrete barricades in two-man railgun teams. A sergeant stood in the middle of them, directing their shooting at a pack of hovertanks. 'Front rank, fire! Second rank, fire!'

A sudden flash of metal between two buildings; a damaged walker lurched across the road with a warbot clinging to its leg. Two beetle-people scurried out of what had once been a fire station, hauling a Gatling cannon between them. Injured men and prisoners were dragged away. Fresh soldiers ran through the ruined houses in a half-crouch and dropped into the battle-line. The night stank of fire and dust.

Jones waited for them a little further on. 'This way!' he called, pointing, and they headed for the main HQ, Smith slowing so as not to leave the women behind. Now he could hear Ghasts, yapping and snarling on the right. Someone screamed, and gunfire rattled off to the south.

Yet it was no panic. The men were ferocious and disciplined. This was their ground, the Empire's ground, and they would fight for it. A wave of giddiness struck Smith and, with it, deep respect for the common people who had come here to fight.

Morgar caught up with them at the entrance to the command building. 'Hello again!' he called. 'And how are we all?'

'Pissed,' said Carveth. She too had availed herself of the landship's medicinal facilities, and consequentially smelt of brandy.

'We're holding rather well,' Morgar said. 'We've drawn back to the second perimeter and we're keeping them at bay. The landships have held the museum and are linked up with us. The beetle-people are reinforcing our defences with – well, you can guess what with.'

'Good stuff,' said Jones. 'Tell the beetles that the defences need as much extra armour as they can manage.'

'I'm sure they'll work something out.'

'Is there anything we can do?' Smith asked.

There was a little pause. Two men ran past, carrying an empty stretcher.

Morgar said, 'You should go.'

Jones nodded. 'He's right. You've got a job to do and

it's not here. It may be a fool's errand, maybe not, but good luck anyway.'

'I suppose so,' Smith said. 'Even if it's a fool's errand, we're still best qualified to do it.'

Morgar led them down the road, and at the far end they started up the ramp towards the landing pads. 'You should be able to break atmosphere without trouble,' he said.

Men were hauling the camouflage tarpaulins off the *John Pym*. Suruk glanced at Smith. 'You should wake its engines,' he said, gesturing to the ship with a mandible. 'I will follow you presently.'

Smith nodded. 'Carveth, go and fire the ship up. Rhianna, you ought to get inside. Jones, could I have a word?'

'Course.'

They took a long step away from Suruk and Morgar. Smith watched the two women climb the ramp to the launch pads. 'Look,' he said, 'Er, there's an awful lot of Ghasts out there. I mean, I don't know if the fleet can help, but if you'd like me to put a good word in—'

'We put a good word in about three months ago,' Jones replied. 'It was *Help*. The fleet's about as useful out here as an Australian in a whispering contest. Listen, you can tell HQ that I'm not wasting good people for nothing. You've seen how our soldiers fight here, and that's all the more reason not to leave them on their own. We'll fight to the last if needs be, but I won't waste men, see?'

'Yes,' said Smith, impressed. 'I see.' He held out his hand, and they shook. 'Good luck, Jones. You're a decent chap.'

'Thanks. You too. Now, bugger off and let me get on with this.'

Morgar took off his glasses and wiped the rain off the lenses with his clan colours. When he put them back on, Suruk was smiling. 'I am pleased, brother.'

Morgar said, 'Oh yes? What with?'

'You.'

'Really?'

'Indeed. You have applied yourself well to the ways of war. You fought boldly at the museum. Of course, I would rather that you used a proper blade than a puny Earth-gun, but there is no denying that you have behaved honourably.'

Morgar pushed his glasses up. Since he had no nose as such, they slid down again. 'Gosh,' he said.

Suruk looked around, 'Perhaps now I should learn the law, to equal you in a profession. It is as Father would have wished.'

Morgar shook his head. 'He would have wanted you to protect your friends. Right now the galaxy doesn't need more lawyers: it needs a maniac with a sacred stick.' He glanced up at the *Pym*, watched steam rise from its hatches, listened to its engines cough. 'I can take care of things here. You'd best go before the elders find some other idiot for you to get engaged in battle with.'

'Well said,' Suruk replied. He lifted Gan Uteki, consecrated spear of the ancestors, as if to brandish it at the whole of New Luton. 'I will stay fast and cunning. No enemy will slow me now, no elder force me into unholy acrimony. To you I say these words: Mimco Vock shall fall by my hand!'

219

'And to you, Suruk, I say these words: have a nice trip. And if you see General Vock – pull his whiskers for me.'

Suruk turned and jogged up to the ship. At the airlock he raised his spear. 'Good hunting, brother!' he bellowed over the roar of the engines, and Morgar waved back.

9

From Museum to Theme Park

Major Wainscott's pod dropped open as it hit the ground and he jumped out into the snow, slapping a fresh magazine into the side of his Stanford gun. He was confronted by a depressing lack of hostile fire, so he threw himself clear of the pod, anticipating an ambush. Nothing happened.

'Hiding, are you?' Wainscott muttered into his beard, setting his backpack cogitator to scan for life as he studied the landing zone through his gunsight. Up ahead, the Leighton-Wakazashi headquarters loomed like a frosted cliff, the tinted windows glistening like black ice.

His Portable Information Transmitter Headset crackled. 'Boss?' Susan said. 'Any contact?'

'No,' he replied. 'They're definitely hiding. Spread out and move up, thirty yard intervals. See any moon-men, do them over. Over.'

Ducking low, he ran across the landing pad. A Ghast shuttle lay beside the company ships, its narrow black nose pointing at the company buildings like a mangled, accusing finger. Nelson was crouched beside its front leg.

'Anything, Nelson?'

The technician shook his head. 'Looks like Gertie headed North.'

'Towards the company buildings, eh? Alright, let's go.'

They ran towards the rail terminal. Halfway there, Wainscott dropped down and prodded something half-buried in the snow. It was a dead Ghast, its coat frozen stiff like beaten lead, body twisted and teeth bared in rage or pain, or both. 'Dead drone here,' he told the intercom.

'Got a few here,' Susan's voice crackled back. 'Someone made a tidy job of their landing-party. Small-arms fire, mainly. There's not a lot left by the looks of it.'

'Bugger!' Wainscott replied. 'Meet me up by the main entrance. There may be some inside.'

He ducked behind a battered sign beside the executive offices. It read: *Welcome to Leighton-Wakazashi, bringing you tomorrow's future today! Access for paupers at side entrance only.*

Wainscott lay down and waited, the snow hiding his outline, Nelson watching his back. Susan, Brian and Craig jogged up beside him and he rose to a crouch. 'If Gertie's here, he's in there,' Wainscott said, nodding at the doors ahead. 'I'll take the doors. Brian, Craig, flanking. Watch our back, Susan. Nelson, would you be so good as to bypass the door controls?'

They ran to their positions. Wainscott nodded to Nelson, and he pressed a device against the doors. A counter spun on Nelson's machine, the lock whined, and the doors slid apart.

A dozen people stood behind the doors: policemen, mainly, and with them a line of young women, all of them armed. A man in a long brown coat stepped forward to greet the Deepspace Operations Group.

'Wainscott?' he said.

'Dreckitt?' Wainscott lowered his Stanford gun. 'What's all this, then?'

Dreckitt holstered his pistol inside his coat. 'The ants sent a mob of gunsels down here. We managed to hold them off. We thought we'd lay low and wait for you.'

'You killed them all?'

'Yep.'

The wide-eyed girl beside Dreckitt gave Wainscott a victory sign. 'Yay! Go ultra robot lady team!'

Wainscott looked them over, sighed and turned to his men. 'Well,' he said, 'there's nothing here to kill. Bloody mission's a write-off. Come along Susan, we're going home.' He stepped back into the snow.

'Wait!'

Wainscott glanced round. 'Well?'

Dreckitt said, 'Major, if you're looking for the enemy, I can help. W's taken a slug and that leaves you and me running this case. Polly Carveth, my squeeze, taught these dames how to pack a piece. She's out there with Isambard Smith, looking for the Vorl. If you want to go help them, I'd be first to ride your running board.'

Wainscott looked at Susan and grimaced. She shrugged.

A tall, elegant android in a long dress and bonnet stepped forward and curtseyed as she reached the door, as if about to welcome them into her home. 'I am Miss Emily Hallsworth, formerly of Mansfield Theme Park. Major, I believe Mr Dreckitt is making you an offer of assistance. He has certain information as to the whereabouts of your colleague – and, I should add, Miss Polly Carveth. Despite his uncouth manner, I would suggest that you accept Mr

Dreckitt's aid and head forthwith to assist Captain Smith.'

'Yeah,' Dreckitt added, 'you said it, sister.'

'Sister? I certainly hope not, Mr Dreckitt.' Emily smiled at Wainscott. 'So, Major, it would seem prudent for you to relieve us of Mr Dreckitt's rather working-class presence. But before you leave—' and her eyes gleamed – 'that's a rather splendid uniform you happen to be wearing, isn't it?'

The *John Pym* rose amid a flurry of flares, decoys and pre-emptive missiles, as if in the centre of a fireworks display. Carveth sat at the controls, following the progress of the counters and dials. A flare burst near them, throwing a green glow onto the brasswork. Below, New Luton was a blur, red flowers blossoming and fading against the blue-grey buildings. It seemed an incongruously cheerful way to leave.

Carveth heard boots behind her. 'Bloody hell, boss,' she said, watching the city. 'What a place. They're knackered down there, aren't they?'

'Most probably,' Suruk said.

She glanced round. 'Oh, it's you – Sorry, I thought you were—'

'Isambard Smith rests in his room. He must be careful with a wound to his head, lest his liver fall out.'

'What? You have your liver in your head?'

'Only my spare one. Most of the space is taken up by my digestive and excretory organs.'

'Weird.'

'We are, you might say, opposites: I excrete from my voicebox, whereas you speak from—'

'Alright, point made. I'm sorry you overheard me just then. I didn't mean—'

'You are correct, though. Most likely they are doomed.' Suruk stood beside her, leaning up close to the glass. 'They will fight bravely, but they will be overwhelmed.'

'I'm sorry.'

'There are worse ways to die.' Suruk looked round. 'A question, small woman. . . can you imagine me in a court of law?'

'Easily, provided the police could catch you first.'

Suruk looked into Gerald's cage and gave his water bottle a thoughtful squeeze. 'I meant as a speaker of law. I would stand before the elder with the ears of a spaniel—'

'The judge.'

'Before him, and say "This man is guilty! Slay him now!" Everybody would wish to employ me then. Do you think I could be a criminal lawyer?'

'Well, you're halfway there already.' She turned to the navigational computer, wondering what had brought on this strange flight of fancy.

'I could execute wills!' Suruk enthused, and Carveth shuddered.

'I'm going to check on the captain,' she said. 'Don't touch the controls – or the hamster.'

She walked down the hallway and knocked on the door to Smith's room.

'Come in!'

He sat at the little table, which was supposed to be for typing vital reports but was covered in Airfix kits and glue. 'Hyperspace Hellfire,' he said, holding up an indeterminate plastic item.

'How's the head?' Carveth asked.

'Right as rain.'

She peered at the model. 'Should the wheels come out of the cockpit like that?'

'Do they? Ah, yes. Whoops.'

Carveth stepped inside and quietly closed the door behind her. 'Suruk reckons we're going to lose New Luton.'

Smith did not say anything. After a few seconds he nodded. 'It's possible, yes.'

'That means Morgar and the rest. . .'

'Quite.'

'Bloody hell. What a waste.' She sat down on the edge of his bed and sighed. 'I quite liked that Jones the Laser.'

'I doubt Rick Dreckitt would have approved. You *are* taken, you know.'

'Only roughly.' Carveth frowned. 'It's bad about New Luton, though.'

Smith stood up, slow and weary. She looked small, deflated somehow. 'Come on,' he said, tapping her on the arm. 'Let's have some tea. We might have some good biscuits left.'

Rhianna was meditating in the living room, making a sound like an old fridge. Her eyes opened at they entered. 'Hey guys,' she said. 'Everything okay?'

'Fine,' Carveth said.

'Fine,' said Smith. There was an unspoken agreement between them never to discuss anything emotional in front of Rhianna, who would only make them miserable by forcing them to talk about their feelings. Smith put the kettle on.

'Is your head okay?' Rhianna asked.

'Should be alright,' Smith replied.

'It's just that I was worried back there. The treatment you received – well, it just didn't seem very holistic.'

'Holistic?'

Rhianna made her spreading-hands gesture. 'Incorporating the totality of the body,' she explained.

Smith dropped four teabags into the pot. 'Well, only my head got hit,' he replied, irritated by her slowness. 'In total I'm fine.'

'Yes, but you could have put your aura out of balance, or blinded your third eye.'

'What?' Smith paused, shocked. 'My aura is quite well balanced, thank you,' he replied. 'And as for my third eye, I don't think that's any—'

Carveth elbowed him in the ribs. 'Magic talk,' she whispered. 'Digging a hole, boss.'

'Ah, I see. Well,' he continued, 'in that case my magic parts are fine. Which reminds me: I think we all ought to thank you for stopping that dessicator beam back outside the museum. Had you not done so, I suspect we all would have bought it.'

'It was nothing,' Rhianna said. 'I'd have done it for anyone.'

'Oh.' Somewhat disappointed, Smith brought the teapot to the table and sat down. Suruk strolled in and they shared out the biscuits.

'Right,' said Smith, as the alien squatted down on a chair, 'I'm pleased to say that we are in a good position. Carveth here has set a course for Lloydland, and once we arrive we can start to search for the Vorl. We seem to have lost the enemy for now, so I can only presume that we have the lead.'

'Which means that we have lost Colonel Vock,' Suruk growled.

'For now, yes.'

'Then this is folly!' Suruk snarled. Rhianna blinked as if awoken. 'Mazuran, I promised my brother that I would singe the fur of the lemming. If we do not face Vock, I shall have broken that promise. I know the pixie here regrets us leaving the soldiers of Jones the Laser behind. Think then how much greater is my regret, living with the knowledge that my father was dishonoured by a rodent! You are a friend, and one I would never harm, but if Vock escapes me my rage will know no bounds. I will have vengeance, or I will have kittens!'

'I understand, Suruk,' Smith said. 'Carveth, I know you're not overly pleased—'

'I know we had to go,' she said. She stared into her tea. 'It's just the thought of leaving all those men behind. All those officers and privates left down there. . . stop looking at me like that. I mean it.'

'No doubt you do,' Suruk observed.

Rhianna was watching, engrossed, slowly twirling a strand of hair around her finger. 'I'm sensing a lot of negative feelings in the room,' she began.

'Amazing powers of perception you've got there,' Carveth said.

'Shush,' Smith said. 'Were you going to say some stuff, Rhianna?'

Rhianna looked down at the tabletop, as if trying to discern a meaning from the tea-stains and dents. She looked at Smith, as if to say something, sighed and said, 'No, nothing. It's terrible about New Luton, but the time for peaceful protest there is over. I can help most by opening communications with the Vorl. I have to go on.'

'You already do,' Carveth said.

'Good,' Smith said, although he felt that something was up with Rhianna. Perhaps it was some strange feminine business, or wind. 'Now,' he said, addressing the whole table, 'pay attention, men. I have listened to your concerns, and I will promise you this: once this mission is complete, or as complete as we can get it without dying, we will return to New Luton. There we will do everything we can to help the troops, whether than involves shuttling them to the battlefield or assisting with evacuation. And while we are there, Suruk, please feel free to resume your quest to defeat Colonel Vock. For it is there that the trail goes cold, and there, if the Yullian mind is what I think it is – i.e. small and nasty – where he will want to stay in order to sate his bloodlust.

'But until then we will carry on. We will keep on going, partly because the freedom of the galaxy depends on us, but more importantly, because we're British, or at least two and a half of us are, and not giving in is what being British is all about. I ask you: did Cromwell, or Nelson chuck it all in? Did Barnes Wallace stop giving a damn? Never!' Full of enthusiasm, mug in hand, he sprang to his feet. 'We will go forward, men, united in our mission to seek out the mysterious being that got Rhianna's mother in the family way. Then, and only then, we will return to the Empire and put our new knowledge to deadly effect! Any questions, men?'

Carveth raised a hand. 'Are you aware that none of us actually *are* men?'

'Not by birth, no. But by extension!'

'What did I extend to become a bloke?'

'He means it as an allegory, Polly,' Rhianna explained.

'Do I have one of those?' Suruk asked.

'We all do!' Smith cried, eyes wild. 'You may not be men, true, but you're doing pretty damned well considering. And with that,' he declared, 'who'll join me in a game of cricket?'

462 sat in his chair on the bridge of the *Systematic Destruction*, admiring his reflection in his newly-polished helmet. Minions scurried around him, suitably busy and afraid. This, he reflected, was the life.

Being Number Eight's chief underling had brought a wide range of benefits. Not least was his new command seat, which reclined and played classic highlights from Number One's speeches. He flicked a control and from speakers in the headrest a voice yelped 'Crush! Smash! Lightning! Ruthless!' 462 settled back, put his pincer arms behind his head and folded his hands over his thorax. 'Complete annihilation of mammalian life!' bellowed his chair.

Heels banged together at the side of his seat. 'Commander!'

462 opened his sole, beady eye. 'What?'

An orderly looked down at him. 'Request from. . .' it shuddered, '—Number Eight's personal ship. He seeks information as to our next move.'

'I see. Tell his pilot to keep back and follow us. Our enemy will lead us to the prize.'

The orderly saluted. 'Puny human craft *John Pym* is on course for Lloydland, a human planet. Lloydland has one main settlement: a "theme park".' It scrutinised its clipboard, perplexed.

'A pathetic source of amusement for decadent weaklings,' 462 explained. 'True amusement comes from unity, strength and standing in lines shouting!'

'Freedom is unity! Peace is shouting!' the orderly quoted. 'Glorious commander, sensors have picked up traces of what may be another craft, entering the system on a tangental approach.'

'I see. Can you confirm its identity?'

'No, Commander.'

'Proceed with our mission. Continue to monitor. Dismissed.'

The orderly saluted, spun round and strode away. 462 activated the screen on his armchair and flicked through the various spy cameras on the ship. In their quarters the Yull were watching a propaganda film. This film was of caged Guinea-pigs which, the voice-over claimed, were Yullian infants that the British intended to ship to the Andes and feed to ravening pan-pipe musicians. The Yull were nearly berserk, eyes bulging as they screeched promises of mayhem and butchery at the screen. 462 chuckled, reflecting that the Yullian government would say anything to keep its moronic lackeys sufficiently enraged.

462 flicked the switch and saw Colonel Vock staring at his suit of polished red armour, apparently in a trance. His axes lay on his lap and there was a cruel smirk across his snout. No doubt he was contemplating the tortures he

intended to inflict on Suruk the Slayer and his allies. Vock reached into a bag and stuffed a handful of mixed nuts into his mouth.

462 switched off the camera.

So, the reckoning would happen on Lloydland. With the disposable allied troops and the specially-equipped praetorians delegated to him by Eight, there would be no stopping him. He would capture the Vorl, but far more importantly than that, he would have Isambard Smith.

His scarred face smiled back at him, reflected in his helmet. An eye for an eye, as the Earthlanders said. How very true.

Smith strolled across the hold with a self-mixing gin and tonic in one hand and a cricket bat in the other. Rhianna and Carveth watched him from the sitting room door. Suruk had climbed onto the walkway that ran around the edge of the hold.

The hold contained the remnants of several expeditions. Around its edges were boxes and chests holding a wide range of useless items: a gun-case with no guns, a scanner stand made out of a ravnaphant's leg and a stained, padlocked crate plastered with biohazard stickers, on which Suruk had written 'Imerjency rashuns'.

Smith whirled the bat around cheerfully, rubbing a tennis ball against his thigh. Carveth leaned over to Rhianna. 'I'm beginning to wonder if he isn't slightly concussed,' she whispered.

'I think his chakras may be out of alignment,' Rhianna replied.

'Pay attention, everyone,' Smith announced. 'French

cricket, as the name suggests, is much like British cricket except not as good. However, having no stumps, pads, teams or a scorer, this will have to suffice. The aim of the game is to get the batsman out by hitting him on the legs—'

'Simple,' Suruk said.

'—with the tennis ball. For Rhianna's benefit, it's a little like the traditional American game of rounders—'

An alarm sounded from the cockpit, a miserable howl. 'Spaceship's broken,' Carveth announced. 'See you later!' She ran from the room with evident relief.

Rhianna slipped off her sandals. 'Which one of us is the hitter?'

'Well,' said Smith, 'there's a batsman, and a bowler. Let's see: why don't you bowl, Suruk, and Rhianna, you can bat. Now, come and stand over here. . .'

In a swish of hair and skirt she skipped across to join him by the bay doors. 'Okay, what do I do?'

Suddenly she was close up, and he could smell hair and joss. 'Right,' he said, assuming an appropriate stance, 'you stand like this, and Suruk tries to hit you on the legs with the tennis ball. Suruk: no maiming, understand?'

The alien dropped down from the roof. 'I see we play French cricket the beginner's way.'

Smith passed Rhianna the bat and sat down on the bio-hazard case. Rhianna undid one of the bits of grubby string on her wrist and began to pull her hair back, like a fisherman hauling in his thrashing net. This struck Smith as deeply erotic. Her body was as sleek and graceful as a 'cello, but with better boobs. Desire made him light-headed, or perhaps it was cranial damage.

'Boss!'

Smith looked round: Carveth stood in the doorway. 'Borrow you for a minute, boss?' she said, and she disappeared from view.

Smith followed her through to the cockpit. 'Listen to this,' Carveth said, prodding the radio controls. 'I've picked up a signal coming from Lloydland.'

Smith leaned towards the speaker. 'Bloody hell!' she exclaimed. 'Are you sure Suruk didn't scalp you by mistake? You want to be careful – your brain'll fall out of a wound like that.'

'Oh, it's nothing much.'

'All the more reason to hang on to it.' She closed the door behind them and flicked on the radio. 'This is on continual replay. I've downloaded a map from the digital signal.'

A woman's voice came out of the speaker, a perky voice with a Free States twang, somehow enthusiastic even though it brought no good news.

'Hi! You are now within transmit distance of Lloydland, where the fun never ends. We are sorry to announce that Lloydland is currently closed for the duration of the Galactic War. Don't forget to call back as soon as one side has surrendered, for the adventure of a lifetime! Lloydland: bringing you—'

The radio cut with an ugly screech. Hiss filled the air. 'Weird,' Carveth said, 'it didn't do this last time.'

And then a voice rose out of the hiss, nothing like the previous speaker. It sounded more like some strange anomaly that by coincidence resembled words, more like wind rushing through pipes than the product of vocal chords. The speakers buzzed with suppressed power behind which was the crackle of raw electricity.

'Do not venture into the realm of the damned! If you value your life or your reason, keep away! Keep away!'

A blast of static and the radio was silent. Smith turned to look at Carveth. Her face was white in the dim cockpit, her eyes wide. 'Maybe they've got a ghost train,' he said.

The radio burst: the front of the speakers fell off and sparks rained over them. Carveth squealed and flinched. Smith stood up, hand shielding his face. The door flew open and Suruk strode in, holding a tennis ball. He tore the radio from the console, threw it onto the floor and stamped on it several times. It gave one long, sorrowful moan like a dying cow and fell silent.

'There,' said Suruk. 'Order is restored. All is well.'

'All is *not* well!' Carveth cried. 'You just trashed the radio!'

'Victory!'

Smith looked at the smashed radio, now a jumble of wires and shattered ferro-bakelite casing.

'We can't ring for help,' Carveth said. Her voice seemed very small.

'There'll be a transmitter on the planet,' Smith replied.

'We're going down there? Are you mental? We've just had a phone call from the Devil and you want to pitch up in his back garden?'

'It was the Vorl,' Rhianna said. They looked round: she stood in the doorway looking concerned. 'It was them warning us, wasn't it?'

Smith looked out the window, at the growing spec in the centre of the screen – Lloydland.

'So what now?' Carveth said.

'Carry on,' Smith replied. 'We complete the mission.'

'Are you mad?'

His voice was quiet and cold. 'If we turn back we acknowledge failure, and we really *will* leave New Luton to its fate. We can't call for help, so I can't see what else we can do. We'll land as soon as you can bring us into orbit.' His eyes roved over them. 'I want everyone ready to move out at first light tomorrow morning. I want weapons loaded and equipment stowed half an hour before we make planetfall. Look lively, everyone. No larking around.'

'Sandwiches?' Rhianna asked.

'Yes please.'

The *John Pym* made the final descent with uncharacteristic grace. Smith peered through the dirty green airlock window, watching fire lick the nosecone as they sank into the atmosphere of Lloydland. The ship thrummed and shuddered. In the corridor, dials clicked and whirred.

Rhianna was making sandwiches in the galley. Smith wandered over, the floor rocking a little underfoot. Something in the shelves rattled.

'Making something nice?' he asked.

'Cheese,' she said. 'I'd usually have issues with dairy produce, but I doubt this has ever been near a cow.'

She draped a sheet of Cheddar, Military, One Serving, onto the bread. Smith watched her work. He had never seen anyone make a cheese sandwich with such elegant eroticism. He thought about saying something, complimenting her in some way, but he realised that anything he said would sound foolish and crude.

'Would you like a dollop of my gentleman's relish?' he asked, passing her a jar.

She took it from him and gave the ingredients scrutiny. 'I'm worried, Isambard,' she said.

'It's fine for vegans,' he replied.

'I mean about going down there,' she said, raising her voice over the racket of descent. 'I mean, what will we find down there? Will we find the Vorl? Will they recognise me as their friend?'

'I'm sure they'll see you as one of the family. Though if they're anything like my family, that might not be a good thing.'

'No?' she turned and smiled at him, which made him feel uncomfortable.

'Rum bunch,' he said. 'Best check on Carveth.'

'I—' Rhianna began, but he was on the way out.

Carveth was at the controls, prodding the retro thrusters. Gerald's cage was in the captain's chair. Everything seemed in order. 'Alright there?' Smith asked.

'Pretty good. We'll start the landing sequence in five minutes.'

Smith watched the planet grow larger as they approached. 'What's the terrain like down there?'

She pulled down a screen on a jointed brass arm. 'Have a look.'

'It looks like Bodmin Moor. Careful with those thrusters: we don't want to burn the heather. The National Trust would raise hell for that.'

'Right, boss. We're carrying a bit of weight on the left dorsal. Might have a look at that once we've touched down.'

'Go ahead,' Smith said. He sighed. 'Carry on, Carveth. I'll be in my room.'

Smith wandered into his room and closed the door. Descent had set the model spaceships swinging on their bits of string. He watched them rock, feeling inexplicably glum, and pulled out the chair to sit down at the captain's desk.

It was Rhianna again. He had tried both ignoring her and being friendly, and still he could not escape the fact that he longed to be friendlier yet. There was no getting away from it: he would always want her, and his chance for that was gone.

A strange depression swallowed him, tranquil and deep. Oh well, there was nothing that could be done. As far as the music of love was concerned, he had always been less of a virtuoso than a soloist.

If only he could just forget the whole women thing for good. Better to have Suruk's cheerful company than feel miserable remembering what he couldn't have. He needed a distraction. An idea struck him, and he reached under the desk and pulled out a large cardboard box. The lid depicted a spacecraft flying through an explosion.

Smith opened the box and smiled as he looked over the moulded plastic parts inside. This was no ordinary model kit: this was the Hyperspace Hellfire of the Space Marshall himself, issued with special transfers to celebrate his hundredth kill. He held up the fuselage and turned it round in his hands, simulating the flight of the ship. 'Eeeeow,' he said. 'Akakak.'

'Isambard?'

He looked round. Rhianna stood in the doorway. Smith

lowered the model plane, feeling not so much embarrassed as annoyed that she had to be here. Couldn't he get some bloody peace, escape somewhere where he could forget about it all? It occurred to him that the M'Lak ancients had never been as wise or perceptive as he had been at the age of eight, when he had first made the great realisation that Girls Spoil Everything.

'Can I come in?' she asked.

'I suppose so.'

She stepped inside and closed the door. 'Can we talk for a while?'

'If you like. Don't mind me, I'm listening.' He resumed his study of the Hellfire, without making the noises.

'I meant like adults, Isambard.'

'This is adult. It says "16 and over" on the box.'

'How's your head?'

'Fine.' He shifted position, drawing away from her in case she tried to make him better.

Rhianna sighed. 'Isambard, I'm sensing a lot of negativity from you these days.' She sat down on his bed, knees close together and hands on them. She leaned forward, as if expecting him to whisper. 'Is something wrong?'

'No,' he said, returning to the kit. 'I'm fine.'

'Are you sure?'

'Yes.'

'Is there anything you want to say to me?'

'Not especially. You did a good job back there, on that Marty war-machine. That was good work. Thank you.'

She nodded and forced a smile. 'Okay. Nothing else?' She stood up. 'I'll be in my room.'

He heard the slap, slap of her flip-flops pass behind him. 'I miss you,' he said. It came out without him meaning to, as unbidden as Carveth's wind. 'For what's it's worth. . . I mean. . .' he found himself adding, earnestly and bitterly, 'That's what you wanted me to say, feelings and all that. But it's not worth saying so it's better not said, because that's done and dusted and whatever I think or feel won't alter it.' He wondered if the fumes from the model glue had done something to his mind, but now it was too late to stop; he had pushed the toboggan of truth down the slalom of his tongue and the jangling bells of sexual frustration were speeding it on its way. 'At the end of the day, assuming Gertie or the Furries don't do us in first, I'll go back to my work and you'll go back to being psychic and wearing that colander thing on your head and that's that.'

'I miss you too,' she said.

'Precisely,' he replied. 'So that rather finishes everything, and. . .' He looked around and blinked. 'Really?'

Rhianna nodded in a blur of dark hair. 'I don't really know why, but yes, I do. I mean, you're English, you're a colonialist oppressor, you've got that terrible moustache, and yet – yet I can't help but sense that your spirit has somehow risen above that and blossomed into this pure, noble thing, like a great, big tree. . .'

He watched her, wondering if she had finally taken leave of her mind, and realised that on some odd level this was meant to be a deep compliment. Suddenly he realised what she was banging on about: she meant that he was decent. He had a sudden, glue-fuelled image of the sort of men she had wasted her time on, the sort that he had never thought he could compete with, and it occurred to him that – to Rhianna at least – he was now actually a catch. Well, then. . .

He stood up. 'Rhianna, if we started walking out again, and we had to part company for you to work for the Service again, I could wait. Provided I knew you would, that is.'

She nodded again. 'I can wait,' she said quietly. She stepped over, looked up and kissed him. The whole world seemed to shake as she did and it was all he could do not to fall over. He realised that Carveth was landing the ship. Smith held Rhianna tightly as the landing procedure was completed, partly for the safety of both of them, and after a few seconds they looked at each other again.

The *John Pym* did not move. They were on Lloydland.

'Erm,' said Smith, 'seeing as we're both here now and pretty much in agreement on this, I don't suppose we could – you know – *do it*, could we?'

Carveth picked up the toolbox, switched on the torch strapped to her head, and stepped out of the airlock door muttering. So much for chivalry. Nobody had offered to help her check the ship, even though she'd mentioned it at least half an hour before. Alright, she was both the pilot and the mechanic, but *really*.

She closed the airlock and lumbered down the steps, weighed down by the tools. Suruk had retired to the hold to do whatever Suruk did and Smith and Rhianna had spent the afternoon sulking at one another and were no doubt at it even now. Midges danced in the torch beam like performers under a spotlight. A breeze caught the heather and set it swaying.

The ship had landed on a rocky patch where there was no risk of setting the scrub alight. It was easy to walk across the barren ground and set up under the rear tail fin. She put the toolbox down, crouched and opened it up.

Spooky out here, she thought, looking over the heather. It swung back and forth, left and right, almost beckoning. She half-expected to see some pale nocturnal creature lurking at the edge of the light: the torch did not shine very far. She turned her attention to the sooty side of the ship, singing to keep her spirits up.

'*Oh Mr Turing, whatever shall I do? I only count in binary but I've just got up to two. . .*'

There was a set of collapsible steps in the toolbox; Carveth pressed the button and stood aside as they unfolded. She climbed up and looked over the tail fin.

On the way down there had been an unexpected weight on the port rear, leaving the *Pym* very slightly unbalanced. It was worth examining. On a newer ship such things could presage minor damage; on the *Pym* it probably indicated that the tail was dropping off. She looked under the fin and found nothing, then turned her attention to the thruster.

A strange shiny substance had attached itself to the side of the thruster, gleaming like dried glue. It looked as if a group of snails had raced each other from the flank to the rear of the retro-booster. She prodded it with a gloved finger. It was as hard as plastic.

Carveth took out a pocket-welder and leaned around the back. The ladder wobbled slightly under her. She followed the snail trails around the thruster, watched them get denser and denser, almost a web criss-crossing the rear of the jet, holding in place something like a pineapple made out of snot. Utterly disgusted, she focussed the torch, and a shudder ran through the pineapple.

It burst. Something red and glistening leaped out at her and she yelled, the ladder swung away and she was falling – *thump!* – and the light fell off her head. She sat up, drawing her pistol and in the torchlight she saw a mass of tentacles and jointed limbs scurry into the heath and disappear. The heather rustled as the creature darted through it, then it resumed its gentle sway in the wind.

Carveth was shaking. She sat there for a moment, revolver in hand, watching the patch of light. The breeze set a strand of hair dancing before her eyes.

She stood up and rubbed her aching backside, quite impressed with herself for not screaming. Whatever that thing was, it had fled. She bent down, picked up the head-set and put it back on. Carveth adjusted the lamp, sighed and turned back to the ship.

She looked straight into the face of a ghost. This time she really did scream.

In Smith's room the lights were out.

'A bit gentler, please?' Rhianna said. 'You're not tuning in a radio.'

'Righto. Any better?'

'Much better.'

'Good-oh. Hold on a moment.' The bed creaked. 'One sec – *tadaaah!* No trousers.'

'Give me your hand, Isambard. There. Do that, okay? Mmm. Now then, what have we here?'

'That'll be my todger, actually.'

'It was a rhetorical question. Let's take your shirt off – it's – uh?'

'Ah. It's got tucked in to my underpants. That happens sometimes. Just out of – ah – interest, where's your hand going there?'

'Just trust me, Isambard, okay?'

'Well, alright then, but – oh, I see. False alarm. Fair enough, all above board.' He sighed. 'It's smashing to be with you again, you know. I honestly thought I'd never get the chance. Rhianna, would you mind if I put the light on? I'd like to see you without your kit on.'

'Okay.' The bed moved as she stretched out. 'Sure.'

'Right. Light switch. Should be just over here. . . Hang on, what's this? Who the hell—'

'Hello, Boss.'

'Carveth! What the hell are you doing? Can't you tell I'm busy?'

'Yeah, sorry about that. I came in, and I was kind of waiting for a convenient break in conversation, and then. . . oh, hi, Rhianna.'

'Hey Polly. Um, we're kind've unavailable right now.'

'I know, but I saw something really horrid outside and now I'm scared to go to bed. Can I sleep in here tonight?'

'Was it the enemy, Carveth?'

'Er, no, not really.'

'Then dammit, no you can't sleep here! Use your own room!'

'I saw a ghost. I don't want to go in my room in case it comes up the vent shafts and—'

'Go away!'

'Please, Boss. I could sleep on the floor. I'd be really quiet.'

'No! Sod off! Can't you see I'm getting my—'

'Isambard, maybe we ought to let her. She sounds really freaked out.'

'Certainly not! Carveth, you're a grown woman, not a child. Now go to your room at once. Dear God, whatever next?'

'Greetings, Mazuran!'

'Oh for—'

'Both the females at once? I salute you! When first we set foot on this vessel, I told you that you would have foul couplings with them both, and most modestly you said no. Yet I was right! Truly you shall spawn many—'

'Suruk, Carveth is here because she claims to have seen some sort of monster outside. She wants to sleep in my room, which isn't practical. I'm trying to get her to go back to her own room.'

'I see. That is indeed impractical. Perhaps one at a time, then?'

'Boss, I saw something on the moor. It was this white thing floating around the moor, making this weird, high-pitched sound—'

'Was it Kate Heathcliffe, little pilot woman?'

Smith finally found the light switch. Carveth and Suruk stood at the end of the bed, like a judging panel. 'Right, young lady robot, out. Out we go. Suruk, would you mind leaving too? Please?'

'Fear not,' Suruk declared. 'I shall take the timorous Piglet to my chambers. Come, timid one. Suruk the Slayer shall stand guard over you.'

Suruk's room smelt of ammonia. The bed was folded against the wall to provide more space for trophies. Carveth watched as Suruk lowered the bed and smoothed the covers down with his palm. 'It has never been used,' he explained. 'I do not sleep in a bed.' He pulled the sheets back and gave her an unnerving smile, like Sweeney Todd welcoming a customer. Carveth yawned.

Warily, lest something dead turn out to be under the sheets, she climbed into bed. The bed was clean and the sheets cool.

'Sit forward,' Suruk said. He took the pillow out and, spinning, smashed it into the wall as if to dash out its brains. Then he put it behind her. She settled back.

Suruk opened the chest of drawers – Carveth kept her socks in her own equivalent – and took out a machete. 'A human gave me this,' he said, placing it on the bedside table. 'It may be of use, if an enemy attacks. Now, would you care for some music to assist you in sleeping?' Suruk pulled out a handful of records from the shelf. 'Let us see. . . Beethoven's Ninth, Shostakovitch Moods, Stockhausen's Greatest Melodies . . .'

'Haven't you got anything a bit less classical?'

'I have Anthrax.'

'Thanks for sharing. What about your Minnie Ripperton records?'

Suruk raised an eyebrow-ridge. 'You listen to war music in bed? No wonder you are so strange.'

'Cheers,' said Carveth, 'I'll be alright without.'

'As you wish.' Suruk reach out and turned off the lamp.

In the dim light Carveth saw him spring up onto his stool, crouch down and close his eyes. His hand rested lightly on a blade on his belt.

Suruk's mandibles opened and he yawned, revealing his shining teeth, before his mouth closed up again like a castle gate. Squatting on the stool he looked like a cross between something from the deep ocean and a roosting bat. Behind him, rows of skulls grinned at Carveth, taken from the most evil and savage creatures of the galaxy, a legion of dead monsters drawn up into ranks.

'Sleep well,' Suruk said.

'Thanks,' Carveth said, and she closed her eyes gingerly.

She did not dream. In the morning she awoke to find herself under a heap of soft toys and cushions, that Suruk had fetched from her room.

10

Where the fun never ends!

Smith finished loading his rifle and propped it against the wall. He opened the Civiliser, tipped out the shells and looked down the barrel. Then he pushed six big bullets into the chamber and dropped two speedloaders into his coat pocket before turning to Carveth's guns.

Carveth laid pieces of printout on the far end of the kitchen table as if dealing out huge playing cards. She pushed them together and stood back, admiring the effect. 'It's the best I could do,' she said. 'I blew up the free map from the radio signal.'

Smith loaded cartridges into the shotgun. 'It looks fine.'

Rhianna brought the sandwiches from the galley and looked over Carveth's shoulder. 'Hey, guys.'

The airlock creaked open, then slammed shut. Suruk's boots clanged on the metal floor.

'Find anything?' Smith called, not looking round.

'Only this,' Suruk said, and he dumped something on the table.

It was about two feet long and had a body like a lobster, but much longer legs. Tentacles sprouted from its back, dribbling gluey fluid.

'It's the thing I saw last night,' Carveth said.

'Indeed,' Suruk said. 'I caught it trying to climb onto the ship.'

'Whoa,' Rhianna observed. 'Nature round here looks. . . kind've unnatural.' Smith caught her eye. She smiled, and he smiled back, feeling himself flush.

'It's Ghast biotech,' Smith replied. 'Look.' He took out his penknife, and with the tweezers unfolded a long, thin stem from the creature's small head. 'Extendable antennae. I'm afraid to say this is a bug.'

Carveth shrugged. 'Well, yeah.'

'An engineered bugging device. Somehow the Ghasts stuck this thing on the ship. It must have happened back at Tranquility. Men, I'm afraid they know where we are.'

Carveth seemed to deflate slightly.

'Oh, no,' Rhianna said. 'That's, like, really bad.'

'Excellent!' Suruk chuckled behind his mandibles. 'Then they are coming. Our old enemy 462 and with him Mimco Vock. The ghosts of legend shall return, and the rides of Lloydland shall run red with villainous blood! This theme park shall be ours, and the theme will be doom! I shall battle my enemy in the shadow of the rollercoaster and spear him in the Tunnel Of Love.

'Ouch,' Carveth said.

'Easy, old chap,' Smith put in. 'First things first. We need to move the ship. We'll dump this monstrosity in the heather. Then we need to get inside as quickly as possible. The Ghasts can't be far behind.'

Seen from the air, Lloydland was sleeping. Few lights shone up from the various domes and landing pads; no vehicles moved around the perimeter. It was the size of a small town, its rides, hotels, theatres and entertainment domes waiting for the call that would bring them back to merry, gaudy life.

Up close, its beauty faded. Lloydland was sliding into decrepitude. Lichen gathered on the windows of the domes. There was dirt in the corners of the great embossed signs. Soft rain fell onto long grass.

A small robot had stopped in the middle of the main street. Carveth opened a panel in its front and took out a soggy map. 'Place is dead,' she said, opening the map. 'If you were a psychic ghost,' she added, 'would you go to Medieval Mountain or the Buccaneers of the Ivory Coast?'

Smith frowned. Droplets pattered onto the map. 'Seeing as the place seems disused,' he said, 'the best place to start looking would be the colony records. The main admin buildings are all in the centre, here: Madrigal Mews, Chanson Court – ah, this looks promising. The big building in the middle – Ballad Point.'

Carveth squinted at the damp paper. 'Looks like some sort of high-rise. Offices and luxury hotel, from the looks of it. We should be able to cut through the dome up ahead.'

'Right,' Smith said. 'We'll try there. Keep an eye out, everyone.'

Carveth nodded, shotgun in hand. They set off across the wide, empty street, the wind tossing thin rain into their faces. Smith wondered if Rhianna would like to hold hands; she did not look very happy.

'Alright there?' he asked.

'It's this place,' she replied. 'It's... really terrible.'

'Oh, it's not too bad,' he said, trying to jolly her along.

'Reminds me of going to theme parks back in England.'
They trudged past a dripping sign that read 'Ride Closed'.
'My parents used to take me to places like this when I was
young. I once went to the Imperial People's theme park,'
he added. *Funfair For The Common Man*, it was called. It
was good, but the children's farm was closed. Some trouble with the animals, apparently.'

'Children's farm?' Suruk licked his thin lips.

'Not like that.' Smith pointed. 'We'll go in there, up
ahead.'

They approached a set of grand, airlocked doors,
decorated with geometric designs and swirling lilies.
Smith looked back at Rhianna. 'Well, here we go.'

He took up a position on one side of the door, Suruk on
the other. Carveth stepped back and reached for the
controls. Rhianna reached out and briefly squeezed
Smith's hand.

Carveth pressed the button.

The doors slid open.

It was the scene of a riot. Vases had been smashed,
statues of Andy Atom overturned, libellous comments
about Sally Squirrel scrawled on the walls. Two huge
busts stood on either side of the hall: smooth, stylised
male torsos nine feet high. There were no corpses.
Someone had taken them away.

'Looks like they're closed,' Carveth said. 'Don't
suppose we could go home, by any chance?'

'Something terrible happened here,' Rhianna said.

'Wow,' Carveth said, 'you really are psychic!'

Suruk tilted his head back and sniffed. 'It smells of
blood, and evil, and parties.' He bent down and came up

with a jumble of wood and wire in his hand, like the strings of a smashed marionette. 'A trap,' he said, looking across the room at a steel spike embedded in the opposite wall. 'We must go carefully, lest we find more.'

'Hell of a party,' Carveth said. She stood in the middle of the room, as far away from everything as she could manage, her muscles tensed ready to cower and duck. She took a step towards Suruk, and he raised a hand. She stopped.

'Shush,' Suruk growled. 'Do you hear that?'

Smith was close to Rhianna, in case she triggered something. He paused, closed his eyes for a moment, and then he too could hear it: ghostly and distant, the sound of echoing music.

'The Vorl?' Rhianna said.

Suruk shook his head. 'Stephane Grappelli. That way.'

Slowly, like a drifting gas, 'Blue Moon' seeped into the hall. It sounded as if it had come up from the underworld, from a vault or the bottom of a well. Smith had an image of pale couples in tattered evening dress, dead but waltzing. He shook his head and it was gone. Blue Moon, he thought: Lloyd Leighton's old company.

Smith swallowed and readied the rifle. He bent his legs and, as if stalking an animal, he started down the corridor towards the sound.

Suruk said, 'One thing, Mazuran.'

'Yes?'

'Let us try to take Stephane Grappelli alive.'

'You like him?'

The alien flexed his mandibles. 'Not as much as Django Reinhardt. But I give him honour.'

'Loony,' Carveth muttered from behind.

Smith crept down the corridor. Little chandeliers winked down at him. Scraps of glass crackled underfoot. With each step his boots sank into the thick carpet. Suruk flanked him, spear readied; Rhianna and Carveth followed, Carveth watching the rear.

Smith stopped beside a long photograph on the wall. It showed a hundred rich, dapper partygoers in evening dress. At the front of the picture stood Lloyd Leighton. On his left was a wolfish, heavy-browed fellow in a checked shirt – the caretaker, perhaps. On Leighton's right was Number Two.

The party, Smith thought, the picture he'd found on Benson. There stood Two, an elaborate cocktail in his thin hand, bridling at the camera flash as if the woman behind had just goosed his large red arse. Smith wished he could have traded places with the woman. Two seconds with a cocktail stirrer and Number Two would never have marched again.

'The music grows louder,' Suruk said.

To the left was a pair of large, open doors. Music seeped out from within. Smith looked back and nodded to the others. Slowly, his rifle ready, he looked around the doors.

The room was a dancehall, strewn with the detritus of a party that had never been cleared away. A banner hung across the hall. It said, 'Welcome Ghast Empire! Jive With The Hive!' Streamers lay across the floor like bits of a dead rainbow. The air smelt faintly of ash.

There was a bar at the far end, manned by a mechanical tender. A man in a crumpled suit sat on a high stool opposite the automaton, head so slumped that his chin nearly rested on the bar.

'Another highball, would you kindly?' he said.

Smith coughed. 'Excuse me?'

The man sat up as if jabbed, whirled round and hopped down from the stool. Smith's hands tensed around the rifle, but the drinker was unarmed. The man beamed and raised a hand in greeting, his eyes suddenly bright as if lights had been switched on behind them.

'Well, hello there! I'm Lloyd Leighton, and I'd like to welcome you to Lloydland!'

Leighton was tall and moustached, friendly but strong-looking and masculine. He wore a double-breasted brown suit, cut loosely in the Free States style. Leighton's age was hard to tell; his face looked about fifty, but there was a twinkle in his eye that suggested that his mind was much younger than that.

'How're we doing?' he beamed, advancing. Smith met Suruk's eye and the M'Lak stepped aside, lowering his spear.

Leighton stuck out a hand. 'Sir, pleased to meet you.' Smith shook his hand; its grip was strong and hard. 'Great to see you, Sir. We ought to hit the links sometime. Madam,' Leighton said, turning to Rhianna with sudden seriousness. 'I sincerely hope you'll enjoy your stay here. At Lloydland we take fun seriously, for the *whole* family. And on that subject – hey, little sister!' Abruptly he hitched up his trousers and squatted down in front of Carveth. 'What's *your* name?'

'Er, Polly,' she said, keeping both hands on her gun. 'Why?'

'Polly,' said Leighton. 'That's a nice name. So, who're you most looking forward to seeing here? Andy Atom? Sally Squirrel?'

'The Vorl, I think,' Carveth said.

The smile dropped off Leighton's face. Then, as if a dark cloud had passed, he grinned again. 'Not sure I can help you there. But hey – who's this little guy?'

Standing upright again, Leighton looked left. Carveth followed his gaze. 'That's Suruk.'

'Suruk, eh?' To Smith's horror, Leighton reached out and patted the alien on the head. This was not easy: Suruk was several inches taller than him. Suruk opened his mandibles and snarled and Leighton whipped his hand away. 'Whoa, he's a feisty puppy! I don't recognise the breed. What is he, a cross?'

'Enraged,' Suruk said. 'I will have no dealings with you, demented one.'

'In which case,' Leighton declared, 'how's about I give all you guys your own tour, eh?'

Rhianna leaned over to Smith and whispered, 'I think he's a little – you know – special.'

'He's bloody doo-lally,' Smith replied. 'Best play along for now, though. He may know more than he's letting on.' Raising his voice, he said, 'That would be excellent, Mr Leighton. Perhaps you could tell us a little about how Lloydland is run?'

'Sure!' Leighton clapped his hands. 'Okay! Who wants to see where we make ice cream?

'Me, me!' Carveth cried. She glanced at Smith. 'Keeping up the charade, Boss. Honestly.'

* * *

The *Systematic Destruction* swung into orbit. 462 listened to the transmission coming up from Lloydland, and a minute later received an order for an audience with Number Eight.

462 folded his command chair to the upright position, polished his metal eye, cleaned the propaganda posters and found three particularly evil-looking praetorians to pack into the camera's field of view. After some deliberation he decided to wear his second-newest black trenchcoat and ordered a terrified drone to buff it until it shone like oil. He was saving the newest for his final run-in with Isambard Smith.

The screen squelched into life. Eight was sitting in a massive chair, reading a book that did not appear to have been written by Number One: a privilege of rank. A marble phrenology bust of a drone's head sat on his desk, marked out with the various parts of the Ghast brain: instinct, will and, taking up eighty percent of the mind, orders. Assault Unit One stuck its brutal head into the bottom of the screen and growled at 462.

'All hail Number One!' 462 yelped.

Eight marked the page in his book with a spare death warrant and looked up. 'Quite so. I understand that we draw near the enemy. I take it you intend to strike soon?'

'Yes, Eight! Once we land, I will use the rodent imbeciles to distract any opposition. While they are busy being destroyed, our praetorians will be able to capture a specimen of the Vorl.'

'Good. Once you have the Vorl, bring it to me in my ship. My science-drones are preparing the gene-splicing apparatus as we speak.'

'I live to obey, Mighty Eight.'

'You live to *succeed*, 462.' Eight raised his book. Assault Unit One bent down and came up with something between its teeth. It looked like a huge lobster claw, and it was still wearing the sleeve of a leather trenchcoat. The screen turned black.

It had been a bad morning for Hephuc, Colonel Vock's servant. The Yull used the same word for *civilian*, *serf* and *kickable stress reliever*, and he had spent most of the day dodging the wads of damp sawdust that Vock threw when irritated. While the rest of the horde ran through a camouflage sheep-dip to dye their fur, Vock armed himself for close combat. Vock's suit of armour was so elaborate that it took most of the night to put on: only helping with this saved Hephuc from being volunteered to test the sharpness of his master's axe. Eventually Vock called a meeting of his soldiers and Hephuc gladly stood at the back of the room, munching seeds and reading a dirty parchment.

Vock was happy to be surrounded by warriors. His chest inflated, he swaggered across the hold in a clatter of armour plate.

'Today,' he proclaimed, his squeaky voice ringing around the bio-rafters, 'you are very fortunate! Today, you are privileged to die fighting offworlder scum in the name of our friendly empire and our peace-loving war-god!'

There were cheers. Vock took out a bottle of dandelion wine and handed it to his standard-bearer. 'Pass it round. One sip each, no cheek pouches.

'Now, listen. For too long we Yull have been held back.

For too long we have been forced to stand and watch as humans have crossed the galaxy, conquering and exploiting helpless native life wherever they go. Now, we must stand up and with one voice cry "We want a go at that!" And believe me, if anyone knows how to conquer and exploit, it is the Yull!' He put his hands behind his back and rocked on his heels. 'Remember, the noble, dignified house of Vock has been disgraced. You, the young generation, are fortunate enough to stand at the precipice of history. It is up to you to leap into action.' He turned to the back of the room. 'Step forward, Hephuc!'

Two hundred furry heads turned to the back of the room. The parchment fell out of Hephuc's paws. He froze, seeds tumbling from his open mouth. 'Me?' he squeaked.

Vock smiled. 'You, Hephuc. Your time has come.'

Hephuc gulped, suddenly aware how loud his pounding heart must sound to the vengeful god of war. Very slowly, he finished eating. His eyes flicked upward as if in prayer, looking for any high ledges from which he might be commanded to jump.

'Look at my servant Hephuc,' Vock barked. 'For many years this cowering menial has served me, fetched and carried at my command, ducked when I have coughed furballs at him in rage. Look at him now. He stands ready for battle, with a heart full of pride and cheek-pouches full of sunflower seeds. He is an example to all of you. Today, Hephuc, I shall reward you for your loyalty!'

Hephuc said, 'Re – reward?'

'Of course! You are a faithful servant of the house of Vock. Your obedience is a lesson to all Yull. The Greater

Galactic Happiness Collective could do with more loyal sons such as you!'

A slow, awkward grin pulled itself across Hephuc's face. In stages, as if unfolding, he ceased to cringe. 'Well,' he managed, 'I do try, you know. Thank you, sir, thank you!'

'Not at all. Which is why, Hephuc, I promote you to the rank of squire and give you the honour of wielding the *Xapistic* against our foes.'

Vock slid a weapon from his belt and held it up for all to see. It was a length of metal pole about a yard long. Duct tape was wound around one end to serve as a sort of handle. At the other end, welded on at right angles, was a large cannon shell.

'This is for you, Hephuc,' he said. 'If you see an off-worlder tank, smite it with the Xapistic and blast yourself to heaven as its crew are blown to hell!'

The soldiers cheered as Vock thrust the stick-bomb into the air. '*Yullai!*'

Hephuc opened his hands to the heavens and began to cry. Vock placed the Xapistic into Hephuc's palms and patted him on the shoulder. 'Do not be afraid to weep, good serf. It is not every day one is privileged to wield the *Xapistic*. Once in a lifetime, you might say!'

Vock began to laugh.

'And this,' said Lloyd Leighton, 'is where the fun begins!'

Smith glanced at Rhianna. She looked at Leighton and raised her eyebrows. Carveth tapped the side of her head.

'Don't be shy!' Leighton called. 'Come on in!'

They were in a long, open-plan office. Once, it had been

a jolly place, but disuse made it sinister. Dust clung to the computer screens like snow. Pictures of Billy Beaver and Sally Squirrel stared from the walls like paintings in a Yullian haunted house. Carveth looked at a portrait of Andy Atom and shuddered. His neutrons seemed to follow her around the room.

'Uh-oh,' Carveth whispered.

'Hey, less of the English reticence!' Leighton laughed. 'I'm just joshing. This, guys, is where the fun begins, where my legions of staff labour like Santa's elves to make sure that everybody's having a good time. You might call it the soul of Lloydland – or, Mrs Smith, perhaps you might see it as the sugar you use when you're baking a pie, right?'

'Um, it depends how you define soul. . .' Rhianna began.

'Look, Leighton,' said Smith, 'I need to talk to you. It's a very serious matter.'

'Of course, Sir.' He leaned forward, and Smith suddenly caught a whiff of dust and hair pomade, and under that something stale. 'Is it a member of staff?' Leighton asked, quick and serious. 'You need me to sack someone?'

Smith shook his head. 'Where are all the guests, Mr Leighton?'

'Well, it is the slow season—'

'There's nobody else here, is there?'

Leighton's face froze for a moment – and there was no jollity there, just a sort of blank surprise. 'Perhaps you'd best step into my office.'

He pointed down the corridor. Carveth shone her torch at a pair of wide walnut doors, inset with lacquered stripes. The doors depicted an ocean liner, over which soared a space rocket. One of the panels in the door had been smashed.

'Now this,' Leighton declared, cheerful again, 'is the nerve centre of Lloydland. Who likes cookies? I bet you do, little lady.'

'Are you calling me fat?' Carveth demanded.

Leighton roared with laughter. 'Would you check her out! Fat? Golly no. I'm just making a comparison, see? When your mom here makes cookies, what does she put in them?'

'Marijuana,' Carveth said.

'That's right, cookie dough! Well, this is where the dough gets baked. This office is where the dough of ideas rises in the oven of activity. Come on in!'

Leighton threw the doors open and Carveth walked past him. 'Bloody hell,' she said.

The office was big and empty. It looked to Smith as though someone had dumped a desk in the waiting room of a very prestigious railway. A painting of Andy Atom hung on the far wall. There were no lamps, or at least not in the conventional sense. Instead, four large, glowing objects threw coloured light across the walls. They looked like shapes cut from coloured ice, Smith thought, curving up like incomplete arches, their edges hard and sharp.

Rhianna gasped. 'Crystals!' she whispered.

'Embrace nothing.' Suruk tilted his head, wary. 'This is the doing of the Vorl.'

'You like my ornaments, huh?' Leighton grinned. He rummaged in the desk, pulled out a cardboard box and passed it to Carveth. 'You'll love this!'

'Is it Vorl stuff?' she asked.

'It's a My Little Xenomorph gymkhana set!' He turned, beaming, to Rhianna and Smith.

'Oh, for God's sake,' Carveth muttered. 'Bloody crazy – ooh, there's a horsebox and everything.'

'Very impressive, Leighton.' Smith leaned over to the others. 'Listen,' he whispered, 'We have to find out what happened here. Leighton needs careful handling, men. I think I'd better—'

'Deranged atom person!' Suruk roared. 'How did the workings of the Vorl come to be in your citadel of lunacy? Answer me, or I shall beat you to death with your own feet!'

Leighton stared, his eyes full of horror and surprise. 'Oh my God,' he whispered. 'A talking dog!'

'Where are the other guests? Did you devour them?'

'Easy, Suruk,' Smith said.

'I – no – well, not *many* of them. I had no choice,' Leighton said, and he sagged. He sighed, as if the life was escaping from him like a punctured balloon. Leighton's shoulders drooped, and as the smile fell from his face his youth seemed to as well. He pulled out a seat and dropped into it. 'I had no choice. They left us here.'

'They?'

He nodded, woebegone. 'We did a deal. We'd party out the war here – my guests and me – and they'd leave us alone. I mean, it didn't matter, right? Whoever won, men or Ghasts, they'd still need entertainment, and we'd have enough money to get by no matter what, my guests and me. Right?'

'Wrong,' Smith said. 'Ghasts don't have leisure: they

march. For one thing, I doubt they'd fit their arses in the rollercoasters, but that's beside the point.'

'They cheated us,' Leighton said, talking to the opposite wall. 'They told us they'd leave us alone. And they did – to starve! They didn't bring us any food. All we had was haute cuisine. . . and that never lasts long. We looked for stores, for anything we could eat, and we found caves under the park. That's where I found the crystals. Then the ghosts came. I guess they wanted their crystals back. But by then. . . the damn dirty ant-men sold us out!'

The light throbbed on Leighton's face, striped it with shadow. Leighton was seeing the truth, Smith realised, perhaps for the first time. Smith saw it too, although, mercifully, he did not know the details.

'They must have known what we might find – must have planned to take it back later when we'd gone. Some of us went into the caves – and they didn't come back. By then, we'd split into little tribes, hunting each other through Ballad Point.' Leighton shuddered. 'I ate a fashion model. And then another. One wasn't enough.'

'It is understandable,' Suruk said. 'After all, they are quite small. In such circumstances, I am sure we would all do the same.' He looked right, then left. 'Anyone? Ah. Well, I seem to be in a minority.'

Carveth said, 'Excuse me. Loo break.'

'Down the corridor, on the right,' Leighton said. He watched Carveth go.

'And so the bourgeois, once isolated from the world, turned to savagery to relieve their boredom,' Rhianna said. 'You could write a book about that. Many books, in fact.'

Leighton turned to Smith, and he looked desperately weary. 'You're not a family, are you?' he said. 'And he's not a small dog.'

'Quite,' Suruk observed.

'My delusions dragged you out here,' Leighton said. 'You three and that poor little girl. And now—'

Feet thudded down the corridor. 'Boss! Boss!' Carveth ran into the room. 'Boss, they're here!'

'The Vorl?' Smith rushed to the door.

'No,' she said. 'The Ghasts!'

11

To the Death!

They ran out of the office, ducking low as they scuttled to the window. 'They're down there,' Carveth whispered. 'Hundreds of them.'

Smith unfastened the rifle sight and stood at the side of the window, scanning the avenue below. Empty. 'Where, exactly?'

'The whole damn lot – Ghasts, Furries, all of them, up the far end of the road.'

'Bollocks. Can't see a thing. Are you sure you didn't – wait a moment. That letter box just moved.'

'What's going on?' Leighton stood beside them, jostling with Carveth for a position at the window. 'What's that red thing?'

Smith turned. 'A lemming sentry, Leighton. I'm afraid the Ghasts are back, with help. They have the Yull with them.'

'Yull?' Leighton scowled. 'Goddam it, I'll have no talking rodents in my theme park!'

Figures scurried into the road, jogging beside the buildings: forage-caps flapping, the Yull were moving into position. Ghast support officers strutted among them, thin and scrawny by comparison, directing their advance.

Under a sign that read: 'Tell your friends about us!' a praetorian dipped its head and barked advice to an armoured lemming with a banner on its back. If Hell had theme parks, Carveth thought, their parades would look like this.

'Mimco Vock!' Suruk snarled. 'That banner shows his ancestral sign. I shall descend and challenge him!'

'No you bloody won't!' Carveth replied. Her eyes looked huge. 'You'll stay here, and protect. . . Rhianna. You'll get killed down there!'

'You doubt my skills, pixie? I am Suruk the Slayer, of the line of Urgar! I have the skill of dozens, the strength of ten—'

'The mental age of four,' Carveth said. 'Boss, don't let him go down there.'

'Nobody is,' Smith said. 'If they want us, they can come up and get us. Maybe we can trap them on the stairs. Suruk, old friend, what do you think?'

The M'Lak frowned. 'Well said. When outnumbered, it is best to choose the fighting-ground. Mazuran, put the seer in the room with the crystals. Perhaps she can speak with them. We four will guard the stairs. The Yull will crave a frontal assault: they will lose many soldiers before they reach us.' He grinned, ready for battle. 'You like this plan?'

Smith nodded. 'It sounds good.'

'We must make a barricade on the lower landing. Keep the seer back, Mazuran. Her powers will be of no use against axes.' He turned and took a step towards the doors, then looked back. 'The Yull will not retreat.'

Carveth looked at her gun, as if unable to believe that it would work. 'Oh, *arse*.'

266

'We will have to slay them all,' Suruk said. 'Still, there is at least a bright side to this situation.'

'Which is?'

'We will have to slay them all.'

'Great,' Carveth said.

Smith said, 'Go on. Leighton, you'd best go and give them a hand. I'll be down in a minute.'

He watched as Suruk shepherded the other two out of the room.

Smith turned to Rhianna. 'Well,' he said, 'This is it. See if you can call up the Vorl while we're away. Stay safe, Rhianna. I won't be long.'

'You too, Isambard.' She leaned over and kissed him. 'Go in peace.'

He loosened his sword. 'Something like that.'

The Yullian sentry raised his telescope to his eye and looked left, then right. Nothing. The road was deserted. Content that nobody was watching, the sentry slipped his axe into his belt, pulled down a picture of Sally Squirrel and with a dirty chuckle stashed it in his pack.

Susan punched an inch and a half of stainless steel into the base of his neck. The sentry gasped and shivered, and she lowered him to the ground.

Wainscott stepped out of the shadows. Craig lifted the sentry's legs, Wainscott his shoulders, and they struggled into a storeroom and laid the dead lemming on the floor.

Wainscott tipped his head and listened. 'Right then,' he said. 'You can come out now.'

Dreckitt breathed out; it felt like he was deflating. 'Goddam,' he said. He'd thought he was good, but these people were either brilliant or insane and he was still uncertain which. The Deepspace Operations Group had been very pleasant to him, but to see them at work was unsettling. Susan – who reminded him of Pippi Longstocking as she might have been depicted by Wagner – was talking to Nelson, the unit's computer expert.

'Alright,' Nelson said, turning from his portable set. 'There's two Ghast ships touched down about a mile West of here. The main movement of troops is towards the central building, Ballad Point. The lemmings are flocking to it.'

'Maybe they're going to jump off the roof,' Craig said.

'Doubt it,' Wainscott replied. 'Not while there's someone they could murder in there. Alright, everyone. If our chaps are here, they'll be in Ballad Point. We'll take the main entrance. Susan, you and Brian work up from the flank.' He smiled. 'Cheer up, Dreckitt. As soon as we've dealt with these few hundred maniacs, you'll be with your filly again.'

Smith and Leighton dragged a table to the top of the stairs and laid it on its side. Carveth carried a computer terminal, and while she propped it up against the table the men hurried back for more goods. Soon they had made a barricade of office furniture, stretching across the landing.

'They'll have to come up the stairs,' Leighton said, 'straight into your guns.'

Carveth was pushing a monitor up against the barricade when she heard them down below. Like soft rain onto a plastic roof: dozens of paws on the stairs. Beneath her the ground began to shake, and she ducked down and clutched her shotgun across her chest.

The feet stopped pattering. She crouched there, hearing her own breath.

'*Hephep*!' a voice shouted from below.

'*Huphep!*' the lemming men shouted back.

She closed her eyes. They were down there, no mistaking now. Cold seeped over her skin.

'Humans! This is lieutenant Hephuc, servant of the revered Colonel Vock!'

The speaker did not have an accent, as such, but his voice was quick and straining, like an accelerating moped working through the gears.

Smith glanced at Carveth: she was staring straight at him, eyes wide, small hands locked around her gun. Smith winked at her.

'Is Colonel Vock there?' Smith called.

'Yes!' the voice snapped back. 'He's on the stair!'

'Where on the stair?'

'Right there – ow!'

'Attention, vermin!' It was a new voice. 'I am Colonel Mimco Vock! My stupid minion does not realise that you ridicule him with your cowardly windmill song. Offworlder scum, you cannot stand in our way. The time of man has passed: this is the hour of the Yull!'

Carveth suddenly caught a glimpse of him: Vock was at the very edge of the stairs, back pressed against the wall, and for a second she saw him in profile. He wore bright red armour, polished to a shine, along with a helmet with large, round ceremonial ears. His chin was tilted up, his whiskers trimmed and waxed. The overall impression was of viciousness, pomposity and fur. Then Vock stepped aside and he was gone.

'British, there are four of you and two hundred of us,' Vock called, and Smith could hear the smirk in his voice. 'Perhaps it is time to consider surrendering, eh?'

'Alright then,' Smith replied, 'come out in tens with your hands up.'

'How dare you insult me! It is you who cannot defeat us! I have granted these soldiers the honour of depriving you of your ammunition. Once your guns are dry, I will assault and I will take you alive – screaming, and very much alive.'

Suruk chuckled. 'You will drink deep of your own folly, fools.'

Smith checked his rifle and loosened his sword in its scabbard. 'Listen,' he said quietly, 'these bastards think that because we value our lives, we're not a fraction as good as them. But they don't realise the half of it: when a man fights for what he believes in, he fights twice as hard as a dozen lemmings. Alright?'

Carveth did some mental arithmetic. 'Alright,' she said.

Smith reached into his jacket and took out her war diary. 'You ought to hang on to this.'

'Thanks,' she replied.

Suruk leaned close to Smith. 'There will be many dead lemmings and much fur. Would your breeding-woman appreciate a nice new muff?'

'Probably not, but thanks.'

'Then let us begin, Mazuran.'

'You there, rodents!' Smith called. 'I've got something for you to chew on!'

'Sunflower seeds?' a Yull cried hopefully, and yelped as an officer beat it into silence.

'But if you want it, you'll have to come and get it. You

270

Carveth noticed that the axe handle was lacquered black, beautifully inlaid with gold.

Leighton took a massive, wheezing breath. 'Ant-people left me to die... with ghosts... and now a goddam rodent hits me with an axe.' He swallowed hard, and blood ran from the corners of his mouth. 'Typical!' His chest fell and the axe shuddered as the life sank from his eyes, deep into his head.

Smith reached out and shook Carveth by the arm. 'Carveth? Go upstairs and check on Rhianna. Go on!'

She blinked and looked at him. 'Right. Right, Boss.' She took two steps away and turned. 'What'll you do?'

Smith stood up and readied his sword. Suruk waited on the other side of the barricade.

'Come, Mazuran. We have business with the lemming men.'

'Forward!' Wainscott cried, and he shot out the window and charged into the hall. Dreckitt rushed in behind him, Nelson tossed a grenade and the Yull turned from the stairs and ran at them.

It was murderous. The Yull rushed in like a wave of fur. Wainscott's gun stuttered as he flicked from one target to another. Dreckitt blasted shells into the horde, too panicked to aim properly. 'They'll surround us soon,' Wainscott called, as if pointing out an interesting wild bird.

'What?' Dreckitt yelled back, hoping that he hadn't heard the major right, but by then the Yull were in full attack.

The lemming peasants died fast: in nothing more than forage caps and dyed green fur, they fell in droves. But among them were armoured nobles, hiding in the scrum.

They shouldered their way through the pack, using the peasants as cover, holding up bulletproof shields like riot police. The Yull closed around the raiders.

Wainscott's Stanford gun was dry, so he tossed it to Craig – 'Reload, please' – kicked a Yullian officer in the chest, drew a sword and ran it through. Craig slapped a new magazine into the side of the gun and threw it back – by then in a blue-steel blur Wainscott had cut down three more lemming men. He caught the gun and went straight in, firing with the left, slicing with the right, teeth bared in a mad grin, his men covering him as he carved his way through the squeaking horde.

Figures bounded down the stairs behind the Yull. 'It's Smith!' Dreckitt yelled, pointing.

'Super!' Wainscott raised his sword in recognition.

'We're surrounded!' Dreckitt shouted back.

Wainscott looked mildly perturbed. 'Of course – right where we want them. Hammer and anvil.'

'What?' Deckitt called back, and a bright light arced out of the side of the hall. A low thrumming accompanied it, and as light sliced through the Yull, he realised what it was: Susan's beam gun. Wainscott might be crazy, he thought, but he was smart.

462 lowered his binoculars. 'The allied rabble is being rapidly depleted.'

Eight shrugged. 'Mere serfs.'

They stood several hundred yards away, in the shadow of Number Eight's personal shuttle. A bio-brolly spread its curved wings overhead. Gunfire flickered in the main lobby of Ballad Point.

A praetorian lumbered over to them, dipped its brutal head and snarled into 462's earhole.

'Excellent!' 462 barked. 'I am informed that the psychoscopic scanning has confirmed my suspicions: the Vorl are here. Seismic charges have been placed. All we need is to move clear and fire the main explosive.'

Eight nodded. 'Proceed,' he said. 'Bring specimens to me. I will be in my shuttle, sitting on the biosplicer.' He turned, paced up the ramp and disappeared inside.

Smith stood on the stairs, firing into the lemming horde. The Yull were outflanked, pinned between Wainscott and the beam gun. It was an ugly business, but Vock's men were doomed.

Carveth reached the offices. Rhianna sat cross-legged on the floor in Leighton's room, her hand resting on one of the Vorlian crystals. Her eyes were closed and she was humming. Carveth paused, not sure whether Rhianna was achieving anything or just powering up. She hoped that Smith and Suruk were alright. She sat down and started to reload her gun.

Suruk was having a splendid time. He sprang into the rear of the horde and his spear sang in his hand, felling the enemy on all sides. A Yullian noble charged in, armour glinting, and Suruk dodged his axe, kicked him over and leaped onto his chest. One good push and Suruk shot forward, riding the fallen noble like a skateboard. He whipped his spear left and right, leaving a trail of decapitated lemming men behind him as he headed towards Wainscott's team. Heads for the house of Agshad!

Smith raised his pistol and put two shots into Vock's standard bearer. Wainscott was either conserving ammunition or just enjoying himself, dodging and cutting with his sword, fast and deadly. The Yull still yelled their battle-cry and attacked, but there was despair in their voices now, not glee. Smith lowered his gun and suddenly a Yull stood frozen before him, blinking and astonished. As battle raged behind them it said, 'I give up.'

Smith thought, I could kill him. One less furry bastard in the world—

'Civilian!' the lemming cried, throwing its hands up. The weapon flew out of its grip, whirling end over end like a shotputter's hammer. He gave up, Smith thought, a Yull bloody surrendered, to *me*! – and as the flying mallet reached its apogee, he noticed that the end of it looked curiously like a tank shell. Strange, that—

The ground rippled like a shaken rug and Carveth flew into the air. She floated for a moment and then – *bang!* – the floor hit her and she was lying flat on her back, battered and confused. In front of her a crystal pulsed, queasily out of time with the throbbing in her brain. She sat up, and for the second time in a day looked into the face of the Vorl and screamed.

'Oh, for heaven's sake, not you again,' it said.

She got up. Rhianna was waking from her trance, blinking uncertainly. The crystals glowed brighter than before, and in front of them was the Vorl.

It was a thing of smoke and dust, a bluish, luminescent blur with an upper body that tapered into a genie's tail where the waist should have been. There was a face, of sorts:

the upper lip was very long, the nose a six-inch spike upturned with arch distain. Wispy arms formed from its shoulders and it put its hands on its insubstantial hips.

'What a ghastly place,' it said. It had a very nasal voice. 'So to speak. Very naff, I must say.'

Weakly, Carveth said, 'You're the Vorl?'

'One of 'em.' It gestured to itself with a long-fingered, languid hand. 'C'neth. Very pleased to make your acquaintance. Pardon the not shaking 'ands, but I'm insubstantial and I don't know where you've been. And as for her, goodness knows,' he added, nodding at Rhianna.

'*Namaste*,' Rhianna said. She looked round suddenly, as if startled, and said 'Isambard and the others! What's happened to them?'

She started to rise, but Carveth shook her head. 'It's not safe.' She turned to C'neth. 'Did you make the room shake like that?'

'Me? I thought that was you,' said the Vorl. 'You're the belligerent one round here. Every time we meet you 'owl blue murder at me.'

'Look!' Rhianna said, and pointed at the window.

A chasm ran through Lloydland. The ground had opened down the main thoroughfare, swallowing rides and exhibition domes, leaving broken joists and rollercoaster tracks reaching for the sky like great steel fingers. Carveth saw arches and spires of blackened crystal at the bottom of the hole, delicate structures like frost on spider web.

'Well, good riddance Lloydland,' C'neth said. 'Art Nouveau? Art Nouveau Riche, more like. Nasty place, terribly *gauche*.'

Carveth shook her head. 'Listen. We need your help.

We're humans, from the British Space Empire – well, Rhianna isn't, and she's actually half Vorl and I'm an android, but we'll deal with that later – and we want to civilise the galaxy – not just us two, but the whole Empire.'

'Oh really?'

'Honestly. Out there are our enemies the Ghasts, who are sort of ant-people in trenchcoats: they want to eat the galaxy and shoot everyone. They're bad. And then you've got the Yull, who are lemmings. They're mental *and* bad.'

'Like that one?' C'neth said, pointing.

'Bloody hell!' Carveth cried, and before she could raise her gun a Yullian noble in full plate armour came bounding up the stairs, axe raised above its head, howling '*Yullai!*' Instinct took over: Carveth leaped out the way, Rhianna sidestepped with surprising elegance, and the noble raced past, ran straight through the window and dropped screaming into the night.

'Yes, just like that,' Carveth said.

'What about the grey thing with tusks?' C'neth inquired.

'That's Suruk,' Carveth said. 'He's – well, actually he's mental and bad too, but he's on our side.'

'C'neth,' Rhianna said, 'please help us. Polly's right: our way of life is threatened by oppressive people of alien origin. We seek only to bring love to the galaxy—'

'Oh, we know all about your love,' C'neth said darkly. 'Half Vorl, she says!'

'—and it is vital that together, we unite in the name of peace and freedom.'

'So will you kill all our enemies for us?' Carveth finished up.

C'neth drew back: his wispy face looked appalled. 'You're 'aving a laugh! I'm not going out to fight people!' he exclaimed.

'Please,' said Rhianna, 'just let me talk to you. We can build up a dialogue—'

'Hear her out,' Carveth added. 'Listen to her for five minutes and you'll be well up for violence. Wait – it's gone quiet.' She picked up the shotgun. 'I'm off to check on the others. Stay here, Rhianna – make friends,' she said, and she scrambled down the stairs.

The main hall was ruined, its edges hidden in a soft snow of fallen plaster. The ceiling had partly collapsed, and a bunch of joists jutted through the roof like a massive claw reaching in from above. The Yull lay in the wreckage at awkward angles: the covering of dust made them look like stuffed polar bears.

Smith stood on the stairs, rifle in hand, white with plaster. An unconscious, spectacled Yull lay at his feet. He looked around as Carveth bounded to the bottom of the stairs. 'Boss!' she called. 'Are you alright?'

He nodded. 'Good to see you. How's Rhianna?'

'She's fine. Boss,' Carveth said, 'we've found a Vorl. He's upstairs, talking to Rhianna.'

'The Vorl? Excellent! Is it the arch-Vorl?'

'Oh, he's arch alright.'

'Splendid. Let's go and talk to him.'

'I'll – ooh, it's Rick!'

People waved from the back of the room, Dreckitt

amongst them. Wainscott stood next to him, beside a heap of lemming men, sword in hand. His men wore space armour, Carveth saw, their fishbowl helmets clipped to their packs.

Dreckitt spat out a wad of plaster. 'Hey.'

Carveth embraced him and stepped back looking as if she had fallen face-down into a snowdrift.

'Hello girlie,' Wainscott called, 'how's tricks? Brian's copped a spike in the thigh. The rest of us are good as new.'

Smith surveyed the room. Dead Yull lay around the Deepspace Operations Group, some in pieces, all dusted in a snowdrift of plaster. It was probably a lot like Suruk's idea of Christmas. For that matter, where was Suruk?

He turned as Suruk stepped into the room. 'We've found the Vorl,' Carveth said.

'Indeed,' Suruk replied. 'So have the Ghasts.'

Something hit Vock in the ribs and he came round. The first thing he saw was the sky above him: the second was 462, kicking him lightly in the side.

'You were thrown clear by the explosion,' 462 explained. 'Your legion is destroyed.'

Vock sat up and gazed along the chasm. As he watched, the remnants of his army stumbled out of Ballad point and ran towards the gulf. The war god had revealed a greater destiny to them.

'Get back!' a praetorian snarled as they rushed past it. 'Get back to the battle!' Its voice was lost amidst squeals of glee. 'Anyone jumping into the hole will be shot! Get away from me! I order you to – *aargh!*'

462 watched the lemming-soldiers fling themselves into the crevasse. The praetorian fell with them, screeching.

'You cannot understand our way,' Vock replied. He stared into the sky: it was almost night. 'It is a beautiful evening. Now I will butcher the House of Agshad. That is all that matters.'

Far away, automated lights were blinking into life. Neon dolphins and dancing girls appeared on the sides of domes. A light wind caught the leather coats of 462 and his guards, slapping the hems against their stercoriums.

They walked to the edge of the chasm and stared down into the gulf. Among the crystal spires, nothing stirred.

'Nothing! All across the galaxy – for nothing!' Vock threw back his head and laughed. 'You are very silly off-worlders!'

And then, at the bottom, there was a tiny, distant flash of purple lightning. 462's entourage stepped back from the edge.

Light blossomed down below: blue, cold light that spread like radiation. The edges of crystals appeared in the glow, winking up at them. Things flitted between the crystals like dust-devils, scraps of cloth tossed in a hurricane. From up here they were tiny.

'Commander 462!' one of the Ghast technicians rasped. 'We have readings!'

462 smirked. 'Watch closely, Vock, as we turn mankind's puny technology against itself. My troopers will use modified Earth technology in order to restrain specimens of the Vorl for molecular analysis and gene-sampling. My soldiers are equipped with instruments of cleansing, originally devised by the human secret policeman J Edgar

Hoover, and now enhanced for warfare by superior Ghast engineering. Minions, ready your vacuum cleaners!'

Every second praetorian along the edge of the chasm pulled a long tube into its hands. Each tube had a flattened end, leading to pipes that ran to the tank on its user's back.

Vock gawped at him. 'You mean to capture those devils?'

'Of course.' He flicked a hand. 'Spotlights!'

A dozen massive lamps boomed into life. Suddenly the chasm wall was an angular mass of bleached rock and hard shadow, and across the stone darted the translucent bodies of the Vorl.

'Beautiful,' Vock whispered.

'Mark your targets!' 462 called. 'Three capture-teams to each spotlight! Suck them up!'

'Hey, Isambard.' Rhianna looked startlingly bright against the ruined hall, as if the colours of the room had leached into her tie-dyed skirt. 'Are you okay?'

'Fine, thanks. And you?'

She stood at the bottom of the stairs. 'Cool.' She stepped over and kissed him.

'Good work on finding the Vorl. Have you got them on side yet?'

'I'm kind've working on it.'

'Righto. Keep going. Maybe I should come up and explain why they ought to join the Empire.'

Rhianna frowned. 'Let's use that as a backup plan. Please be careful.'

'Saddle up, Smith.' Wainscott turned from the window

and lowered his binoculars. 'We need all hands on deck. Gertie's turned on the Vorl.'

They stood at the window, passing Wainscott's binoculars and Smith's scope between them. A strange sort of battle raged outside: a praetorian had folded over under one of the searchlights, crackling with static electricity. A second Ghast shook and melted like an ice-cream in an oven, dropping into a helmet and a soggy coat.

'What *are* those things?' Wainscott muttered.

'Ghosts,' Carveth said.

Smith glimpsed a Vorl disappear into some kind of suction-tank on one of the soldiers' backs, hands clamped to its head. It reminded him of an Impressionist painting he'd once seen of a screaming man – Van Gogh, he thought, trying to find his ears. He shuddered. 'Good God. Gertie's collecting the Vorl like frogs in a jam jar. Looks like he's taking them into his ship. . . Men, we have to move fast. This has all the hallmarks of evil science.'

Susan crouched down to check Hephuc's bindings. He was tied to the remnants of the banisters, looking downcast but surprisingly relieved to be alive. 'Let's get going,' she said, picking up the beam gun.

'A distraction is required,' Suruk said. 'Wainscott's men, together with Piglet, must assault the enemy and slow their schemes. Then, whilst their spirit-sucking is hindered, Mazuran and myself will creep into the vessel and destroy it.'

'Destroy an entire spaceship?' Carveth said. 'Is it just me, or are you mental?'

'It is just you. The rest of us are quite sane,' Suruk replied, readying his spear.

'This is *so* amazing,' Rhianna said. 'It's like, two cultures coming together and sharing with each other.'

'The only thing you've shared with me is an odour,' C'neth observed, tilting his nose up still further. 'Are you *made* from joss? Still, it won't matter soon. There are more important people than me to talk to, believe me.'

'Really?'

'Oh, naturally. I am a mere underling. You need to talk to the overlord I under for, so to speak. You'll be hob-nobbing with the big cheese before you can so much as blink.'

'Incredible,' she whispered. 'That is so. . . amazing.'

C'neth shrugged. 'Don't get your hopes up. Still, who knows? Maybe the Archpatron does want to exchange the secrets of the galaxy for the Clannad back catalogue. Oh!' C'neth paused, head tilted. 'He's right here!'

Rhianna glanced at the window. Something swirled outside, like smoke, and in the smoke, a face. Wispy fingers tapped the glass; a hand like mist made a sign.

'He says to meet him on the fire escape,' C'neth explained.

Wainscott opened the door and the night air rushed in, close and warm, and with it the sounds of battle. He pushed his targeting monocle into place and grinned. 'Shall we?'

Smith finished loading his gun. 'Now, remember the plan, everyone: we all run to the toilet block over there, then you chaps cover Suruk and I as we get to the enemy ship.' They nodded and checked their weapons. 'Everyone ready?'

'I was spawned ready,' Suruk said.

'Wait.' Dreckitt raised a hand. 'I just want to say how honoured I am to serve with you. You guys may all be off the track and, Mister Suruk, I'm not sure you were ever on the track at all, but it's been a pleasure. And as for you, sister,' he added, turning to Carveth, 'you're the most straight-up dame I never croaked.'

Carveth slapped Dreckitt's bottom. 'Really?' She pulled his head down and kissed him while the others looked away.

'Let's get cracking,' Smith said. 'Please.'

Outside, lights crackled and flared. The wind carried howls and screeches back to them. Gunfire and search-lights crossed the sky.

'Alright then,' Dreckitt said. 'Let's nail these antsy bastards.'

Smith cocked his rifle. 'To us, and to victory!'

'To the toilets!' Wainscott cried.

Guns blazing, they ran into the night.

12

Giving Eight the Finger

For the first time ever, Mimco Vock felt respect for something other than himself. As he watched the handful of humans rush out of the storage buildings, guns blazing, he experienced a twinge of admiration that surprised him. For stupid dirty offworlders, they were brave. The humans reached the toilet block and took up positions, shooting into the praetorian flank. Distracted from their Vorl-catching, the Ghasts returned fire.

But Suruk the Slayer was nowhere to be seen. Vock cursed. Gunfights and demon-suction did not matter now. Honour needed to be satisfied, as slowly and viciously as possible. His hand strayed towards the axe at his side.

Something shoved him: he spun round, ready to fight, and a praetorian strode past, a steel cylinder under one arm. 462 was waiting for it at the bottom of the ramp that led to Eight's ship.

Taking hold of the cylinder nearly floored 462: staggering under its weight, he turned and lurched awkwardly up the ramp.

Vock ran to 462's side. 'Where are you going, disgraceful ant? You must assist in locating Suruk the Slayer!'

462 stopped. 'I think not,' he said. The airlock slid open

at the top of the ramp and a science-caste drone ran down to help him with his burden. 'This is *my* moment, Vock,' 462 said. He stepped inside the ship. The airlock, slammed shut and he was lost to view.

Vock realised that now his soldiers were dead, the Ghasts no longer had room for him in their plans at all. He stood on the ramp, shaking with fury. 'Come back! Come back, insect-scum! May Xitipoxispot strike you down with plague!'

He spat, turned and stomped down the ramp. His vengeance, his cruel, beautiful vengeance, had gone dreadfully wrong. 462 had betrayed him, Suruk the Slayer had disappeared and his minions had jumped into an enormous hole. Without Suruk his revenge was gone, his disgrace permanent. Even if he were to seek atonement at some high precipice, Popacapinyo would tear him apart in the afterlife. Grief welled up in his furry breast: he sat down on the ramp and tried not to cry.

Something moved under the ship. Behind the rear legs, something tall wobbled and flexed. Vock leaped up as if on a scent and ran to the leg, flattened himself against it and peeped round.

A man was being pushed into the rear waste-ejection port. He wore a long coat, and he was standing on his comrade's shoulders to reach the port. Half of his body was in the vent already, and his legs kicked as he was shoved inside.

But it was not the man that mattered. Vock slid his axe from his belt and stepped into view.

'Pig-face M'Lak!'

Suruk glanced round, saw Vock and gave Smith a

massive push. Smith shot up into the ship and the ejection sphincter closed behind him. Suruk lifted his spear. 'So,' he said, 'You have come at last.'

Vock threw back his head and laughed. The grief was gone: his mind swam with bloodlust and evil glee. 'The time has come, dirty pond-dweller! Your father disgraced me and now I shall have my revenge upon his line. Now I shall deliver your heart to Popacapinyo. . . nice and slow.'

'Truly, then, the game begins,' Suruk said, 'for now the soccer mascot approaches. You killed my father. You know what happens next.'

'Lies!' Vock snarled, setting his whiskers twitching. 'I am entirely innocent and nothing like a soccer mascot. I have crossed this galaxy to avenge the insult done by your father, and to offer your beating heart to the war god to atone for my failure. I, Mimco Csinty Huphepuet Vock, noble warlord of the honourable Yu—'

Suruk yawned. 'Less prattle, more battle.'

Vock thrust out his axe in both hands and screamed a warcry. For a moment he stood there howling, shaking, gripping his weapon like a live cable, and then he charged.

Suruk ran to meet him, spear raised.

One huge boost from underneath and Smith shot through the hole. The bioship gave a convulsive shudder and he was inside, lying in an unimportant hold beside the air-lock, glistening with sealant gel. For a moment he caught his breath – then he remembered that he was covered in slime, and ripped off his coat and leather flying helmet and tried to kick them aside until the goo stuck to his boot and he overbalanced.

He lay in the dim, empty room, surrounded by pulsing biotech. A door slid open beside him. As he drew back into the shadows a Ghast technician emerged, twitching and muttering. Its white coat was lilac in the sickly light: the lenses of its goggles winked and glimmered.

Smith jumped it from behind. It was hardly sporting, but neither was Gertie. He swung the Civiliser into its bulbous head, and the technician dropped into his arms like a swooning maiden of exceptional ugliness. Smith grabbed a couple of its appendages and hauled it into the shadows. He slipped into the doorway and found a set of spiral stairs. Promising. Gun and sword at the ready, Smith climbed.

Wind whipped around the fire escape. The night air was cold and, far below, lights flickered around the chasm. The sound of gunfire joined the pattering of the rain.

The Archpatron of the Vorl waited. Little whorls of smoke rose from his dark body as the rain passed through him. His empty sockets turned to Rhianna.

'Hello, patron,' C'neth said. 'This here's Rhianna Mitchell, some sort of human being. She claims to be a hybrid: half Vorl, half organic cereal bar, from the looks of it. Downright bizarre, if you ask me, but there you go.'

'It is true,' the Archpatron replied. 'I know it to be so.' Its voice was partly psychic, a rasping whisper that cut straight into Rhianna's mind. 'You came here for truth, did you not, to learn about your origin?' It extended a hand to her like strands of toxic smoke. 'You wondered for so long as to the nature of your father. Now I will show you. Take my hand now, Rhianna. Stand beside me, Rhianna, and know the truth.'

Whoa,' she said, taking a step back. 'This is getting a little bit freaky. I'm not sure. . .'

'Take my hand, Rhianna, and we will face our destiny together. *This* is your father.'

'Ooh, I *never*!' C'neth exclaimed. 'Oh, patron! I don't know how you can say such things. Lies, awful lies! Don't believe a word of it, dear. Innocent as a lamb, I am!'

Vock ran in howling and cut at neck-height for a trophy-kill. Suruk darted back, testing him; Vock jumped and whipped the axe down and Suruk rocked aside. Screeching to his bloodthirsty god, Vock rushed on, cutting and cutting, and Suruk gave ground.

Vock was good, no doubt about it. This was no mere *Mechi'chu'en*, no praetorian: this was an expert, a mighty enemy. Vock might have tested his weapons on prisoners, but he had trained with the best fighters of the Yull. Yet my father drove him back, Suruk thought, and with the thought came fury, and he attacked.

Suruk jabbed the spear like a bayonet and Vock darted aside, but Suruk had anticipated that and he whirled Gan Uteki so that the shaft cracked Vock across the ear.

Vock was thrown over and his armour clattered as he rolled into a crouch. Squatting he looked more like a letter box than ever. He stood up quietly, arms by his side.

'You fight well,' he said, 'for a disgraceful furless coward. Come. Surrender now and no slow killing. Promise.'

Suruk backed away and raised an eyebrow-ridge. 'Is that so?'

'Oh, absolutely, mangy offworlder. I would never—'
Vock screamed and leaped. He sailed through the air,
his axe swung down. Suruk dropped onto his back
and slammed his boot up into the Colonel's groin.

Vock paused for a moment, held in the air by Suruk's
sole, and he gave a little squeak. He sprang away, yelped
his war-cry and charged back in, and suddenly they were
carving and dodging, raging back and forth, the air
whistling with the sound of blades.

Smith reached the top of the steps and looked out into a
massive hall.

The air buzzed with power: it sounded even louder than
the electric toothbrush Carveth seemed to keep in her bed-
room; a dull thrumming that unnerved the brain, coming
from somewhere high above.

Tubes dangled from the roof like roots into a cave. The
tip of each touched the rounded end of a cylinder the height
and width of a man: translucent things like a forest of
mushroom stalks, all linked to some machinery above.

Smith took a step into the hall, between the rows of tubes.

Technicians moved through the room, cackling as they
checked their clipboards. A little party of them drew near
and Smith pressed himself against one of the tubes, listening to them pass. They carried a metal cylinder between
them. Whatever it was, Smith knew that he had to take it
from them. Anything Gertie wanted that badly needed to
be retrieved, or at least destroyed.

He turned to follow them, and something in the tube
beside him moved.

Smith recoiled, his gun raised, and a moment later saw

that the praetorian was in no state to fight him. It was not awake, not even finished. The monster was comatose, its limbs bobbing in nutritious sludge, its muscles knotting together under a half-formed exoskeleton. It looked like a peeled, evil prawn. A trenchcoat was growing next to it.

Smith looked at the next tube down, and the rows of tubes after that. 'Good God,' he whispered. 'It's a bloody ant farm!'

Towards the front of the rows, the praetorians were more complete; at the rear they were little more than bundles of veins and insignia. The tubes must spit them out by the platoon, Smith thought.

He had heard the stories, but he had never imagined what a Ghast soldier-factory would actually look like. Thousands of years ago, the Ghasts had decided that females were inefficient and, instead of putting up with it like proper people, had shot them all and turned to applied genetics instead. He crept out, weaving between the tubes, following the scientists.

There was a mezzanine a little way ahead. At the top of the stairs coils of pipes ran into a monstrous bio-machine suspended from the roof; a maggot-shaped organ the size of a blimp. It looked like a very old sausage.

Smith ducked back as the scientists connected the cylinder to the pipes. The head scientist turned a dial and the air crackled with static. The blimp wobbled. The scientists stopped for a group-cackle and Smith slipped past them and up the stairs, onto the mezzanine.

Vock got first blood, a gash across Suruk's arm. Suruk went low, tripped Vock and put his knee into the lemming's snout.

Then their blows started to strike home: a kick to Vock's chest that buckled his breastplate, then a raking claw to Suruk's face that missed his eyes by half an inch.

To the left was a row of maintenance sheds and Vock backed away between them. Suruk was taller and had a longer reach; the tightly-packed sheds would stop him swinging his spear. Suruk knew that trick: he stepped out of view and sprang up onto the roof of the nearest building, ran across and jabbed at Vock's head as if to spear a fish. Vock dodged, yelled and slammed his shoulder into the corner of the shed and it collapsed in a thundering pile of plastic sheets.

Suruk crouched behind the wreckage, waiting. 'Where are you?' Vock snarled. Suruk heard the Yull toss a heap of plastic aside. 'Come out, offworlder!'

Suruk listened: not to Vock's words, but to work out his location.

'Being with these humans shames you, Suruk Son of Agshad. Think of what you could become under the General Galactic Happiness, Friendship and Co-operative Collective.'

Suruk waited.

'These mangy British bleat about kindness. They love the weak. They lack our fighting spirit. We Yull have been warriors for a thousand years!'

'So have they,' Suruk said, and he drove the spear through the wall. The blade sliced Vock's thigh and he yowled and twisted free. The wall fell – Suruk cartwheeled back and Vock swarmed over the wreckage, an axe in either hand, feinting and cutting so fast that it took all Suruk's skill to avoid being hit, let alone counter-attack. Vock threw his smaller axe at Suruk and leaped after it.

Suruk knocked the axe away and, just in time, raised his spear to block Vock's battleaxe. The blade whirled down and Gan Uteki broke in two. Suruk stumbled back, half of the sacred spear in each hand, and tripped. Vock loomed over him, squealing with glee, his axe raised to strike the killing blow—

Smith reached the mezzanine and stopped, incredulous with disgust. Ghast biotech was always distasteful, but this took it to new depths of scatology. Strange, pulsing cables lead from thrumming machines to the far end of the mezzanine, where they fused like veins, reaching up to a sort of elevated throne. On the throne sat a huge Ghast, leafing through a copy of *Exchange and Martian*, humming a marching tune. Beneath the throne the blimp began, like a monstrously swollen abdomen.

The seated Ghast sighed and behind it the blimp quivered. Smith's stomach followed suit. He was still gawping at the spectacle when the Ghast lowered its newspaper.

'You,' it said.

'Me,' Smith replied.

'Well, well,' said Number Eight. 'You must be the good Captain Smith. I congratulate you for getting this far. Sadly though, your quest is over. In two minutes' time my DNA will be spliced with that of the Vorl and a legion of psychic stormtroopers will be mine to command. Your decadent race is finished, Smith.'

'Decadent? I'm not the one with no toilet door, you bloody freak. What do you think this is, Holland? Put the paper down and no sudden movements.'

'Silence!' Eight snarled. 'Do you not know who I am?'

Smith looked at Eight's vast back end. 'Some sort of queen?'

'I am Number Eight, the first of my kind, the genetic pinnacle of the Ghast Empire. I am the new master of the galaxy. I will—'

'Oh, shut up,' Smith said, and he rammed his sword into the side of the machine.

He was thrown back in a flurry of sparks. The explosion launched Eight from the throne, hurled him through the air and dumped him in a tangle of limbs and leather twenty feet away. Smith staggered upright, blinked and shook his head.

Eight lay on the ground, propped on all four elbows, shaking his head groggily. Smith's sword was wedged in the machine, electricity crackling along the blade. He patted his jacket: the Civiliser had fallen out. Bugger. Eight's own pistol lay on the ground: Smith picked it up between thumb and forefinger and tossed it over the railing.

'Not so fast, Captain Smith!'

He turned: 462 stood on the stairs, grinning through his facial scars. His metal eye glinted as he took a lurching step forward. There was a gun in his hand.

'Shoot him, 462!' Eight barked from the ground.

'All in good time, my glorious master,' 462 said, and his smirk widened. 'So, here are both of the great leaders, unarmed. No doubt you both had some romantic notion of a duel to the death: warrior on warrior, champions of either side.'

'Not really,' Smith said.

'What are you waiting for?' Eight yelled. 'Kill him!'

'You see, Number Eight, I made a little alteration to the machinery. Oh, the Ghast-Vorl crossbreeds that result will be the fruit of your abdomen, have no fear. But they will be programmed to be loyal only to me. A legion of perfect warriors at my command, and all I need do to restart the process is to remove this sword – like this!'

462 grabbed the pommel of the sword – and screamed. He frothed as the current ran through him, his collar and antennae standing up on end. Smoke rose up from his palm. 462 staggered back clutching his hand, turned and fled down the stairs, coat and stercorium flapping behind him.

'Super,' said Smith, and Eight stood up.

The Ghast cracked its knuckles. 'To the death, then?' it said.

'Right!' Smith replied, and he drove a neat punch straight into Eight's nostrils. Eight blinked. Smith waited, and he began to suspect that something was not working here as it should. When Eight tossed him one-handed across the mezzanine, he realised that his suspicions were indeed correct.

The world froze. Vock towered over Suruk, ready to strike, and Suruk gazed up at him, unable to move.

A shadow stepped into view. It was a silhouette, a misty outline the same shape as a M'Lak, but made of darkness. Two eyes were holes in its head. Black mandibles opened from its jawline, and it spoke.

'Come, Suruk. It is over.'

Suruk said, 'Are you. . .? You are no Vorl, are you?'

'No. I am the Dark One, come to lead you from this world to the hunting-ground of the ancients. Come with me. It is finished.'

'No!' Suruk cried. 'Vock was mine!'

The Dark One sighed. 'He is about to strike the blow that will murder you. Better that you come with me now and avoid the pain he longs to inflict. Come, Suruk. The light in your eyes no longer shines so brightly. Run with me to Ethrethor.'

'Curse you!' Suruk growled. 'I will not leave my father unavenged!'

'There is no choice,' the Dark One hissed, and his arm shot out. As it did, a hand slapped down on his shoulder and dragged him back. A second ghost stood beside it, a broomstick in its free hand.

'Hello, Suruk,' Agshad said.

'Father?' Suruk glanced left, then right. He lay before a semicircle of his ancestors, those who had wielded the spear before him and, now that it had been broken, had been freed from within: Agshad Nine-Swords, Urgar the Miffed, Brehan the Blessed, King Lacrovan. . .

'Unhand me!' the Dark One snarled as Agshad pulled him backwards. 'This warrior is dead!'

'Dead?' Brehan the Blessed chortled. 'Suruk's alive!'

Agshad opened his mandibles and smiled. The Dark One thrashed in his grip. 'Promise me one thing, son.'

'Name it, father.'

'Go and get a proper job, would you?'

He vanished. Vock screeched in triumph as Suruk sprang into a crouch. The axe whipped down and he darted under the blade and caught the shaft in his left hand. For a moment they stood there straining, strength against strength, and then Suruk drove his right fist up and punched Vock in the jaw.

Vock was lifted clean off his paws, tossed ten feet and dropped in a clattering heap of armour plate. His limbs flailed and he whirled upright into a fighting-stance, paused, frowned, and patted the end of his snout. Alarm spread across his face.

Suruk raised his right fist. Wedged in the back of his hand were two long teeth. 'You seek these, rodent?'

'Bathtard!' Vock screamed. 'Dirty offworlder bathtard! Die!'

Suruk felt no fear as Vock sprang. He leapt to meet him, the axe flew past, and Suruk hit Vock's breastplate – grabbed it – turned him upside down and drove him head first through the lid of a wheelybin.

Suruk landed in a crouch and rose slowly to face the wheelybin. Vock's legs protruded from the top of the bin, kicking furiously. Arms pinned to his sides, he could do nothing but howl with rage into his echoing plastic prison.

'Let me go, offworlder! I am the dignified and honourable Mimco Vock! You shame me with your cowardith!'

Suruk chuckled. As he strolled over, he cracked his knuckles. 'Greetings, Colonel.'

'Offworlder, you die slow! You will beg for merthy—'

'I think not. Now, Colonel, you are my prisoner. Listen and understand. Your war is over, as it shall soon be for all the Yull. I shall take this bin to my people and, when they crave your skull, I will plead clemency, so that you may remember this moment for as long as you live, when

I drew your teeth and – what is the phrase? – dropped you into the shit. Not for you a death in battle, but a life of captivity and shame. This I do in honour of my father, whom you murdered like the coward you are when he bested your men.

'*This*, however, I do for fun,' he said, and he punched Vock in the groin. Vock's head made loud contact with the bottom of the bin. Suruk smiled

Eight bent down and lifted Smith up by the collar. 'So,' he said, 'to the death. How amusing. Tell me, Space Captain Smith, what gave you the impression that you could defeat me? I am *most* intrigued.'

Smith drove the side of his hand into Eight's temple, a blow that would have floored a praetorian. 'What do you say to that?'

Eight frowned. 'What's that? Oh, I *see* – you were trying to slap me across the face.' He raised his pincer arms. 'Amateurs. Believe me, Smith' – and his arm flicked out and knocked Smith's head to one side – 'when it comes to slapping people across the face – I – wrote – the – book! And – the – appendix!'

As if batting aside flies, Eight whacked Smith's head left, right, left and right again. Then he tossed him onto the ground: Smith slid along the floor and into the wall. Eight sighed.

'It is too bad that I will not be able to listen to some opera while I rip you apart, Captain Smith. Then this moment would be almost as perfect as myself.' He brushed a spec of dirt from his lapel. 'Why do you people bother? Tell me, captain, can you wrestle an ant-wolf?

Plan an invasion? Write a piano sonata – *before* breakfast? I don't think so. You humans are utterly outclassed. I mean, is there *anything* you have that I don't?'

Smith hauled himself upright. There was blood at the corner of his mouth. 'I have a nose, you alien bastard,' he snarled. 'Beat that.'

'Not quite what –' Eight began, but Smith roared and charged straight into him. His shoulder slammed into the massive Ghast, he snatched something from Eight's belt while his left hand shot up and grabbed Eight's singed antennae. He yanked them forward and with his right fist he punched the monster once – twice – three times in the jaw. He pulled back his arm for a fourth massive blow – and Eight opened his mouth. It was a mantrap, a tunnel lined with fangs, and Smith's hand disappeared into it. Eight slammed his jaws together, bit down and shook his head like a terrier killing a rat. His head tore free in a bloody flurry and Smith staggered back, clutching the half of his right arm that remained.

Eight tossed his head back and, gannet-like, swallowed Smith's hand. He drew himself up and struck a pose suitable for a raconteur. 'As I was saying,' he began, smoothing his trenchcoat. He paused and looked down at his belt. 'Odd. Where's that grenade gone?'

Smith's face was white. The world lurched and flickered before him like a badly-tuned television screen. Eight's question only just reached him, but he smiled nonetheless. 'It was in my hand,' he said.

'What?' Eight's eyes widened: his mouth fell open. Like a toddler he thrust his fists into his mouth, stumbling around as he tried to reach his gullet. '*What?* No, no!'

Eight bellowed around his hands. 'You can't do this! I'm better than you!'

With the last strength left to him, Smith raised his left arm. Slowly he folded his fingers, and gave Eight the ancient gesture his people had bestowed upon invaders for a thousand years.

Eight burst like a dropped egg: strange organs and leather scraps spattered the ceiling and the walls.

'Pillock,' Smith said, and he passed out.

Smith woke up in his bed on board the *Pym*. His room was quiet and dark, and the model spaceships hanging from the ceiling looked as tranquil as soaring birds. He felt numb and a little sleepy.

The last thing he could recall was giving that big Ghast the V-sign. He smiled. Yes, he'd shown that bugger. He could remember the thing bragging about its genius. Not anymore, he thought. Eight wouldn't even be able to play the spoons, let alone write a sonata.

Smith paused, vaguely sure that there was some fly in the ointment of victory. Nope, it was gone. He yawned and stretched, and noticed that he was not stretching quite as far as he'd expected.

'Balls,' he muttered, remembering. 'He bit off my arm.'

The right arm of his pyjamas was neatly folded and pinned just above the elbow. Or the place where the elbow would have been. A drip stood beside the bed, wired to Smith's other arm.

Suruk stepped out of the corner of the room. 'Wainscott's medicine woman fixed you to that tube,' he said. 'I assisted as best I could, but your biology is strange

301

to me. Besides, I dislike needles almost as much as I dislike bees.'

'Thanks. Damned nuisance, this. Rhianna and Carveth – how are they?'

'Bizarre and futile, respectively. They are well.'

'And yourself? Did you. . . ?'

Suruk smiled. 'I did indeed. My father is avenged. The warlord Vock lingers in the hold, pinioned within a plastic bin. Now we take him back as our prisoner, for trial.'

'Good work, old chap! Excellent stuff.'

Smith realised that he could hear the hum of engines. An, ugly crunching noise from the cockpit told him that the *John Pym* had just gone up a gear. 'We're moving,' he said.

'We travel to New Luton with our new comrades. Major Wainscott follows us in his craft, warlike and probably nude. I like him. The Ghast vessel and its spawning-factory are no more. Now we shall conclude our mission.' The alien frowned. 'As your medic, I advise you to rest. Your arm is growing back much too slowly.'

'I see. Look, I know the Yull are bastards, but I don't want you roughing Vock up too much, or the prisoner—'

'I shall not injure the prisoner; there would be no challenge to it. Besides, for Vock a long life in captivity will be far more satisfying. In the meantime I shall do nothing more cruel than play him *Les Fleurs* – several hundred times. Per day.'

'Well, as long as we don't have to listen to him banging on about his honour all the time—'

'I doubt it,' Suruk said. 'Sooner or later he will either go mad or hibernate.'

'I ought to check on things,' Smith said. 'Could you help me get dressed?'

'Gladly.' Suruk bent down and came up with Smith's trousers. 'Tell me, which side do you dress on – front or back?'

Carveth opened the airlock and they stepped out into chaos. The black sky throbbed with explosions and laserbeams: gunfire hid the roars and cries of Ghasts and men. Aresian walkers were tearing down the barricades at the edges of the Imperial compound. Praetorians swarmed around their legs like piranhas. Yet Jones' men fought on, hard and disciplined, the railgun teams covering each other, the fire from small arms and landships holding the waves of attackers at bay.

Smith heard C'neth's nasal voice behind him, 'Gawd, what a dreadful place. You could have at least taken us somewhere nice, not this crap'ole.'

Jones ran up to meet them. 'Alright, Smith! God, what happened to you, man?'

'I had a run-in with Ghast Number Eight. Turns out he bit off more than he could chew.'

'Good – bloody hell, man! What's that?'

'Oh, and this must be the charming local welcome,' C'neth observed.

'This is C'neth of the Vorl,' Smith replied. 'Good to see you, Jones.'

'You too, mate. So you found a Vorl to take back, eh? Rescue party, is it? I'll give orders to fall back by squads: there's too many Ghasts to stay here.'

'Nobody's falling back. We've brought reinforcements.'

Smith looked over his shoulder, at his friends. Suruk was twirling the two pieces of his spear. Carveth was preparing to advance behind Dreckitt. Rhianna was smiling vaguely. Behind them, loading up a fresh magazine, Wainscott stood grinning and fully clothed. His men checked their weapons, looking like dangerousness made flesh. And behind them all, the great ranks of the Vorl rolled out of the two spaceships like a bank of mist, their faces grim and deathly, tendrils of smoke stroking the air like the scarves of a thousand Morris men.

'Bloody hell,' Jones whispered. 'This is a turn up for the books. I wasn't expecting this!'

'*You're* surprised?' C'neth said. 'You're not the one who's just found out he's got a daughter – and she's solid!'

'Well,' Smith said, 'only one thing for it. Could someone help me draw my sword, please?'

Carveth helped.

Smith lifted the sword above his head. 'Right then,' he called, 'you all know what to do. Ladies, gentlemen, Suruk, Jones, Morgan, strange ghost people and Rhianna's dad – for the Empire, *charge!*'

* * *

'And that's how the battle of New Luton was won,' Carveth finished up. 'Or at least the bits I saw. I was hiding under a table for quite a lot of it.'

'How. . . er. . . very interesting,' King Victor replied. He gave Carveth a short bow, and she responded with a curtsey that nearly put her on the floor like a broken deckchair. Smith held his breath and forced himself to remain calm as the king moved down the line.

Although their mission would stay secret, W had arranged for the king to meet Smith, Carveth, Rhianna and Suruk before he knighted General Young later in the day. The four of them stood in a smartly-dressed row in the Great Hall of the Imperial Palace on Ravnavar Prime, the Emerald of the Empire.

The hall was the size of a cathedral nave, the walls decorated with polished brass and racing green. Lances jutted from the vaulted ceiling and from them hung banners from a hundred campaigns, many little more than tattered rags. High in the rafters, like a preserved shark, there hung the Hellfire used by the Space Marshall in his first hundred missions, donated to the people when he ran out of room on the fusillage to tally up his kills. The hall was empty apart from a pair of guards at the far end and a prim man in a morning suit who looked entirely dull and was probably a bodyguard-assassin of extreme lethality.

The crew were very excited to meet the king. Rhianna had pretended to be disinterested in the whole procedure, but she was wearing her smartest flip-flops and a skirt tied-dyed in the official colours of New Francisco. Carveth had reached a level of prattling nervousness that made Smith deeply uncomfortable and Suruk was intrigued by the whole idea of meeting King Victor, 'son of Elvis, of the line of Arthur'.

King Victor's vague, pleasant eyes met Smith's. The King smiled gently and said, 'Erm. . . so, what do you do?'

'Captain Isambard Douglas Winston Smith, Your Majesty,' Smith said, nervousness sending his gut and bladder into an alarming whirl. 'I'm in charge of the *John Pym*.'

'Splendid. Good work,' said the king as a mechanical cherub hovered past, belching out a cloud of lavender essence as it disappeared into the galleries. King Victor put out his hand and they shook. Smith had acquired a bionic arm on the National Health Service to tide him over until his new arm could be attached and it had developed a number of minor twitches from its last user, a commando. Today it was holding out and King Victor's neck remained unbroken. 'Um. . . keeping well, are we?'

'Mustn't grumble, your Majesty.'

'Yes, er. . . absolutely. Of course.'

Smith was not sure what to make of Victor Rex, ruler of two dozen sentient species, figurehead of three hundred worlds and organic farming enthusiast. It was an open secret that he and Queen Kylie – who was currently visiting Proxima Centauri to open an orbital sports centre – were simulants, grown to specification. So far, Victor had been unfailingly polite but rather awkward, only showing real interest when he had got into a discussion with Rhianna about the possible sentience of the local foliage. Still, he seemed harmless enough.

'Well,' said the king, 'carry on, er, Captain Smith. Now then, who might you be, my good green fellow?'

'Greetings! I am Suruk the Slayer, and I bring you this.' Suruk was adorned with some of his most impressive trophies, one of which he quickly unhitched from his belt and dropped into King Victor's outstretched hand. 'It is the skull of a Procturan ripper. May his death-howls prove sweet music to your noble, if somewhat protruding, ears. May you make soil organically enriched with the bones of our slain foes! In its jaws I have put a list of rewards I would like.'

'Um. . .' said King Victor. 'Yes, very good. And what do you do on board the ship?'

'I kill everything! If I might inquire,' Suruk added, 'which battles exactly are you the Victor *of*?'

They left with the honour of having been thanked by the King himself. A wallahbot gave them picnic hampers and guided them to a gilt lift, and they were whisked up through the centre of a spire, hollow like a scrimshawed horn. The lift's scrollworked doors clattered open and they stepped onto a balcony that curved around the top of the tower.

'I shall arrange for your transport, gentlemen,' the wallahbot grated. It rolled back into the lift and, with a rattle of motors, descended from view.

The view from the palace was astounding. Below them lay the garden city of Ravnavar. The roofs of greenhouses winked at them in the sun. The parks looked almost luminously alive: in one of them the Colonial Guard were drilling; and in another a placid Ravnaphant was giving children rides, forty at a time. An airship drifted past, advertising war savings. Tiny red oblongs rolled through the streets: buses bringing wellwishers to watch General Young receive her knighthood.

'Ooh, biscuits,' said Carveth, peeking into her hamper. 'Now then: who'll give me a Cumberland sausage for two pots of the King's Own Jam?'

A hundred yards below, the first wellwishers were arriving to cheer the general to the palace. A huge banner had been hung between the mighty Arcadian veen-trees on Imperial Avenue, saying: THREE CHEERS FOR AUNT

FLO. Quite right too, thought Smith, looking down at the gathering crowd. Had Young not halted the Yullian invasion, the city would be burning by now.

The sun was shining and the pavements looked almost white. The forests glowed at the edge of the city. A light wind blew across the spire, rustling Carveth's dress and forcing Suruk to push his top hat down over his ears. The smell of roast beef drifted up to them from a kitchen in the palace below.

'Nice day, isn't it?' Smith said, holding out his arm for Rhianna to take.

Carveth looked out across the glistening city. Somewhere out there, past the towers and minarets and the shining forest, there were Ghasts and Yull who hated everyone, and a war that still needed to be won. But on a day like this it seemed as if even nature was on the Empire's side. God, she decided – not the brutal god of the Yull, but something subtler and more intelligent – was indeed in his heaven, and if all wasn't right with the world, it could have been a hell of a lot worse.

'You know,' she said, 'on days like this, I think we will win.'

Smith waved for an air-taxi. 'Of course we'll win,' he replied. 'We're British, aren't we?'

The taxi halted beside them, thrusters humming. 'Where to, guv?' it asked, opening a door.

'Hospital, please,' Smith replied, and he stepped in. 'See you this evening,' he called as the door closed behind him.

There was a small television in the corner of the hospital waiting room. On it, General Young was climbing the steps to the imperial throne, where King Victor waited in fleet uniform. He knighted her and, as the Scourge of Yullia stood up, *Jerusalem* parped out of a choir of hovering trumpet-bots.

W sat on the far side of the waiting room, looking hard and thin. He wore his usual battered tweed jacket, which made him look like an impoverished schoolmaster, but there was a plastic collar around his neck and two wires ran from his temple to a speaker mounted beside his throat. The room smelt of cough mixture.

'Hallo, Smith,' W's speaker said.

'Hello, sir.' Smith sat down. 'How's things?'

'Could be worse,' W rasped. 'The metal missed my jugular and most of my nerves. The doctors're putting in a new voicebox this afternoon. Apparently, they're going to whip my lung out while they're at it. How about your arm?'

'This afternoon, too.'

'Did you meet the king?'

'Yes, indeed. He seemed a nice enough chap. We're having a bit of a do tonight. Want to come along?'

'I may well do. Have to eat ice cream for a few days, what with the new neck.' The long, solemn face turned to him. 'Well done on Number Eight, Smith.'

'Thank you, sir. Just a shame he ended up in so many bits. He'd have looked good over the fireplace.'

'You don't know the half of it. Eight was one of the smartest buggers Gertie's ever bred up. We think he was planning to take over from Number One. With him at the helm, God knows what evil they could have done.'

On the television, General Sir Florence Young was holding aloft the axe of a Yullian general, addressing the attendees. 'This is for you!' she declared, and the crowd's cheering drowned her out.

'The tables have turned on the Yull,' W said. 'They fear mankind now – and they know full well what the Morlocks will do to them once they get the chance. Now we get our own back.' His eyes half-closed, and he reclined in his battered chair, surrounded by the smell of medicine and dust. 'They've had their last migration,' he said. 'It'll be a hard fight, but our men are the equal of anything they can put into the field. And then the Ghasts – but still, all in good time.'

'W,' said Smith, 'what will happen to the prisoner we took?'

'Vock's slave? Oh, he'll be fine. We keep the few we capture on a farm, under guard. They'll go back to Yullia once we've won the war. After all, it wouldn't make much sense for the lemming homeworld to have no lemmings on it, would it?' He leaned forward, his big hands resting on his knees. 'Tell me, Smith, what will you do with yourself when the war's over?'

'I don't know. I'll probably go down the pub.'

W raised a thick eyebrow. 'And after that?'

'Curry.'

'Good choice. But the space war's not over yet, Smith, not by a long way. There's plenty for us to do. The secret war is going to get pretty damned busy.'

'Quite,' said Smith. 'There's a lot of work ahead. We've got a lot of Ghasts to deal with, and the lemmings aren't just going to kill themselves, either.'

'Actually, Smith—' W began, and he sighed. 'Anyhow, it's going to be a tough few years for mankind. And while the army moves on, wreathed in glory, we chaps in the Service will have our own clandestine struggle to win: fighting unseen, relying on skill, secrecy and cunning to see us through – subtle and crafty, known only by our deeds.'

The door opened and a nurse looked into the room. 'Mr Lint? Your lungs are ready.'

She looked at Smith, who shook his head.

'Eric Lint, please?'

'Oh, bollocks to it,' W said, and he stood up.

'Come on, you buggers, sing up!' Wainscott stood on the dining table, waving a mug above his head. For his size he had an impressive voice and he bellowed across the room like an enraged ruminant. His eyes had a terrible aspect and he looked like the sort of man who could have wooed Boadicea. Unusually, though, he was still wearing his best uniform – all of it – which was all the more surprising as Emily the android kept trying to finger his epaulettes.

Around him stood, sat and lay the Deepspace Operations Group, Morgar, Tormak the Rune Reader, Jones the Laser, Grocer Green, W (testing out his new lungs with a roll-up and a sing-along), the Grand Archivist and George Benson, who wore a bandage on his head and was in charge of the drinks. And on the wall beside the table, next to the stuffed praetorian's head, soon would hang the two sacred axes of Colonel Mimco Vock.

'*Who am I? Who am I?*' Wainscott roared, and a ragged set of yells joined him for the refrain. '*I am the Berkshire huntsman and this is the Berkshire hunt!*' The song broke down into cheers; Wainscott stumbled off the table, Jones climbed up after him, promising to show them all how it was really done and Tormak the Rune Reader punched both fists into the air and roared 'Glorious!'

It seemed like a good moment to slip out and change Gerald's water. Smith stepped over one of Carveth's android protégées who had passed out in the doorway like a schoolgirl-shaped draft excluder.

On the way to the cockpit he passed Carveth's room. Dreckitt lay sprawled across Carveth's bed, looking as if he had dropped into it from a great height. He stirred in his sleep. 'No more,' he said weakly, 'Not again, Polly, please.' Smith ignored him.

Smith wandered into the cockpit, thoughtfully flexing the fingers of his new right hand. The light was on and the slow, steady squeak of Gerald's wheel pulsed through the room. Smith dropped into the captain's chair, the sound of merriment filtering up the passage behind him. The mock leather creaked as he made himself comfortable: drunk and oddly calm, as if he had staggered into the eye of the storm.

He did not feel triumphant. With tranquillity came an odd sense of sadness that he could not have explained even if he had been sober. He looked across the cockpit at the row of novelty items on the dashboard, and remembered the first time he had seen them over a year ago. They had taken off from New London as beginners, and now they were – well, if not elite as such, at least approaching competence.

'Hey, Isambard.' Rhianna slipped into the room with an enticing hiss of tie-dyed skirt. She perched on the arm of his chair and looked down at him. 'Chilling out?'

'Yes, I suppose,' he replied. 'How's things?'

'Pretty cool.' She sighed. 'It's been kind of heavy though. All those lemming people, then meeting the Vorl, then finding out one of them was my father – Mom must have been so stoned,' she added, with a kind of awed pride. 'Crazy.'

'Still,' said Smith, 'you did get to go to a theme park.'

'Yeah,' Rhianna said. 'You do take me to some amazing places.'

'Seeing as we were on a mission, I thought it was pretty good,' Smith began, a little hurt.

She laughed and patted his shoulder. 'I'm kidding. It's cool; just relax. Okay?'

'Righto. I'll do that. I'm. . . ah. . . hep to that, daddy-o.'

'I think I like you better uptight. Want some?' she added, holding out her hand. A tiny joint was wedged between her fingers; it looked to be largely made of yellowed paper and spit.

'Fine with the beer,' Smith replied.

'Where's Suruk?'

'Out in the forest, communing with the ancestors. I would help him, but this is something Suruk has to do on his own,' he said. 'After all, no-one else would understand a word of it. Goodness knows how he's planning to fit all those ancestors back into his spear.'

'I really hope he can,' Rhianna said. 'After all he's been through. . .'

'I suppose so,' Smith said. 'You know, when it comes down to it, we've not done too badly – so far.' He picked up the novelty paperweight from the dashboard and turned it over in his hands. A storm raged around Parliament inside the plastic dome.

Rhianna stood up. 'I'm going outside for a moment,' she said. 'I think I could do with some quiet. I never realised Major Wainscott's folk singing was so. . . *authentic*.'

'Straight out of Agincourt,' said Smith. 'I'll see you soon.' He listened to her leave the room and sat back in the chair. He felt inexplicably weary. The stitches in his arm ached. He sighed, tired and contented, and thought: well, we actually did it. We fought the lemming men, rescued New Luton, and we've even got the Vorl on our side. And here I am, with my crew – my friends. How could things have ended better?

A light flickered on the dashboard.

A little drowsy, Smith pulled himself up and leaned forward to get a good look at the panel. It was not the self-destruct light – Carveth had shown him that a while ago – so there was probably no immediate problem, unless it was some sort of missile detection system. No, he realised, it was the long-distance intercom.

Tape clattered out of the slot. Smith watched it emerge like a snake from a burrow and ripped off a length. The message read: 'Turn on the television.'

The television took a bit of finding. Puzzled, he sighed and heaved it onto the main console, found the plug and wired it up. His apprehension slowly rising, he switched it on.

With a sudden click, he was looking at a Ghast officer. It sat at a desk, a row of flags hanging behind it like dangling wire. Martial music played in the background: a band accompanying a Ghast warbling in heroic treble.

The scarred, one-eyed face turned towards Smith and smiled.

There was something wrong with 462, something beyond the usual facial scars and metal lens. His working eye was slightly unfocussed, and he seemed to have slumped a little in his chair. There was a brightly-coloured paper helmet on his head and a tube of liquid before him.

'Well well,' he said, his voice slightly less crisp than usual, 'we meet again.'

'So it seems,' said Smith. 'But if you've come here to threaten, Gertie, I can tell you that—'

'Threaten you? Nonsense.' 462 waved his antennae dismissively. 'I would not dream of it. In fact, I seek only to share your moment of victory.'

'What?'

'I thought I would congratulate you. Shake your hand, as it were.'

'With a serrated pincer, no doubt.'

'Not at all. For once I have no desire to snip off your puny appendages. It is most amusing: once again your weak Earth-mind is unable to fully appreciate the irony of your situation. Neither of us has lost out from your last little adventure. The death of Eight has left, shall we say, a vacuum of power here. Nature may abhor a vacuum, but I myself do not.'

Slowly, like a crocodile breaking the surface of a lake, a long, bestial head rose above the level of the desk beside 462. There was a conical party hat wedged between its antennae.

'This is Assault Unit One, the former property of the glorious Number Eight. Now that Eight has been killed and the pieces regrettably devoured by his own praetorians, Assault Unit One belongs to me. You see, the

Ghast Empire required someone to take over Eight's duties and, as his assistant, it was assumed that I had the ruthlessness and skill to take his place. My superiors suspected that I had assassinated Number Eight and promoted me for my initiative.'

Smith stared at him. He did not feel anything much, only a vague, exhausted contempt. He would never be rid of 462, he realised – not until he killed the monster himself. 'I suppose you let them believe that?'

'I dropped the odd hint.' 462 smiled and took a sip of liquid. 'Mmm, that tastes effective. You know, we Ghasts do not indulge in many frivolous celebrations.'

'It probably comes from living in a one-party state.'

'Quite so. And this, as you can see, is the party.'

'And you're in a state.'

462 adjusted his paper helmet. 'Well, perhaps so. After all, my unfortunate predecessor did keep an impressive cellar of nine-percent sucrose solution.' He raised the liquid tube. 'So thank you, Captain Smith. You have saved me a lot of unbecoming dirty work. Number One needs a personal assistant to help him with Number Two. Perhaps I shall become his deputy.'

'So you'd be clearing up after Number Two? It sounds disgusting but, for you, pretty appropriate.'

462 shrugged. 'Ah, who knows where inexorable destiny will carry us? But at any rate, I think we shall meet again. It may not be for some time – I have other business to attend to. But I will see you again and then, Smith, I shall have the pleasure of destroying you for good.'

'Just bugger off, would you?' said Smith. 'Go and dance round your trenchcoat or whatever you chaps do.'

'As you wish. But I suspect that you have not seen the end of me.' 462 gave a mocking wave.

'Yes I have; it's big and re—' Smith began, but the connection was gone. 462 was still on the screen, his hat slumped over one antenna, arm frozen in mid-wave. His hand was scarred from where he had grabbed Smith's sword. As Smith stared at the screen he made out the words 'Made in Sheffield' seared across 462's palm.

'I'll bag you yet,' Smith promised the image. 'My crew and I will not rest until you are defeated. We—'

A huge robot suit danced past the nosecone.

Smith leaped up, ran out and hauled the airlock open. Dwarfed by the twenty-foot Leighton-Wakazashi fighting suit that danced around it, the *John Pym*'s stereo stood on the tarmac, pumping the greatest hits of Queen into the warm night air.

Nearby Yoshimi Robot-Pilot watched, horrified. 'Oh, Captain Smith!' she cried. 'Polly Pilot wanted to borrow my fighting suit, and now look!'

The robot's head spotted him and the speakers boomed: 'Look at me, boss! I'm tall! Can you see me, world? I'm the tall one now!'

'You bloody idiot!' he yelled back. 'Stop that at once!'

The fighting suit paused, shocked, and straightened up. For a moment it stood there, hands on hips, looking curiously offended – and then it raised one vast hand and blew him a mighty raspberry.

'Oh, what the hell,' Smith called back. 'Carry on, Carveth.' He looked at Rhianna and smiled. 'Care for a dance?'

Epilogue

A Message from the Ancestors

The trees closed over Suruk's head, almost hiding the sky. The forest was damp and hot and its smell seemed to wrap itself around him. A fine night for battle, he thought, and a fine night to make peace with his ancestors.

He knew when he had found the right tree, a mighty alien pseudo-conifer with a trunk as broad as a watchtower. He swung the rucksack onto his back, bent his legs and sprang onto one of the lower branches. He flexed his fingers and jumped again, and in a moment he was springing from branch to branch, bouncing off the trunk and limbs, leaping ever upward until he cleared the forest canopy as if bursting from below the waves.

Suddenly he was looking at the moon. Light rain tapped his skin. Under his boots the branch on which he balanced swayed gently with the wind, and Suruk swayed with it.

'Greetings, Father,' he said. 'It is I, Suruk the Slayer.'

The sky was silent.

'Morgar has become a good warrior,' Suruk said. 'He has slain many of our enemies. Dozens of Ghasts have fallen to his hand. Soon he shall join those taking vengeance to the foul Yull and teach them to fear the House of Urgar. I am sure you are proud, Father.

'And I wish you to be proud of me, as well. When last we spoke you said that I should get a proper trade, and you lamented that there were no lawyers or doctors in our family. I have remedied that. The fight with Vock was great and terrible, as you saw. In return for my work in shaming Mimco Vock and revealing the Vorl to mankind, the greatest scholars of the British Empire have forged a helm and cape for me, and anointed me by post Doctor of Law. And not just any doctor, Father, but an *honorary* one!'

Suruk reached into his bag and took out a mortar-board hat. It would not fit easily on his head, but with a bit of shoving he managed to wedge the mortar-board in place. The rain grew in force, pattering down on his hat. Thunder rippled through the trees and, a mile away, lightning broke the sky.

Perched on the branch, Suruk drew two last items from the bag and raised them in his hands. 'See, Father. I swore to follow you and to bring vengeance and honour to our line. Let the ancestors know that this I have done! In this hand, the axe of Mimco Vock: in the other, the scroll of learning of the University of New Stoke. Look closely now, my Father: are you not avenged? *Are you not avenged?*'

He threw his head back and bellowed into the rain, arms raised as if to hold up the head of a mighty beast for the ancestors to see. The thunder roared back at him and a bolt of lightning shot into the axe, down the shaft, into Suruk. He shuddered and frothed, frozen mid-cry, and dropped like a rock into the forest below.

Suruk awoke stretched out on his back, surrounded by the smell of singed mane. He flexed his limbs; they still worked, but he did not get up. The rain was warm around him and he smiled up at the sky through wisps of smoke.

'I shall take that as a yes,' he said.